ᴏᴏᴛʜ Tarkington's newest heroine is one of those fascinating creatures you don't know whether to love or hate. At first glance, Josephine Oaklin seems to have everything—great beauty, wit, wealth, and an impressive knowledge of all things except herself. Yet in the small midwestern city where her grandfather had been first citizen and leading benefactor, she manages to make herself thoroughly despised.

For Josephine, lonely and spoiled, twists her shining qualities all out of proportion and presents to the world not her true self, but a hard, grating outline. Bailey Fount was to discover the real Josephine, but not until her image had made a lot of trouble.

As the story opens, Lieutenant Bailey Fount, back from the Pacific with shattered nerves and a string of medals, has been ordered to rest and recuperate at the Oaklin Art Museum. It happens that Josephine is the real force behind the museum which her grandfather founded. Also she's badly in need of a fiancé, having just been jilted for the second time. And so it comes about that a somewhat broken young man becomes engaged to a desperate, headstrong girl whom he doesn't love.

This brief summary cannot convey the customary grace and subtle humor with which Mr. Tarkington endows his story. Image of Josephine is a worthy addition to the Tarkington library of American classics (*see back of jacket*).

IMAGE OF JOSEPHINE

BOOTH TARKINGTON

IMAGE
OF
JOSEPHINE

Doubleday, Doran and Company, Inc.

Garden City, New York

1945

To

MAJOR BOOTH T. JAMESON, A.C.

IMAGE OF JOSEPHINE

I

B<small>OASTING</small>'s the vulgarest thing there is," the fair young girl, Josephine, informed her three guests as they came out of the big brick Oaklin house after lunch. "Boasting's practically the same thing as bragging, and both are incredibly vulgar."

The guests, two girls and a boy, all three of their hostess's age, fourteen, were already depressed, though well fed, and they became gloomier as she used what they thought a show-off word. " 'Incredibly,' " the boy repeated. "That's about the hundredth time to-day you've said something was 'incredibly,' Josephine. You've said about a thousand things were 'vulgar,' too. Besides that, you can deny it all you want to; but you were boasting or bragging, or both or whatever you call it, just as I taxed you with."

"I did not!" young Josephine cried. "You're incredibly mistaken! There! I'll say it as frequently as I wish to and I'd like to see you endeavor to stop me because I'll throw you down and rub your face in the grass if you do, the way I did yesterday. Want me to show Ella and Sophie I can?"

In heated response he used an expression still permissible to youthful fashion that year, 1932. "Can it! Can that stuff!"

Young Josephine Oaklin, slim from small feet to broad shoulders, was an athlete and as precociously active bodily as she was mentally. Jamie Elliston well knew she'd not hesitate to manhandle him. "Go on and incredibly yourself sick," he said. "It'll sure be swell, so have yourself a time. *I'm* through objecting."

" 'Sure'! 'Swell'!" Josephine taunted him gayly. "Those two foul old words are fifty percent of your vocabulary, my dear. The other fifty consists of 'guy' and 'gal' and 'can it.' Take those away and you'd be denied all utterance."

"Oh, I would? Then listen to this: Skip it, you heel! Suit you any better?"

Sophie and Ella, each boredly skewering a patent-leather toe into the newly April-green grass, looked on coldly. "Always tangling with the boy-friend, isn't she?" Ella said. "I don't deny you gave us a nice lunch, Josephine; but who couldn't with all those servants, and if you think always picking on Jamie to prove he's yours is interesting, it simply isn't."

"I'm not hers," Jamie began. "I'm not any——"

Sophie agreed with Ella. "Yes, Josephine, you're supposed to be having a luncheon party for us; but now we've eaten it, what do we do next?"

"Well, I'll see; but there's an important event going to happen here this afternoon." Josephine made her pretty fourteen-year-old face as mysterious as she could. "Of course I don't mean anything important about you three or anything like that. The importance is going to be on the adult scale. It's essential I keep within call of the house, so we can't go anywhere else, soda-fountaining or anything. Fortunately we've got plenty of room to do whatever I decide till I get called in, since our yard happens to be the only one in town that comprises a full block."

"Oh, no! No vulgar boasting or bragging!" The Elliston boy

became loudly sarcastic. "Never missed a chance yet to holler you got a yard that covers a whole block and's got your family's private art gallery in it besides the house and all the old bushes and trees! Listen, what's this adult scale you claim you're going to mix up with? Adult scale! That's a cute one."

Josephine moved toward him dangerously. "Asking to get your nose rubbed in the grass?"

He backed away. "You let me alone!"

Josephine leaped, caught him about his middle, threw him and did what she had threatened; but her two other guests remained apathetic. "If you think you're giving Sophie and me a good time at your luncheon party," Ella said, "you're mistaken, Josephine. Can't you two lovers do anything but fight? It's pretty boresome for us spectators."

Jamie Elliston, prone, cried out thickly against the word "lovers," whereupon Miss Oaklin rubbed the grass with his face again; then let him rise. "I'll tell you what we'll do," she said. "I'll show you three some new basketball shots I've worked up. Come on."

She ran ahead and they followed slowly round the wide house. Jamie, muttering moroscly, used a white handkerchief upon his face and the green-stained knees of his trousers. "Doesn't care whose clothes she destroys! Got a basket in front the side wall of their old art gallery. Wants to show us she can make more baskets than we can, just because your old Miss Murray's School for Girls' basketball team's got her for its captain."

"You're not up to the minute, Jamie," Ella informed him. "Nobody can deny she's a good player and everybody thought the team'd elect her captain this year; but the girls on it all simply declined and elected Amy Keller instead."

"Good!" Jamie cheered up a little. "So our proud and mighty old gal's just a humble member of the team."

"Not so humble," Ella said. "Practises hour after hour all alone by herself so's to prove even if she isn't captain she's anyhow the best."

They'd come round the house to an open space before a building of pale limestone, the "old art gallery." It wasn't old. Jamie had used the term in the instinctive manner of the young, for whom "old" naturally defines anything uninteresting, difficult or contemptible. Attached to the Tudorish brick house by a stone passageway, the skylighted gallery, a single story high and windowless on this side, made a convenient backstop. Josephine was already poised with a ball in the center of the open space and facing a "basket" set up before the wall.

"Watch this shot!" she called. "Notice the new way I use my wrist and——"

Ella interrupted her drearily. "What's the use your having that four-thousand-dollar tennis court back yonder? There are four of us and we could all get our rubber-soles and——"

"No. The court's covered on account of spring rains. You watch this shot; it's different. Zing!" As adroit as she was graceful, Josephine "shot" the ball accurately. "Basket! Got a basket! Run get the ball for me, Jamie; I appoint you my retriever." She glanced at his face, and laughed. "What's the matter? Insulted speechless again?"

The discontented Ella made another protest. "Josephine, is it entertaining guests they just get to stand around while you shoot baskets? Hostesses are supposed to afford pleasure from the background, aren't they?"

"Well, I'll tell you," Josephine said, assuming a confidential air. "I haven't got much time to think up anything until later.

You see, this important event on the adult scale I mentioned may begin to take place almost any instant and I've got my mother on my mind because she's out at a big female luncheon at the Country Club. She always gets absorbed, especially if there's contract; but I impressed and impressed it on her that she had to be on time. She ought to be here right now and I can't get a second's peace of mind till I see her car on our driveway."

Jamie Elliston spoke with pain. " 'Impressed it'! 'Impressed it on my mother'!"

"She does," Sophie told him. "That's exactly what she does. Josephine absolutely runs her mother. Everybody in town knows Mrs. Oaklin does everything Josephine tells her to."

Josephine listened to this with a matter-of-course complacency; then "I hear a car now!" she cried, and ran back by the way she'd come. When she reached a corner of the house she stopped and looked toward a porte-cochère that sheltered a side entrance. There a taxicab had just halted; a preoccupied man carrying two thick brief-cases stepped out, rang the doorbell and disappeared within the house. The taxicab drove on till it reached a graveled space before a large brick garage at the end of the driveway. The driver stopped his car, lighted a cigarette and waited. Josephine ran back to her guests.

"It's commencing," she said. "Mr. Oscar Glessit's got here. He's Grandfather's lawyer; but look, I've got a little time left, so I can show you some more of my shots. When I haf to go in the house the rest of you can practise 'em till I come out again, so it stands to reason I'll do all the shooting up to then. Fetch me the ball, Sophie, since the princely Mr. Elliston's so ungracious about it."

Sophie Tremoille went for the ball. "Oh, all right!" she said almost admiringly, as she brought it. "Always got to have your way! You think everybody else are just your mere attendants, don't you?"

"Well——" Josephine laughed, and in this contortion her daintily shaped features were prettier than ever. "You ought to keep remembering who I am, oughtn't you?"

"Well, honest to gosh!" This was Jamie appealing to Ella. "She means it!"

He was right. Young Josephine laughed, amused by her own egregiousness; but she did mean it.

II

WITHIN THE HOUSE, meanwhile, the "important event" had
begun to take place, and it was even more important than
she'd said. The passageway from the art gallery led by a door
now closed into a large and lofty oblong room, at one end of
which stood a splendid Jacobean mantelpiece of carved and
blackened oak. The great fireplace, wherein small logs burned,
was flanked by its proper antique adjuncts, part and parcel of
the same despoiled Manor overseas: paneled high wainscotings
similarly blackened by time, smoke and dark wax. Further aged
panelings along the southern wall of the room separated the
diamond-paned, deeply recessed windows of seventeenth-cen-
tury glass that laid yellow rhomboids of sunshine on the broad-
planked floor. The other sides of the room displayed books
almost to the high and elaborate plaster ceiling—books on long
"set-in" shelves, rows of tall thin books, rows of massive shorter
books, rows of books in "special bindings," tooled and gilded;
and almost all of these books bore upon the arts of painting,
sculpture, music and architecture. More books, as well as portfolios too large for the shelves, were stacked upon heavy
Jacobean tables; but that there should be comfort in the room,

7

however incongruously, the chairs and a couch against the north wall were of to-day and done in scarlet leather.

This was Mr. Thomas Oaklin's library. Manorial himself, black-coated and wing-collared, with a beautiful Cashmere shawl over his knees, he sat in an easy-chair near the fireplace —a white-haired, finely withered old man palely handsome and still commanding. As he talked to his lawyer, Oscar Glessit, he sometimes made a gesture with a long, bony and old-veined white hand; but the movement was always so consciously suave that it took care not to disturb the inch-and-a-half ash of the cigar held between the first and second fingers. The picture he presented to the eye conveyed flawlessly the tradition in which he loved to live—connoisseur patron of art, grand seigneur—easily possible to an eighth-generation American, fastidious and scholarly third-generation mid-western millionaire. So neatly, in his rich surrounding, he made this portrait of himself that his knowing he made it is little to be doubted.

"You have it all in order now, Glessit," he said graciously. "I've no further criticism."

"Yes, it'll do at last, Mr. Oaklin." The lawyer sat at one of the Jacobean tables, and upon it his open brief-cases revealed a dismal quantity of legal papers. "Broadly, it all sounds simple enough, sir; but in detail it's a rather staggeringly elaborate affair. The amount of securities involved and not leaving them to the natural heirs——"

"Just a moment." Mr. Oaklin slightly lifted his long-ashed cigar as a middle-aged tall colored man entered the room. "What is it, Harvey?"

"Mr. Horne on the telephone, sir. Ask me find out how soon you expectin' him, sir. Say he ready come now if you want him."

"I do. Tell him so, Harvey."

The colored man departed soft-footedly, and Mr. Oaklin's grey eyes denoted pleasure. "We've got a surprise for John Constable Horne, I think, Glessit, what?"

"No question, sir. I hope Mr. Horne'll have the patience to go through these papers as he ought to, considering what you plan for him; but, knowing him, I doubt it. By the way, until I drew them up for you I never knew his middle name was Constable. Is that a family name?"

"No, Glessit. His parents—rather 'arty' people in their day —naïvely named him for the greatest British landscapist, perhaps the greatest of all landscapists; but from boyhood John Horne's admired that painter so much he's always thought it would be pretentious to use the name. Probably he thinks it's more American, too, to call himself John C. Horne; he's notional. He's a dozen years younger than I—at my age I find that my friends are all my juniors, otherwise they wouldn't be alive—but John Horne's life, like my own, has been a continuous devotion to the Fine Arts. He's spent almost as much time as I have, myself, in my gallery of paintings and sculptures, and he's a genuine authority upon Oriental art, in particular upon the Northern Wei stone sculptures. I fear this doesn't much interest you, Glessit." Mr. Oaklin smiled faintly and with his left hand rang a small steel bell beside him upon a squat old black table.

The colored man, Harvey, reappeared in the doorway. "Yes, sir?"

"Harvey, has my daughter-in-law come home?"

"Yes, sir. Few minutes ago. Upstairs changin' her dress again."

"And Miss Josephine's where you can find her when I wish her to come in?"

"Yes, sir. Basketballin' right outside."

Harvey waited a moment; then, seeing that his employer had fallen into a meditation, departed. The lawyer, rearranging though not rustling certain of his papers, glanced up from time to time during the next fifteen minutes, but refrained from speaking. Mr. Oaklin not infrequently went into these silences—contemplations concerned with the past or with art, or with God knows what, Oscar Glessit thought; men as old as Thomas Oaklin seemed to live mainly in their own old dead worlds. The old dead world at present engaging Mr. Oaklin was shattered by the noisy voice of his friend, John Constable Horne, who walked into the library already talking. He was followed by Harvey, bringing upon a tray a decanter of sherry, thin wine glasses and a porcelain basket of small cakes.

"What, what? What's all this?" Mr. Horne asked brusquely. Somewhere in his sixties, he was a thick, short, baldish, bustling man, pudgy in feature but with noticeably sparkling small blue eyes. "Oscar Glessit and a barrel of his horrible documents? Scene from one of those extinct genteel melodramas: the Duke changes his will."

Mr. Oaklin smiled at him. "Sit down—I'm never comfortable till I can get you to sit down, John—and don't go leaping up every moment or so while I'm explaining what you're here for. Let the sherry alone; I'll offer it later. That's all, Harvey. I ask you to sit down and listen, John."

"I'll sit," Mr. Horne responded, and did so. "It's against my nature but I'm doing it. What for? My soul, but you and Oscar Glessit look ponderous! If you're not changing your will——"

"No, I've just been making one, the first and last."

"I see," Horne said. "You want me for a witness, which shows you're not leaving me anything, thank God!"

"I am, though." His old friend regarded him gravely. "I'm leaving you a responsibility; I'm putting it upon you."

"I decline. Whatever it is, Lord help me, I refuse!"

"You can't." Mr. Oaklin's thin but mellow voice was slightly tremulous for the moment. "It's what I'd have asked my son to do for me if he'd lived until now. It's a great thing; but since Tom's death there's no one except you I'd trust with it. My daughter-in-law wouldn't do at all. I make no complaint of her; I merely say she won't do. My granddaughter is remarkable, highly gifted and precociously advanced in mind and character; but obviously she's still too young. So I turn to you."

"Why to me?" Mr. Horne looked seriously disturbed. "Don't like responsibilities. What about your niece, Mary Fount? She's your own brother's daughter. She's still alive, isn't she? You know where she's living, don't you? Certainly used to take a great interest in her and——"

"I did, and I suppose of course she's still alive or I'd have been notified. Mary Oaklin had a genuine feeling for the arts and I'd taken great pains to cultivate it in her —until she threw it all away to marry that migratory fellow, Fount." Mr. Oaklin, though remaining scrupulously formal, looked cross. "Why bring it up, may I ask?"

"Oh, just a passing thought," Mr. Horne explained. "A bit surprised by your saying you had no family except your granddaughter."

"For this purpose I have not." Irritation lingered in Mr. Oaklin's voice. "I don't say but that if my niece still lived here —and were not Mrs. Fount—I mightn't have somewhat associated her with you and my granddaughter in this project;

but I know almost nothing of her nowadays. She's not available, John; she's out."

"Out of what?" Horne said testily. "Let's get to it. What do you want done?"

"I think you already have an idea. The surprise for you is that it's you who'll have to do it. First I want you to understand why I want it done. I'm afraid the root reason is that in my old age I've discovered how abominably selfish a life I've led."

Oscar Glessit displayed a protesting hand above his open brief-cases. "Oh, no, you can't say that, Mr. Oaklin! A man who's already made such a magnificent gift to his city as the Thomas Oaklin Symphony Hall—yes indeed, and provided for the orchestra's annual deficit as you have and——"

"No." Mr. Oaklin smiled ruefully. "I've done all that for my own personal pleasure. During most of my life, in order to hear a symphony orchestra I had to travel to larger cities. I'll go abroad on a boat any day; but in my old age I hate trains and I hate automobiles. I backed a symphony orchestra here simply to avoid going away and for my own convenience. It's been expensive, yes; but not compared to what I have in mind now."

"To it, man!" the lively Horne suggested. "To it!"

Thomas Oaklin was not so to be hurried. "No, I'll have my say my own way, no matter how it bores you and poor Glessit." He disregarded another protest from the lawyer. "How many centuries and how many men tried to find the Philosophers' Stone?"

"Asking me?" Horne said. "I think the search for it began before the Middle Ages; but I'd have to look it up, and as for how many alchemists spent their lives——"

"Never mind," the old man interrupted. "We know it was

supposed to change base metals into gold. In other words, it was to turn hard dull life into happiness. Well, I found the Philosophers' Stone when I was young; but I never handed it about, just kept it to myself. It's a real thing, Glessit, though I don't expect you to believe it. What's more, I shouldn't say I found it, because it was presented to me by my father. My grandfather had given it to him."

Oscar Glessit looked indulgent. "I understand, Mr. Oaklin. Everybody knows how largely and wisely you've increased what you inherited from your father and grandfather."

"I'm afraid you're speaking of money, Glessit." Mr. Oaklin was amused. "However, most people would. They don't know they may all possess the Philosophers' Stone if they will."

"Prosier and prosier in his old age," the lawyer thought. "Always got to talk as if he'd written it first!" The spoken words were, of course, "Very interesting, Mr. Oaklin."

"No, it isn't. Not to you, Glessit, because you don't believe me; you think I'm just mooning—and yet what I say is literally true. Any human being can find the Philosophers' Stone for himself and by means of it transform his life. Even if it's the dullest and most sordid, he can bring a golden happiness into it and keep that happiness as long as he lives. The Philosophers' Stone isn't what this nasty new slang calls 'escape'; it's a magic ready to anybody's hand; yet it's a secret from most of the millions of people on this earth. Strange, isn't it, that such a secret should be as plain as day to anybody who chooses to open his eyes? The Philosophers' Stone, Glessit, isn't philosophy, isn't science, isn't even religion—it's what we call art."

"I see, Mr. Oaklin. Yes, of course, we all know that an appreciation of art is——"

"No, you don't all know." The old man became more emphatic. "Only a few people in this city of ours know what art could be to them, even though it can intimately be almost everything to almost everybody. Myself, I have known from my boyhood because right at home in the old house down on Madison Street there were my grandfather's and my father's collections surrounding me. They were of an earlier, sometimes naïve taste but had noble items among them, and thank heaven they got to me when I was young! Well, until now I've been a pig about them and all the splendid things I've added to them. I've kept to myself the pleasure they could put into other lives. Yet I love my city as well as any Florentine of the Renaissance loved his. Of course you see what I'm up to, John Horne."

"I suppose so. Going to open your gallery to the public and _____"

"No, that's not a tenth of it." Thomas Oaklin leaned forward and a pinkness appeared upon the old grey-white of his cheeks and temples. "I've been asking myself what it was the Florentines did to make their city a shrine of art for the whole world. What would a devoted Florentine have done with resources like mine? He'd have built something beautiful. I've said to myself, 'Here's my own town, a city of close upon a hundred and eighty thousand people now. I've given them an orchestra for their ears, yes; but what about an art that their eyes can see?' John Horne, I want to build a great place. Call me romantic, call me sentimental; all right, but I want to build a Temple of Art. It will be the people's and in it they'll find the Philosophers' Stone I've kept so long to myself. I want it to be for all the people of my city."

"Bigger than I thought," Horne said. "You're having your will drawn to provide for a real museum, are you?"

"That guess goes only half way, John. I'm leaving the funds

to carry on the life of a museum amply; but I intend to see the building itself with my own eyes. The small gallery I built a few years ago is so crowded it hurts me to go in there—great paintings almost frame to frame, Whistler and Manet and Sargent in the next alcove to Rubens and Dobson and Van Dyck; Mino da Fiesole and Amadeo sculptures within ten feet of a Chinese room; Île de France Gothic ivories and Renaissance bronzes on shelves of the same cabinet, and some of my father's darlingest Seventeenth Century Dutch pictures with no place to live but the cellar. Worthy canvases even pack the attic of this house. I intend to last until I've seen my masterpieces with the right space about them, John Horne; I mean to see them myself in the setting they deserve!"

"Easy come, easy go," Horne said; but his laugh was a little excited. "Going it, aren't you, rather?"

"I am indeed." Mr. Oaklin still leaned forward, and the thin flush deepened upon his cheeks and brow. "That jumbled gallery of mine is to be only the lower story of one wing of the palace of art I'm going to build, and I'll show you the blueprints next month when my New York architects bring them out here to be passed upon. You'll have to look over those blueprints with me, and pretty critically, because you're going to be President of my hand-picked Museum Association and Chairman of the Board of Trustees of the Thomas Oaklin Museum of Art—and for life, Jonathan, my Jo-John."

"I am not!"

"You are." The old man sank back in his chair, relaxed and smiling. "The will provides for the carrying-on of the museum after I'm gone, staff salaries, maintenance and all that, with also a fairly considerable fund, upwards of two hundred thousand dollars a year, for the continuing purchase of works of art—an item you'll not be able to resist, not if I know you, and I think I do."

"I'm afraid you do," Horne said, almost in a whisper. "I'm afraid you do."

"What a man!" Mr. Oaklin spared another glance to his lawyer. "Glessit, notice this fellow. When I spoke of bringing happiness and beauty into the lives of our fellow-townsmen he had no enthusiasm; but now when he understands it's a chance for him to spend the rest of his days haggling with art dealers and winking at auctioneers, why, he's all on fire!"

"At least starting to scorch and smoke," Horne admitted. He jumped up and began to walk about the room. "President? Chairman of the Board of Trustees? Ex-officio on all committees, what? Dealers bringing Franz Halses, Bellinis, Sung porcelains, Gothic chasubles to make my mouth water—me that's never had but one chipped Shansi head and one Pontormo drawing and one Winslow Homer watercolor to my name! I feel myself on the way to accept. Damn my old soul, I *know* I'm going to accept! Time for the sherry, ain't it?"

"No, it isn't. Sit down."

Mr. Horne didn't sit; he came and stood before Oaklin's chair, serious. "See here, though! This is a fairly colossal cobweb you're spinning, ain't it? It's a prospect removing a good big hunk of your assets out of the reach of your family, ain't it?"

"Yes, more than nine-tenths."

"Well, see here, then." Horne's seriousness increased. "What are Mrs. Thomas Oaklin, Junior, and her young daughter going to say to it? The time may come when they——"

"No. I was just getting to that—if I could induce you to sit down again."

"I'm down," Horne said, and was.

Mr. Oaklin leaned forward once more. "I'll show you presently; but first I want to ask you to begin to interest yourself rather earnestly in my granddaughter."

"But I——" Horne looked polite as if with certain inner reservations. "Oh, I do, I do! A very, very pretty child, Josephine. Precociously advanced, too, as you say. A nice confidence in herself; willing to be talkative with older people and on almost any subject under the sun. Only the last time I was here she told me all about El Greco."

Mr. Oaklin laughed fondly. "Yes, she's a bit that way and I'm glad she is; youth ought to be sure of itself. I want you to learn to understand her better, though, John. I'm not just a doting grandparent when I say she has a feeling for art and a comprehension of it far, far beyond her years."

"Oh, no doubt, no doubt! I'm sure——"

"She's sound, John. Volatile, yes; but sound underneath. That lovely child's companionship in my tastes—why, even two years ago, when she was only twelve and she and I had a month together with the Prado, her love of the great masters there was as deep as mine and her knowledge of them almost as thorough. Last year it was the same in the Louvre and the Uffizi. It's her human quality I want you to know better, though."

"Oh, yes, certainly! I'm sure I——"

"I want you to know her generous heart, John. Isn't it rather remarkable that she's enthusiastic over my plan for a museum? She's for it heart and soul, in spite of the plain fact that it'll keep her from being what people call a great heiress. Isn't it a pretty rare thing, John Horne, that she'd actually rather see the museum built than have the money, herself?"

"She would? You're sure she understands what she loses?"

"Perfectly. I've been all over it with her and she wants it my way; but for what she gives up I intend that she'll have the compensation of identifying her life with that of the museum. I've been over it with Glessit and it's provided that when she comes of age she'll be a member of the Board of Trustees, herself, and I know you'll regard my wish that along with you she'll always have a decisive voice in the museum's control. I've promised her that and I know I can trust you to see the promise kept."

"Yes—certainly, certainly." Shadow again lay faintly upon Mr. Horne's brow. "But young people—and their mothers— do change their minds sometimes about inheritances that go to great public benefits. You're sure you're not afraid that some day——"

"I said I'd show you." Mr. Oaklin once more rang his bell and spoke to the prompt servitor. "Harvey, ask Miss Josephine and her mother to join us now. Then go into the gallery and tell Mrs. Hevlin and her sister-in-law I'd like them to come in."

"Yes, sir."

Mr. Oaklin turned a smiling face upon his old friend. "Now, John Horne, you're going to see how a child in years can have the mind and heart of a woman whose love of art—yes, and of art for all our people—is greater than her love for self."

III

JOSEPHINE came into the room quickly, and, against the background of dark paneling and the tiers of books, her fair head was a charming shape of light. Her face wore an expression entirely different from that she'd shown to her young friends outdoors; a fully grown-up dignity, not unlike a schoolteacher's, was displayed and yet she hurried gracefully to sit upon the arm of her grandfather's chair somewhat as if she'd been a favored page.

"How do you do, Mr. Horne," she said in a sweetly hushed voice. "How do you do, Mr. Glessit. Grandfather dear, I'm quite ready to perform my part in this affair. Ceremony perhaps we should all more appropriately call it? Yes, ceremony, I think."

Her grandfather beamed upon her, took her hand; John Constable Horne looked appealingly at Oscar Glessit as if to ask, "Don't you want to help me kill her?" but the lawyer kept his eyes to the contents of his brief-cases.

"Ceremony if you prefer, certainly, dear," Mr. Oaklin said. "Is your mother going to keep us waiting?"

"No." The young girl laughed. "No, just stopped for a last

touch before our Cinquecento silver mirror on the stairway landing. I gave her a yell, so she's practically here."

Mrs. Thomas Oaklin, Junior, came in slowly, a prettyish blonde woman too-plumply forty-five, not over-dressed or over-hairdressed but almost so, and self-pamperedly though languidly all in the top of the latest moment's fashion. She didn't speak to anybody; she nodded discontentedly at the room in general, sat down and looked toward the windows.

"That's right, Mother," Josephine said. "Just rest and listen, please. I think we can all begin now. What papers do I sign, Grandfather?"

He patted her hand. "Your signature's mostly garniture, I'm afraid; you're still legally a minor, dear. Your mother's is more important." He spoke to his daughter-in-law. "Folia, you understand that of course I don't need your consent or Josephine's to the building of a museum or anything else I choose to do during my lifetime; but Mr. Glessit thinks it might be useful, in view of any future contingencies, if you and she sign a statement. It's to the effect that you fully understand the museum project and approve of it, and also that you're both aware of the provisions in my will for the future maintenance of the museum and of the symphony orchestra, too. You agree that you and your daughter are provided for by separate deeds and bequests; that you fully consent to all provisions in the will, have no wish to alter any of them, and will never attempt to do so. You realize, don't you, that the will would stand anyhow and this is only an extra precaution of Mr. Glessit's?"

Mrs. Oaklin didn't answer, nor did she move; she continued to stare toward the sunlit windows across the room. Josephine, still upon the arm of her grandfather's chair, spoke warningly.

"Mother!"

Mrs. Oaklin's expression altered slightly, trending more toward the sulky, and Josephine spoke again.

"Mother!"

Mrs. Oaklin gave her a resentful glance but consented to speak. "To me it all seems rather peculiar. I don't ask anything for myself, I never have; but when I'm expected to sign away much the greater part of my only daughter's prospects in life——"

"Mother!" Josephine jumped from the arm of the chair, stood ominously stiff, facing the rebellious lady. "Didn't I tell you you're not signing away anything, because it's going to be done anyhow willy-nilly whatever you say and you'll only make an exhibition of yourself? Didn't you give me your consent, only last night when we had that argument, you'd accede to my absolute wishes in this matter, and Grandfather's? How many times have I got to tell you this museum is the object of my life and I'll carry it out to the last iota? Have I got to tell you again that——"

"No." Mrs. Oaklin suddenly looked whipped. "Don't tell me again. I've been very nervous ever since I lost your father, and I can't possibly go through any more of these scenes with you."

"Then step straight around that table and sign where Mr. Glessit shows you!"

Mrs. Oaklin, with an emotional heave, got herself up from her chair, went round the table and stood sacrificially beside the lawyer. At the same time the door opposite the fireplace was opened and a stout, horn-spectacled elderly woman, amiably expectant, stepped into the library from the passageway that led to Mr. Oaklin's art gallery. She was followed hesitantly by an older woman plainly in a state of awe.

"Mr. Glessit, this is my curator, Mrs. Hevlin," Oaklin said. "She's kindly brought her sister-in-law and they know the purpose of the statement they're to witness. So of course do my granddaughter and her mother; but I think you'd best read it aloud and let all four of them examine it for themselves before they affix their signatures." He was silent, looking tenderly and admiringly at Josephine as this process was followed.

She took full charge when the time came for Mrs. Oaklin to sign. "Sit right down here, Mother," Josephine said. "Write your name in full where I put my finger. You're supposed to sign even before I do, myself." Mrs. Oaklin, still reluctant, stood motionless. Josephine gave her a pat on the shoulder that was more a push than a caress. "Mother! I'm the person most concerned, not you, am I not, if I voluntarily and of my own act gladly make this sacrifice for the sake of art and Grandfather? You're only his daughter-in-law, not a blood-relation at all; so what are you hanging back for?"

Mrs. Oaklin sat and wrote. "Very well," she said badgeredly. "I only hope a day won't come when you'll bitterly reproach me for what you're making me do."

"Never!" The enthusiastic child's uplifted face was radiant. "Never! This is for the ideal that Grandfather and I both live for. It's for art. I'll never regret what I'm doing to-day if I live a thousand years!"

"Nobly spoken!" Her grandfather's aged face was almost as inspiredly brightened as was her youthful one. "Isn't that nobly spoken, John Horne?"

"Very, very," Mr. Horne replied, trying not to imply that he was aware of any grandfatherly infatuation. "I suppose the signatures of the witnesses complete this—this safeguard?"

Josephine smiled at him. "Aren't you forgetting something

rather important, Mr. Horne? The witnesses are only supposed to guarantee my and my mother's signatures, aren't they? So naturally both of ours would come first, wouldn't they? I haven't affixed mine. Such matters ought to follow in their proper order, oughtn't they, Mr. Horne?"

"Certainly," he said, and for a moment seemed to look into the long future wherein he was to be associated with Josephine in the management of the Thomas Oaklin Museum of the Fine Arts. "Certainly you sign before they do, my—my child."

Josephine took the pen from Oscar Glessit. "I do this, glorying in it!" she announced, sat, wrote her name; then sprang up, ran to her grandfather and threw her arms about him. "There! Are you happy? I am! Are you going to put it in the newspapers, Grandfather?"

"I suppose so—some sort of formal announcement within the next day or two."

"So it won't hurt if I mention it to people?"

"No, not at all, dear."

"Then——" She looked thoughtful. "I've got a few luncheon guests, you know, and as they're still probably around somewhere perhaps I better go back and try to keep them amused—unless there are some more documents I ought to sign? Of course if there are any other documents that ought to have my signature——"

"No, no; that's all," the old man said. "Run along, but come back to me here in the library later, after your young friends have gone."

"I will." She reached the door at a hop-skip-and-jump; then checked herself, turned and spoke, not only to her grandfather but to her mother, Mr. John Constable Horne, Mr. Oscar Glessit, Mrs. Hevlin and Mrs. Hevlin's sister-in-law. "This is a day long to be remembered by each and every one of us," she said; and went forth, walking solemnly.

Outdoors, near her practise "basket," she found two of her guests in a state of complaint while the other enjoyed himself. "He's just as big a pig as you are, yourself, Josephine!" Ella cried. "He hasn't given Sophie or me one single chance at the ball ever since you went in the house."

"Why should I?" the Elliston boy inquired. "You're neither of you any good. Look, Josephine, here's that shot you were braggin' about, how you used your wrist and everything. It's nothing. Watch me. Yippee!"

He threw; but Josephine didn't watch him. "To me," she said, "compared to the ceremony I've just performed my part in, shooting baskets is rather less than infantine. I've just been through a pretty emotional ceremony, so I feel pretty emotionally exhausted. I might tell you about it some time; but not now." She placed the tips of the fingers of her right hand against her forehead and tried to look wan. "No, not now, not now."

"Why not?" Sophie asked.

"Well—it seems almost years ago since I went in the house." Josephine let her forehead alone and became brisker. "It's been pretty exhausting but if I decide to tell you I give you my permission to let your fathers and mothers know about it and everybody you like, because now it's an open secret and's going to be in the newspapers practically right away. It changes my whole life, so——"

Sophie Tremoille interrupted. "You're going away to boarding school?"

"No!" Josephine was annoyed. "Boarding school! Diable!

Quelle bêtise! Jamie Elliston, put down that ball!" She ran at him, knocked the ball from his hands. "Listen, can't you?"

"To what? To you tryin' to squeak first-year French?"

Josephine pointed to the stone steps leading up to a side entrance in the wall of the art gallery. "Sit down there, all three of you." Then, when they'd gloomily obeyed her, she stood before them, clasped her hands upon her breast and looked at the sky. Jamie didn't care for the pose.

"Whatch doin'?" he asked. "Tryin' to look like Joan of Arc at the Battle of Bunker Hill?"

"Be quiet," she said dreamily. "I've given my life to a cause. That's what the ceremony was. Sophie, you and Ella can have love in your lives and bright homes and children and firesides. I used to think those things might be for me, too; but not any more."

The effect failed upon Ella. "No love? You mean you're giving Jamie the brush-off; he isn't to be the boy-friend any more?"

"I didn't say that exactly," Josephine admitted. "I don't mean I couldn't like any boy I want to or'd haf to stop Jamie from preferring me; but I've undertaken a terrific responsibility. Grandfather's going to build a tremendous Museum of the Fine Arts. It's going to fill almost the whole of our yard, from here clear across to North Walnut Street, and's going to be the intellectual center of our whole city and state."

"What?" Jamie asked listlessly. "Is that all? If your grandfather wants to go building buildings nobody's going to stop him."

Josephine became more natural. "I admit I get a kick out of you at dancing-class, old kid; but I've always known your brains are in your feet."

"Oh, are they?" he retorted. "So you say!"

"Can't you listen, Jamie? I haven't told the important thing yet. It's I've just officially done the biggest thing in my life so far. I voluntarily and of my own act and free will surrendered practically my whole fortune, and you being my three best friends I'll tell you the reason. It's because of how I love art and it ought to be brought to the public—and I'd rather run an art museum than be anything else in the world!"

Here she spoke with a sincerity that seemed to uplift her; but her friends didn't respond as she expected. The one she liked best was forthrightly disagreeable.

"Run a what?" Jamie said. "Look, you couldn't even run a little old gals'-school basketball team; they threw you out."

That hurt. Josephine's voice shook; but she faced the issue stoutly. "This is my reply: my grandfather has created me practically the head of the whole immense institution to be carried on from now through all the rest of my life. I'm practically almost in charge of it right now."

At that, the three guests, seated somewhat squirmingly in a row, showed more interest; but it was of the noisily incredulous kind. They didn't believe her; they frankly said they didn't.

Josephine looked down upon them angrily. "Did I claim I was officially the President of it yet? Grandfather's appointed Mr. John Constable Horne to be Chairman or whatever the title is; but that's a mere legal form because who's the one that's made the sacrifice of a whole birthright and fortune? Old Mr. Horne's only going to be practically a figurehead."

This brought but another demonstration of unbelief. "Josephine, you're only fourteen years old." Jamie, now upon his feet and gesticulative, tried to speak judicially. "Look, your grandfather's a respected old man all over the city. Why try to put it over that a man in his position would ever appoint a child of fourteen in charge of——"

"Not if you were the child!" Josephine said. "Nor Ella nor Sophie. No, I don't expect any of you children of fourteen to comprehend there's a pretty striking difference between fourteen and fourteen. Look at Lord Macaulay at fourteen, look at Mozart at fourteen, look at Schubert and Giotto and Milton and Leonardo and Juliet and——"

"Look at who?" Jamie had already lost his judicial poise. "Look at Old Dog Tray at fourteen! Look at a cage of fourteen chimpanzees all fourteen years old!" Abruptly he was morose, lowered his voice. "This is the sourest luncheon party I ever got sucked into. Thank you for the pleasure, I'm going home." He began to walk away.

"Wait!" Ella called. "So'm I. Excuse me, Josephine; but I scarcely believe a word you say, and kindly stop looking at me as if I was some low form of zoology."

"Ella," Josephine said thoughtfully, "you're quite the belle at parties and our dancing-class. The way you do it is you make the boys think all you think about's themselves, they're marvelous; so they admire you the most. Instead of being yourself, which'd irritate them, you please them to get them excited about you. It's cunning; but it's ignoble. That's my reply, Ella. Since you're going, good-bye."

"Thanks for your divine permission!" Ella produced this helpless retort and trotted after Jamie.

Sophie Tremoille lingered a moment. "Thank you for the nice lunch and everything, Josephine. I think they're rude; but I guess I better catch up with 'em. G'bye."

IV

Sᴏᴘʜɪᴇ ran to join the others, and, as the three walked down the curved driveway of crushed stone, she was a little regretful. "Listen, Jamie and Ella, look, she *is* an awfully important girl and terribly talented and everything. Maybe it's true her grandfather's doing all this, whatever it was about her and these art buildings and all that, so maybe we oughtn't to've——"

"Yes, we ought," Ella said crossly. "I don't care whether it's true or not, who cares about any old art museum and I scarcely like her at all any more."

"Don't you?" Sophie looked pensive. "I think I do, sort of. Anyway I'm always going to stick up for her. She can do awfully nice things. You know that gold-and-green enamel pin she had on last dancing-class we all admired so? Well, I was here next day and happened to begin talking about it again and she ran in the house and got it and gave it to me, and I knew from her looks she'd like to've kept it, herself. All these servants they keep around here, you can see they like her, too."

"Who pays 'em?" Jamie asked, and answered himself. "Her own grandfather—that's who—so they got to. She can order

'em around all she likes; but not me, no soap! The more you
go with her the more she acts like she's fifty or sixty Queen of
Shebas, and I don't care what she invites me to she makes me
so tired I'm never going to set another foot in her grandfather's
old grounds again!"

"What? You aren't?" Ella cried. The two young girls exchanged sensational glances. "You mean never? You mean
actually, Jamie?"

"That's what I mean. You bet!"

"But, Jamie, you can't say that," Sophie said. "Why, that's
practically terrible! Why, you're supposed to be practically her
own special!"

"Not from now on." He was dogged. "She's too much for
me and it's got so I just can't stand her. I just can't *stand* her,
I tell you! I'm through. I'm not going to be dragged around
at any old girl's chariot heels!"

The deserted Josephine had stood looking after them until
they passed round the far corner of the house on their way to
the street. For a time after they disappeared from her sight she
remained near the gallery steps, lost in a hurt wonderment, unable to understand why Jamie and Ella had taken so offended
and offensive a departure. Even the humbler Sophie hadn't
been very nice. Josephine didn't care terribly much how Sophie
or Ella behaved; but Jamie Elliston—that was different—and
he'd been outrageous throughout this whole memorable afternoon.

She knew of course that art was beyond Jamie, and the noble
conception of the museum above his understanding; but even
so he needn't have been too dumb to be proud of her, need he?
Perhaps she hadn't explained enough about her sacrifice of

all that money. After the triumphant scene in the library this was a pretty mean anti-climax and she couldn't fathom its cause. She took the problem to her grandfather, found him alone in the library with a half-empty glass of sherry on the table beside him. He was still a little flushed by recent pleasurable excitements and smiled upon her happily.

"I was waiting for you, Josephine. You and I have had a great afternoon, haven't we?"

"Yes, I suppose so." She sat upon a stool before him; but her lovely grey eyes were downcast.

"What's the matter, dear? You ought to be on tiptoe after what you and I've been doing together to-day. What's gone wrong?"

"Nothing." She clasped her hands about her knees but still looked at the floor. "Grandfather, why are people so queer?"

"What people?"

"Well, I mean people my own age."

"Oh, I see!" He was sympathetic. "You told your young guests about the museum, did you?"

"Yes, I did."

"And told them something of the costly difference it makes in your future, Josephine?"

"Well—I sort of——"

"I see," he said again. "So now you're wondering why our contemporaries usually aren't delightedly enthusiastic about us when we do something rather splendid? Your young playmates didn't respond to the news as you thought they would?"

"No. You'd almost have thought—— Why, you'd really have thought I was telling 'em something they didn't like."

Thomas Oaklin laughed sadly. "Yes, poor child. You'll have

to learn that people, especially our contemporaries, are seldom generous enough to warm up to us when we're shown to be their—well, let's frankly say their superiors. The crowd'll cheer the jockey who wins a race for them; but if they suspect any-one of being intellectually or artistically, or even morally, of a higher type than they are, they turn churl. I'm afraid that's what your young friends did with you."

"You think so?" At this, Josephine looked up and her eyes brightened suddenly. "I bet you're right; I bet that was the matter with 'em! You always understand things, Grandfather."

"No, I don't," he said. "I don't understand why envy and jealousy were put into this world. I only know they're here and that such people as you and I have to learn to seal our hearts so that they can't injure us."

"Seal our hearts? I like that idea, Grandfather. Yes; seal our hearts."

"Defend our heads, too," he added. "It's true that the higher you lift your head the more they'll throw bricks at it. You've just been finding out a little about that, haven't you?"

"I certainly have!" Josephine was more and more pleased. "They showed the most despisable sides of their natures—yes, and their awful dumbness, too. Why, Grandfather, intellectu-ally they're just the mere young of the animal kingdom. They've learned how to read and write and begin conjugating; but there they stop flat. Compared to what I know about art, for instance——"

She let a widely waved hand finish the sentence for her; but her grandfather took up the theme. "Compared to what you know about art, Josephine, you needn't expect even many grown people to show much competence. Think of all these books you've read—rare ones, by no means at everybody's disposal—and of all our discussions of them and our long talks together. Think of your life among our collections and our pilgrimages to galleries abroad." He sighed wistfully. "You'll be one of the true brand of connoisseurs by the time you're fully grown, dear—critic, expert and art historian all put together. I wish I could live to see it."

"But you will, Grandfather. You surely——"

"No." He lifted his right hand and let it fall resignedly upon the varicolored shawl over his knees. "My feeling for art, though, and my ideas will live on in you. You must remember that. I think I may last to see the building finished and my collections placed in it as I wish them; but—afterwards—well, you're my hope of survival."

"Am I, Grandfather?" He'd spoken with such gentle pathos that she was moved, almost tearful. "Am I truly that?"

"How else could it be, child?" he said. "My name will be over the portals of the museum; but the name only proves my pride that I loved art and my pride that I loved my city. The name's only stone; you'll be a living part of the museum—my granddaughter. You have a great heart and great talent—a great heart or you wouldn't have wished me to go ahead with the plan; you'd have wanted the inheritance all for yourself."

"No! No, I never wanted that." Josephine's emotion was still genuine. "I want to be a living part—oh, the very living spirit!—of the museum. It's exactly what I want, Grandfather."

"You'll find it your reward. Don't let anything interfere with it. Your experience of to-day may repeat itself, Josephine, because you're made of finer fibre than other people. You mustn't ever let the envies and jealousies of your inferiors affect you."

"No," she said softly. "I must remember that. Grandfather, it's like the quotation I found the day Mother called me a miserable snippet on account of what I said to her about her not appreciating our full-length Goya. Whenever I'm hurt I'll always seal my heart and—and I'll always 'sing high and aloof, safe from the wolves' black jaw and the dull asses' hoof.' "

The grandfather was thus given a moment of æsthetic and ancestral rapture. "Unbelievable!" he said. "No wonder your commonplace young companions don't understand you, Josephine—a girl of fourteen quoting dear Ben Jonson like that on the very subject of themselves! I began to hope for this when I lost your father. Now when my time comes I can depart in peace."

Josephine spoke in a whisper. "You mean because of—because of——"

"Yes, because of you. My museum is safe." He leaned forward and lightly touched the top of her head.

This was his blessing upon her —and upon their high and generous enterprise, too—and he let his fingers linger. During some moments the two held that pose, with the lozenges of sunshine falling upon them through the old glass of the Jacobean windows and gilding the aged white hand among the glowing fair curls of the granddaughter. The attitudes were of such traditional perfection that neither the aged man nor the young girl could have been wholly free of satisfaction with the tableau. Not alone the artist, even in his truest emotion, must be his own audience; those who live mainly in the light he sheds must share that histrionic lot.

"Oh, Grandfather!" Josephine still kept her voice to a whisper; tears were now full upon her lashes. "Art is sanctuary.

Our museum will be that, and I—oh, I'll be what you want me to!"

Thomas Oaklin gently withdrew his hand, leaned back smiling upon her in a profound content. "I know what you'll be," he said, and sublimely believed he did.

V

HEAT CENTERED UPON THE CITY as if through a vast yellow burning-glass. Noon was dangerous anywhere out of the shade, and, toward two o'clock on this airless day of the thunderous summer of 1943, August reached its hottest. The passengers who'd sagged into the trackless trolley-car downtown were sorry for themselves; but one of them extended some of her compassion to a fellow-sufferer.

"Look at the poor thing!" this Christian woman said. She was one of a pair of housewives who sat, baskets on laps, fanning themselves with Noon Editions. "Thank goodness he found a seat when those children got off. I was afraid if he didn't he'd drop flat and die on the floor."

"Who you mean, hon?"

"You hadn't noticed him? That poor soldier—the one four seats in front of us. See how thin the back of his neck is and between his shoulder blades. Must be terrible to come back wounded and limping to all this heat. Got quite a cultivated look, too, and see that nice brown hair. If he gets off before we do, you notice his face."

35

Thus, when the car stopped at Twenty-first Street, both stared at the young soldier who came down the aisle trying not to limp. "Did you see, hon—that expression they get from what they've been through?"

"I'll say! Those dark eyes all sunk back in his head looked as if he couldn't get away from it even back here at home." The car resumed motion. "Was he a lieutenant? I didn't get his insignia or service ribbons, I was so busy gandering at his face. He certainly had that look, poor soul!"

The pitied young soldier had been left at a street corner in a neighborhood of elderly houses, some of them smelling of recent noon meals for boarders and all of them less important than they once had been. He stood staring about him uncertainly; glanced back over one shoulder, then over the other with the pathetic distrust a lost dog shows upon ground always more and more perilously unfamiliar. Then, seeing that the two metal signs at right-angles on the corner lamp-post displayed each the name of a street, he peered at the names, sighed heavily and set off westward, limping more than a little upon the hot cement sidewalk of Twenty-first Street.

At the next corner he came to a north-and-south boulevard, crossed it and walked on before a lawn a full block in breadth. This lawn, shaped between bordering shrubberies, was the green approach to the stately long façade of an imposing building of pale grey limestone. A smoothly flagged path forty feet wide led from the sidewalk and across the lawn to the building's great pilastered and pedimented central entrance; the soldier came to a halt, wiped his neck and forehead and looked long and troubledly at the architectural magnificence before him.

The noble edifice faced south, and its classic effect was enhanced by corresponding pediments and their supporting tall pilasters at the eastern and western ends of its front; but at the eastern end an incongruity puzzled the eye of a stranger. Here, umbilically attached to monumental grandeur by a short stone passage, stood a dwelling-house older than the great building apparently its parent, and this paradoxical house was not only brick but most illegitimately of a Tudor-like design often in favor among millionaires at the turn of the century. The young man, easing his lame leg by his halt upon the sidewalk, gazed plaintively at the inappropriate mansion, plainly making nothing of it. Then his eyes slowly turned again to what had first held their attention when he'd stopped. Above the superb central portal and below its crowning pediment there was an eternal-looking inscription carved in stone:

THOMAS OAKLIN MUSEUM OF THE FINE ARTS
Anno Domini MCMXXXVII

As the soldier again read this uncontradictable announcement his lips moved, though not as if following those formidable stone words on high; he was whispering to himself, "Get on with it, can't you? You've *got* to! Get on!" He limped forward upon the flagged broad path, ascended the wide steps of the museum, passed between open ponderous bronze doors and found himself in a vast and stony hall floored with varicolored marble.

Before him, in the center of this space, there rose upon a black pedestal a single work of art: the sculptured stone figure of a youth, deeply pitted, footless and noseless but Archaic Greek. The museum, extending cavernously beyond open archways, seemed void of life; then in the wall at his right the young man perceived a cubbyhole with a narrow strip of lettering above it: PLEASE CHECK CANES AND UMBRELLAS. He went to the cubbyhole, looked through and saw a fragile old man asleep in a stiff chair. The soldier coughed deferentially; then more loudly, and, as this exertion produced nothing except itself, he spoke, though timidly.

"I beg your pardon. May I trouble you, please? Would you kindly tell me where——"

The slumber of the custodian continued to be sound. The soldier, thus easily disconcerted, turned away, glanced toward the sunshine beyond the bronze doors as if considering a retreat from the building; but again urgently whispered to himself and walked toward a majestic stairway opposite the entrance. He seemed about to ascend to a skylighted region where sculpture in marble could be glimpsed from below, white figures set against mellow tapestries; then more uncertainty prevailed and he went to an archway at his left.

Here he examined a small bronze tablet set into the wall, ORIENTAL ART, before he limped dubiously through the archway and was in a great room that disturbed him with its contents—human-like shapes, large and small, in scarred gilt bronze, in stone, in marble, in glazed baked earth and in carven wood. Many retained color and some of them were bland; others were illimitably ominous. They stood spaced against the walls, and after he'd advanced a few steps he stopped with a physical flinch, stood irresolute. He flinched again as a tremulous voice spoke to him and a stooping but fat old woman, with a soft feather dust-brush in her hand, came out from behind a life-sized Kuan-yin.

"Is there something I could show you?" she asked, beaming upon him through horn-rimmed spectacles. "We're delighted

to have soldiers interested in our collections. Maybe you've
been in the Orient, so this gallery especially appeals to you?
I'm Mrs. Hevlin, Curator of Oriental Art nowadays. I used
to be——" She paused and laughed apologetically. "Well,
that's neither here nor there. Was there something in particular you wanted to see?"

"I was looking for—for——"

"Maybe something in the gallery beyond this one?" she
asked with a hurrying eagerness. "It's so seldom I have a
chance to show anybody our treasures nowadays. You see, I
was in retirement; but the war's got the museum so short-
handed they've had to send for me." She renewed her apologetic laughter a little cacklingly. "Oh, yes, even for *me!* We
have a beautiful room just beyond, if you're looking for ceramics or—or jade? Our jade is heavenly—all in glass cases of
course; but if there's any piece your soul just screams to touch
—well, you're one of our soldiers and I'd gladly open the case
and——"

"No. Thank you very much; but I'm trying to find Mr.
Rossbeke."

"Oh, I'm sorry! I didn't understand. If you're a friend of
Mr. Rossbeke's——"

"Well—no," he said. "I don't—I've never met him. I have
an appointment with him, though."

"Oh, I'm sorry!" Mrs. Hevlin repeated this flutteringly and
in a vague way seemed agitated and a little soured. "Of course
I don't mean I'm sorry you have an appointment with Mr.
Rossbeke—the great Mr. Rossbeke! Of course as he's the Director of the Museum we all have to think he's a great man!
No doubt he is; I scarcely know him. You see, when I was retired and he took charge of everything—well, I needn't go into

that. Visitors to the museum aren't expected to be interested in these details."

"Well, I——" The young soldier looked helpless; this fat old woman-curator seemed as nervous and scatter-minded as he was, himself. "I found the museum all right—a hotel clerk told me how to get here; but that old man in the checkroom's asleep and I didn't like to—I mean, as you say, that's another of these details not expected to—I don't know why I'm talking about it—not important." He paused, aware that this conversation between two strangers in a gallery of Oriental Art was becoming too peculiar. "I—I believe I ought to be finding Mr. Rossbeke if I can."

"Oh, certainly!" Mrs. Hevlin was abruptly prim. "Go straight back, cross the big vestibule, then go through the Gallery of Mediæval Art—you'll see the tablet—and you'll come out in the east corridor. The first door in that corridor will take you into the Director's office."

"Thank you."

The young man returned by the way he'd come, crossed the vestibular hall, passed through an archway tableted MEDIÆVAL ART and was again among disturbing shapes. They were as exotic as those he'd just left but more angular and austere. Traces of ancient red and blue and gilding lingered upon some of the carved grim Madonnas, gaunt saints and narrow angels; color was even violent upon a few of the embossed panels and framed mosaics here and there on the walls. Then, as the soldier limped along, he came less uneasily into an area of monastic benches, old black choir stalls, stained glass, and glass cases displaying browned illuminated manuscripts and marginally illustrated psalters and missals. Beyond loomed another archway, and, passing through it, he was in a transverse corridor and saw in the wall opposite him a paneled old oaken door somebody had left ajar.

He knocked upon the door but had no answer. Venturing to open it more widely, he found before him what seemed to be a short hallway leading to another oaken door, which also stood ajar as if somebody'd lately passed through both of these doors in haste. Beyond the second a strip of fine interior could be seen—darkened wood panelings, diamond-shaped leaded panes of glass in a deeply recessed window, rising shelves of richly bound tall books. Evidently this farther door led into somebody's library.

He advanced, knocked again, and an angry-looking girl appeared in the aperture. He had an impression of blonde hair, lipstick, a diamond clip near a tanned throat, grey eyes that didn't look upon him as a person.

"Haven't you sense enough to know nobody's permitted through this way?" she said fiercely, and she added the sound "*Uff!*" as if the public's stupidities were spoiling her life.

The door was banged—at his face—and there was the intentional clatter of a bolt upon the other side. He comprehended that the hallway in which he stood was the stone passage he'd seen from outdoors, the link between the museum and that attached incongruity, the overshadowed brick mansion.

He went back, and, again in the corridor, saw facing him a more office-like door, half of opaque white glass. Small-lettered upon the glass was the name "Mr. Rossbeke." A woman's voice, "Come in," responded to his abashed tap here, and he entered a spacious room dominated by a long table laden with big books and portfolios; but what he saw first, through wide windows, was an inner court just outside where trees grew and a fountain played—a pink marble old Italian fountain that sprayed iridescence coolly high into the hot air. He wished that he could stand in the falling water, stay in it till after dark.

He glanced but flickeringly at the middle-aged woman who sat at a desk in sole occupancy of the room. "I think—I think Mr. Rossbeke's expecting me," he said in a low voice. "I—— My name is Bailey Fount."

She was a pleasant-looking woman and proved affable. "Yes, Mr. Fount. There's a caller; but I think he's about going."

"Thank you." Bailey Fount, already made aware by vehement sounds from an open inner doorway of the office that there was indeed a caller, went to a spindle-legged settee against the wall, sat and fanned himself with his cap.

The excited voice from Mr. Rossbeke's private room grew louder. "I am beink made seek! Can I go on liffing in a such atmosp'ere of bossness? Rossbeke, I comed to spik a little with you as a colleague in the arts and poum-bang! *who* boops in, sees me, what happens? I would not comed here except I think they are out of town all summer."

Another voice, also a man's, uttered a melancholy laugh and spoke. "She's only home for a day. That's a great advantage. She'll be off for the St. Lawrence again to-morrow, so——"

"Rossbeke, Rossbeke, one day is too long! You heard. Shouts me, 'Parannik, Parannik! Parannik, take care; last season you played too much classics.' Too much classics! Is it a persecushion!"

The other voice was placative. "Oh, well! You heard what she just said to me, too."

"Did I hear? You, Rossbeke, the Director of the Museum,

how can you listen and still be patient? Me, I can't do it; I can't be polite. I must conduct a symphony orchestra in a city only two-hunder-fifty-souzand people and when it's war. If I play what she tells me, who comes? Can I play wizout somebody listen? Is my orchestra for her alone? I say no; I say no like hell! Where is my hat?"

"You're going, Parannik?"

"Home to my bass-tub. Crazy people doctors put in bass-tubs to quietenate them. I was crazy hot and now I am crazy crazy. I am runnink to bass-tub! Good-bye!"

Parannik, a lean blond man in limp white clothes, his hair disordered, brilliant eyes agonized under imperceptible eyebrows, came forth stampingly, strode through the outer office, paused at the corridor door to shout "Oh! Oh!" and departed.

The middle-aged woman at the desk glanced companionably at the young man upon the settee, hoping that he was as amused as she; but he was looking into his cap, unaware of his privilege in being witness to an intimate mood of a celebrated personage. "Ah, yes," she thought. "Coming out of it must be harder for too many of them than even getting into it was." She spoke cordially: "I'm sure Mr. Rossbeke'll be glad to see you now, Mr. Fount."

VI

HENRY ROSSBEKE, a stoutishly handsome man of fifty, had the look of slightly wearied scholarship that is sometimes like a frosty coating upon lifelong probers into the arts; but there was no frostiness in his reception of Bailey Fount.

"Hurrah, so you're here!" He came forward, almost shouting, hand outstretched, as the young soldier entered the inner room. "Sit down; sit down. I'm delighted to meet you and so'll we all be. We'll do our best to make you comfortable among us." He went to the doorway. "Mrs. Williams, please call up Miss Jyre. She'll be in the upper southwest gallery, or perhaps among the Primitives. Tell her Mr. Bailey Fount's arrived. You had a pleasant journey, I hope, Mr. Fount?"

"It—it was all right, sir," Bailey Fount said in his jerkily hesitant way. "Yes, I—well, I—— Of course I know I *look* pretty queer, so probably anybody in the train that noticed me must have wondered what was the matter with me. They must have thought——"

"Nonsense! Of course they didn't. The uniform—if nothing else—answers that idea, Mr. Fount."

44

"Well, I——" The young man seemed to have forgotten the invitation to sit; then saw another spindle-legged settee, abruptly went to it, sat, and began to twiddle with his cap, keeping downcast eyes upon it. "No, thank you, sir," he murmured, responding to the offer of a cigarette. "I mean—I mean not now, thank you."

"I'll be glad to have you come here whenever you do care to smoke." Rossbeke sank into an easy-chair near his desk. "It's the only place in the building where one can. Another thing I believe I ought to mention at once, Mr. Fount: we'll see that your work in the museum shan't keep you on your feet too much of the time. One of the letters about you I've had from my dear old friend, Frank Bedge, explained that your wounded leg——"

"It's coming all right, sir." Bailey Fount glanced up for an instant. "Colonel Bedge is a great doctor as well as—as well as a lot of other things."

"Isn't he, though!" Rossbeke agreed heartily. "A grand old soul, Frank Bedge, and his particular interest in you turns out to be a bully thing for what's left of us here. We had a rather youthful staff; the war's taken nine-tenths of the male side of it, and the Waves and Wacs have left us almost as under-womaned as we are undermanned. Don't make any mistake, we look upon you as a godsend."

"What? Oh, no! I—I'm afraid——" This disjointed mutter from the settee was almost inaudible. "I don't know if I'll do at all. Most likely not."

"Oh, but you will!" Rossbeke remained cheerful. "I've gone into all that with Frank Bedge by letter. You'll get onto things here easily; don't worry. Most of your work'll be simple routine and you'll be associated with a delightful woman, Helena

Jyre. She's our Curator of Paintings and, as Assistant Curator, you'll be under her wing. I think you'll find that agreeable. In fact, I'm pretty confident you'll like all of us—the staff, that is." The Director paused, flushed a little, spoke impulsively and with feeling. "We hope so because we're proud—very proud, Mr. Fount—to have you with us."

"No! No! Oh, no!" The young soldier glanced up again and his right hand left the twisting cap to make a zigzag wave of protest. "Not that! No, sir, not——"

"We are, though. We're all proud to have you here. It may be hard on your modesty; but I must say it. War heroes don't grow on every tree and——"

"No! No! I'm not one! I can't——"

"Don't fear, I won't press it," Rossbeke assured him. "I just had to say it once, for all of us; but it's done, so be easy. Besides, I think you'll begin to like your new job right now because there's Miss Jyre's voice saying hello to Mrs. Williams."

Helena Jyre, already entering, brought the briskest friendliness with her. About thirty and of a dark comeliness, she had the decisive manner of a competent woman made certain of herself by a thousand successful experiences. She reached the settee before Bailey Fount could get to his feet, though he tried. Her hand on his shoulder stopped him. "Don't ever get up for me. All those rules are off for you and me, Mr. Fount, we'll be so constantly together. Now perhaps Mr. Rossbeke'll introduce me to you."

The Director explained that this had already been done as a prelude to her entrance; she said that then she'd no doubt been described as a slave-driver, and for a few minutes she and Rossbeke maintained a light chatter to which the young man on the settee was no party. He seemed detached from everything except from an inner distress that he struggled not to reveal—and his two new friends shared the sympathetic embarrassment of people who try to brighten things up but know they're not succeeding. Miss Jyre turned from the Director to the silent settee.

"Mr. Fount, I hope you feel the rightness of your being here as much as Mr. Rossbeke and I were just telling each other we do. What could be more appropriate than your becoming Assistant Curator of Paintings precisely here? Except for Thomas Oaklin, this city wouldn't have an art museum at all—no more than it would have a symphony orchestra, for that matter. Except for Thomas Oaklin, the museum wouldn't exist. So for you to join a staff of people who wouldn't be doing this lovely work except for your family——"

"My family? Why—why, no. They didn't have anything to do with—I mean I didn't—I'm not——"

"Oh, yes, you are!" Miss Jyre insisted gayly. "This is the Thomas Oaklin Museum, and Thomas Oaklin was certainly your uncle, wasn't he?"

"No, he was my—my great-uncle."

"Exactly!" she cried. "So of course you ought to be just where you are—on the staff of the museum he built. It adds to our prestige; we're going to brag about it."

The young soldier's thin hand was protesting again. "He was only my great-uncle; I don't think I ever even saw him. Besides, I—I think I—— Didn't Colonel Bedge write you I haven't had any museum experience? I told him he'd better. You see, I keep thinking I mightn't—mightn't do."

Miss Jyre laughed. "No fear! We know all about it—for instance, that before the war you'd begun to do pretty well at painting, Mr. Fount. A one-man show in New York at the age of twenty-five has never been very usual, has it? Colonel Bedge's letters also went into details about your art-courses in college and——"

"Yes, I know, but——" He was only the more doubtful. "There are other things, too. Did Colonel Bedge make it clear that I might have to leave at—at any time—without previous notice? I'm to report back to him for examination as soon as I feel pretty sure, myself, that I could pass one, and if Mr. Rossbeke, too, thinks I can. Is that——"

"All understood," Miss Jyre assured him. "Colonel Bedge knew what he was about in sending you here, and Mr. Rossbeke and I know what we're about, too. Trust us for that, can't you?"

"I hope so—thank you," he said humbly. "When would you like me to begin to try to see if I'll do? I suppose I ought to get started. To-morrow?"

"To-morrow's splendid," Rossbeke said.

"Well——" Bailey Fount glanced at the door. "I'd better get ready. I'll be moving along. I thought perhaps if I could find a room somewhere near here——"

"You can," Miss Jyre informed him. "You see, as we've been expecting you, we thought you wouldn't mind if we rather arranged for that. There's a pleasant sort of *pension*—I suppose it's really a boarding-house—only three blocks from the museum, and the food isn't bad. It's called The Cranford and I live there, myself, if you don't mind."

"No, I'd be glad." His wasted cheeks flushed. "I mean——"

"Don't take it back! Here, I'll write the address." She took a memorandum book from her skirt pocket, sat down beside him, wrote with a pencil, tore out the slip and gave it to him. "They have a room waiting for you, if you like it. The town's rather crowded, so I took the liberty of asking them to hold it, to see. The windows look out into nice trees."

"You're very kind. Thank you. I——" He rose, stood hesitating, again examining his cap. "Perhaps you could tell me— I've never been in this town before. I believe I still have some relatives living here. My mother used to speak of them when she was talking about my great-uncle. They were the widow of his son, my mother's first-cousin, Thomas Oaklin, Junior— Cousin Folia, my mother called her, and I think she had a daughter. If you happen to know them——"

"Yes, we do." It was the Director who spoke, and the glance he exchanged with Miss Jyre wasn't seen by Bailey Fount because of the preoccupying cap. "We both know your cousins, Mrs. Oaklin and—and her daughter—very well."

"Then will you——" Bailey interrupted himself. "I've never met them; but I've thought perhaps they'd think I ought to call on them. I suppose it's a sort of duty. Maybe as I'm starting the work here to-morrow—maybe I'd better go this afternoon and get it over with. If you'll tell me where they live——"

"Yes, right here," Rossbcke said, and for the moment his cordial aspect and that of his colleague, Miss Jyre, underwent the almost imperceptible stiffening that takes place when self-controlled people share an effort to withhold a mutual emotion from expression. "They live almost in the museum itself."

"They do?"

"Yes. As you came in from the street didn't you notice that house—unfortunately brick, with half-timbering and stucco for the gables? Didn't you notice that it's fastened to the museum by a passageway?"

"Yes, I did. I wondered how it'd happened."

"It happened because your great-uncle lived there," Ross-beke said. "A part of this eastern wing we're in was originally his private gallery; but after he'd built the museum and dedicated it to the public he still wanted to come in and browse among the works of art whenever he liked, so he kept the passageway. When he died he left the house to his granddaughter for her lifetime. After that it's to be torn down; but she and her mother still live there."

"They do?" The response was listless. "I think I must have got into that passageway, trying to find your office. Somebody told me not to come through there."

Miss Jyre laughed. "Yes; it's strictly a limited thoroughfare. They can come in to see us; but if we museumites have to see them we're supposed to go round outside to their front door."

"So that's how I'd better go?" Bailey asked. "If I'm to get through with this call on them perhaps I——"

"You don't need to bother with it." Miss Jyre spoke quickly. "The house is practically closed and there's nobody there but a caretaker. Your cousins have a summer place on the St. Lawrence and they usually don't get back here till the end of September. So you can postpone——"

Rossbeke intervened, somewhat as if his conscience made him do so. "It just happens that Miss Oaklin is there. I believe only for to-day. In fact, a while ago she was in here and——"

"Oh, she was?" Helena Jyre said, and added reflectively, "She was, was she?"

"Yes." Rossbeke looked at her as if casually. "Parannik had dropped in and there was quite a talk. So I suppose she'd probably be at home now if Mr. Fount feels that he ought to——"

"Well——" The young man's forehead showed a vague distress; he may have been remembering the girl who was brusque with him in the passageway. "If it's only the daughter that's home I might postpone it, mightn't I?" The appeal was to Miss Jyre. "Some other afternoon I could just ring the bell and leave my name with the caretaker, couldn't I? That would look as if I'd tried to see them, wouldn't it? Do you think that would be all right, Miss Jyre?"

She spoke brightly, covering a throb of compassion. "What could be righter? Of course it would."

"Then maybe I'd better be getting along to go and see that room and bring my things from the hotel. I—— You've both been so very kind I——"

"No, we haven't," Miss Jyre said as she saw his hands return to their persistent work upon his cap. "I've got enough gas in my car parked behind the museum. I'm going to take you to The Cranford, then to the hotel to get your things, then back to The Cranford."

"Oh, no, I couldn't let you!"

"Yes, you could," she said. "You'd better begin to get used to my being your immediate boss, hadn't you?"

"I know; but *I* mustn't begin by being a burden. You're both so very kind I——"

"Not we!" She filled the gap his faltering left. "You're going to be a life-saver in an almost manless museum." She cosily took his arm. "Come along. Thank heaven we'll get at least a breath of coolness in the car, if we don't melt on the way to it!"

Prattling of the hot weather she led him forth, and Henry Rossbeke, alone, sat in smoking meditation until he'd finished a cigarette; then he left his office, attended to small duties in various parts of the building, wherein were not half a dozen visitors, and returned to the desk in his private room. He was slowly re-reading a letter when Helena Jyre came in, dropped into a chair, tried to fan herself with a handkerchief and moaned, "The poor thing! Oh, the poor thing!"

"Did you get him established?"

"At The Cranford? Yes, he liked it and he'll rest there all afternoon. It's a nice room; but he'd have said he liked anything, I'm afraid. Pathetically grateful. This museum's been too much a shelter from the war—for us; he brings it home. He must have been an alert and vigorous man before this happened to him."

"Or he wouldn't have survived at all," Rossbeke agreed. "Pretty shattered. I wonder if he was always as shy as he seems to be now. I don't think I've ever met a shyer young man."

"That wasn't shyness!" Miss Jyre spoke with sudden vehemence. "It's fear—fear he'll go to pieces! I tell you, when I sat down on that settee beside him I could feel it trembling. You don't see the tremble when you look at him; yet all the time he's holding himself in so tight that he's shaking. Yes, enough to vibrate that settee. I felt it!"

Rossbeke took up the letter he'd been reading. "Here's more from Frank Bedge in my morning's mail: 'Young Fount will probably be along about the time you receive this. Do get him into the museum work as soon as possible and see that it runs placidly for him. No excitement, no shocks, not even little ones. For his particular case I'm relying on you to furnish the best therapeutics in sight. It ought to come out all right.' You see, Bedge is confident, Helena."

"What else does he say?"

Rossbeke read again. " 'Don't let the museum's publicity department star Fount's special military exploit. After he began to get better he found out there'd been an account of it in some of the American papers, and it upset him. Like a good many thus glorified, he thinks it makes a fool of him; they're jumpy about it.' " Rossbeke looked up. "I discovered that, myself, Helena. I was indiscreet enough to say something to him about our pride in having a war hero here. He showed acute distress."

"Naturally he did. So would you or I in his place."

Rossbeke went on with the letter. " 'Fount has acquired a hypersensitiveness about eventually getting back into active service. He thinks that if he doesn't it makes him a quitter who can't take it. Amounts to an obsession. He understands that my hospital's right to send him off like this for a recuperation that'll need an indefinite time; but he's got the fixed idea that if it doesn't fit him to return to combat duty he'll never be fully a man again. That's why I didn't insist upon his accepting a disability discharge. He was so stricken when I suggested it——' " Interrupted by a sound from the sympathetic Helena, the Director looked up. "What's the matter?"

"Nothing." She controlled her voice. "Go on with the letter."

Rossbeke resumed his reading: " 'So stricken when I suggested it I decided he should have his chance. Regulations require a renewal of leave every thirty days; I've arranged those details with him. I want him to think about the war as little as possible. In public, of course, he'll have to be in uniform; but if he wears it in the museum visitors are likely to ask questions, talk about the war and set him back. Arrange for him to do his work—that is, all the time he's inside the museum—in civilian clothes. What Fount needs is tranquillity, tranquillity, tranquillity! No emotional jolts but precisely the cheerful busy background, quiet atmosphere and congenial work of an art museum. I trust him to you.' "

" 'Tranquillity'!" Miss Jyre uttered a sardonic gasp. "Dr. Bedge puts the cure up to our cheerful background and quiet atmosphere, does he? It's a pity he never saw the place. Tranquillity! When summer's over, heaven help us!"

VII

A THUNDER SHOWER CAME UP out of the southwest late that afternoon, and Bailey Fount, shiveringly despising himself, lay on his bed at The Cranford, face down, his head under a pillow. The uproar and the flashing passed, leaving the air temporarily cooled; he rose, sat by his window and stared blankly out at the glistening leaves of the trees Miss Jyre had promised him. The room was pleasant, even cheerful, had been done by somebody with an eye for color and for furniture; but to the cowering mind of its present occupant it was a foxhole. After the shower had passed he felt temporarily safe there.

As long as he could be alone in this room, with the door closed, he wouldn't have to talk to anybody and nobody could look at him. He could even sit by a window and nobody could look at him, for the wet branches were thickly leafed and came close to the house. The trees rose from the side yard; he was glad that his room wasn't a front one where he'd have had to see the street if he looked out.

He was afraid. One reason was because he couldn't be sure of what he might do or say. The strain of this special fear relaxed when he was alone, but didn't leave him because pretty

55

soon he'd have to be again with people. They'd speak to him and there was no counting upon what he'd say in return—or even upon what he might say to somebody who didn't speak to him. He'd said something queer to the colored porter on the sleeping-car—he didn't remember precisely but it was something about stopping the train till it quit making all that noise —and the porter had looked at him, then hurried away down the aisle. This morning, moreover, what was that talk he'd had with the odd old fat woman, the museum's Curator of Oriental Art, and how well or ill had he got by with the kind Mr. Rossbeke and the even kinder Miss Jyre? He couldn't be sure.

Bailey Fount didn't know himself to be as a matter of course Bailey Fount; he didn't seem to be just one person. It was as if within him were unreliable strangers who couldn't be trusted to say the right, ordinary things but might at any moment become irresponsible, babble, startle listeners. He had carefully to think beforehand of every word he was going to say, almost of every movement before he made it. He didn't feel himself to be a natural part of human kind; he felt out of the herd, disqualified for fellowship, and just to shake hands with anybody seemed a false pretense. Apparently he was made of many separate pieces that weren't holding together—like a watch that couldn't keep time any more, and what's a watch for?

One part of him was all the while bitterly contemptuous of the condition in which the other parts of him were. Those weakling parts, the strong and contemptuous part of him thought, had made him unfit to face what other men were standing up to; he'd never again be a man at all unless he could go back, a soldier, to stand beside them again. To do that he had indeed to pull himself together—or be pulled together by somebody else. The main thing—the first thing—was to get over this eternally apprehensive thinking about himself. If he couldn't do that he was gone, and most humbly he wanted all the help he could find. Mr. Rossbeke and Miss Jyre, no doubt well coached by letters from Colonel Bedge, had seemed to understand—anyhow a little. Perhaps with them, afterwhile, he needn't be afraid of himself.

Within the trees there was a quiet sound of diminished dripping; airless outdoors grew warm again and shiny leaves took rosiness from the western sun. There came a tapping upon Bailey's door. He started, muttered at himself for doing so, and opened the door. Miss Jyre, cool in a pinkish print dress, was smiling upon him from the hall.

"I've come to give you a choice, Mr. Fount. We Cranford-ites all eat at small tables in the big dining-room downstairs and I've arranged for you to sit at mine. The others at that table are only a comfortable elderly couple and one of my fellow-spinsters, a librarian—all of 'em easy to get on with. So if you feel you'd rather, you'll hear a dinner gong pretty soon and I'll be waiting for you in the lounge downstairs."

"Thank you. I——"

"Wait," she said. "I promised you a choice; but I'm afraid it doesn't include an escape from me. Before I came home this afternoon Mr. Rossbeke remembered he'd asked the head of the museum to dine with him to-night—our boss, you know, Mr. Horne. He's been just as much interested and pleased by your coming to join us as the rest of us are. Mr. Rossbeke thought it might be pretty nice if you and I'd come along and have dinner with them, especially as Mr. Horne's anxious to meet you."

"To meet me?" Bailey looked dismayed. "I don't think I'd better——"

She laughed quickly. "Nobody needs to worry about meeting Mr. John Constable Horne. He's the best old soul alive and as easy as an old shoe. He's a terrific talker, so all that the rest of us need do is eat and listen. Besides, he said he knew your mother and she was a grand woman."

"Yes, she was; but I'm afraid—I'm afraid I'd better not——"

"I think you'd like it," Helena Jyre said. "I know how you feel about meeting people. I often feel that way, myself, all jittered up and just wanting to hide."

"You do? You—you feel that way sometimes, Miss Jyre?"

"Why, of course! Everybody does—sometimes." She was persuasive. "We've all got to get used to being with people, though, don't we?—even when at first it seems a little appalling. There'll be only one other guest, an amusing man, Mr. Parannik, our orchestra conductor, and the food'll be the best in town. Mr. Rossbeke's a widower, you know. The restaurant's on the ground floor of the apartment house where he lives, and his table will be in a sort of alcove where we can be pretty private to ourselves. Probably we'll have coffee in his living-room upstairs. It's only a step or so from here and really might be less bothersome than going into The Cranford's dining-room and meeting the people at our table. Still, I said I'd brought you the choice, so it's up to you."

"No—I'll—I'll leave it to you."

"I hoped you would! We'll join Mr. Rossbeke. I'll be waiting for you downstairs in ten minutes."

"Yes—I'll come."

At the table in the alcove Bailey sat with his back to the main part of the restaurant; but he could hear the murmur of

numerous voices behind him, and, though he knew that the
diners were busy with their own concerns, he didn't feel much
protected from them. At first, when he sat down, he felt an
actually quivering need of shelter even from Miss Jyre and
Mr. Rossbeke, as well as from Mr. Parannik and that un-
formidable old personage, the Chairman of the museum's
Board of Trustees.

"Fine boy! Fine boy!" Mr. Horne had said at once. "What
I'd have expected from knowing your mother—yes, and your
father, too; though I never had much chance to see anything
of him before they moved away. No wonder you turned out to
be a painter—until the Army got you. You'll get back to the
gummy old color tubes some day, of course."

Bailey stammered that he thought not; but Mr. Horne returned to the subject as they were finishing their jellied gumbo.

"I saw one of your landscapes reproduced somewhere two
years ago, young fellow," he said. "Looked promising. Maybe
better than promising. About the age of poor Bonington when
he did his best, aren't you? Oh, yes, you'll go back to it! Never
knew of any landscape painter that quit cold, unless it was
Hobbema. Of course you'll be at it again some day. Not now,
not now. Take it easy a while, what?" He laughed as if at some
inner information. "Nothing to disturb you much in the way
of visitors to our museum, I promise you! That uncle of yours'd
be surprised, wouldn't he?"

"You mean my—my great-uncle, sir?"

"Who else? Old Tom Oaklin, certainly. What's an art museum for, Rossbeke?"

The Director shook his head. "Ask Helena. She's got it all
set—in her own mind."

"Yes," Helena Jyre said. "I think your question's wrong,

Mr. Horne. You say, 'What's an art museum for?' I think you
should ask, 'For whom is an art museum?' "

"Oh! Oh! Always the museum!" This was Parannik. "You
talk museum, museum, museum! Better ask for whom is my
orchestra? I tell you they both are for avverybody, all the people—and how many take what we want to give them? Don't
answer or you are goink to distress me."

"At that, you do better than we," Rossbeke said. "You've
just heard our President telling our new Assistant Curator of
Paintings he won't be bothered by many visitors to the museum.
Our attendance for the whole of last month was about four
hundred. Of course it was July and wartime—but four hundred out of a population of two hundred thousand—call it two
hundred and fifty thousand now, with the war plants—four
hundred out of something like a quarter of a million! Think
of it!"

"I do," John Horne said cheerfully. "I suggest to Mr. Fount
it's a joke on his uncle. Some people think a museum's purpose
is the preservation of works of art. All right; but as this finicky
gal just said: Preserve 'em for whom? Some people think art's
for an élite; some think it's for the general vulgar and some
think it's for both. Well, since nobody can intelligibly say, except to himself, what art is, who the devil's entitled to decide
either what or whom it's for? Care to answer, Rossbeke?"

"No, I don't." Rossbeke drank cold white wine from a
chilled glass. "Too hot."

"Too hot a subject!" The old man grunted chucklingly.
"People are scared to talk about art unless they know beforehand you agree with 'em—afraid they'll get their feelings
lacerated. Funny thing! We're jumpier about our own peculiar
little art tastes and opinions than about the condition of our

souls. Oh, yes, me too! Disagree with me about a painter and I'll be madder at you than if you aspersed the honor of my grandmother. Are you like that, too, Bailey Fount?"

"I suppose so, sir."

"Why, certainly! Let's get back to your uncle. Old Tom Oaklin didn't give much of a damn whether or not students of art history came to dig in his museum or if a few æsthetes might wander in, either—no, nor for schoolteachers to hustle gangs of children to get bored and romp in the Oaklin galleries. Your uncle had a rarefied old vanity, young feller. What Tom Oaklin wanted was to perpetuate himself in a gift to the populace."

"Was that all, sir?" Bailey was able to look up from his plate. "Just to perpetuate himself?"

"Oh, there was generosity in him, too! He knew that art's a sort of secret from the public; but that anybody—anybody at all—can discover the secret if he lets himself look at works of art a little attentively and that thenceforth he'll live much more happily than other people will. Poor old Tom! He called art his Philosophers' Stone because his own discovery of it transfigured his life. Knew it could be the same with anybody else; so he thought all he had to do was to put his collected art into a magnificent setting, give it to the people and they'd rush to take the gift. They didn't, Mr. Fount. They didn't and they don't. They——"

Helena Jyre interrupted. "Sometimes they do. They come to our special exhibitions and they like our lectures and chamber music concerts. Then remember that Renaissance Loan Exhibition we had——"

"Miraculous!" Mr. Horne laughed loudly. "That exhibition had forty-one hundred visitors in four weeks, about two per cent of the population! Why did even that poor many come? Because our newspaper publicity mentioned that the paintings and sculptures in that exhibition had cost the owners three million dollars. Anywhere in America a lot of people'll go look at anything that cost three million dollars. I would, myself. No, Mr. Fount, our museum's a joke on your uncle."

"Did he see it?" Bailey surprised himself by finding voice to ask this. "I mean—I—— Was he able to see the joke, himself, sir?"

"Didn't live long enough to be killed that way. We had a tremendous opening—Governor, both Senators, Mayor, a crowd from all over the state. Then it slacked off and he died thinking that was only temporary. Just as well, wasn't it? So what's the answer to the great question and to the joke on the poor old fellow? It's this: art is for those who can take it, and anybody can take it who's willing to expose himself to it. If the people don't care to put that interest and happiness into their lives, we can't force 'em or even coax 'em to it. It's their loss. We don't repine."

Parannik looked gloomy. "You will some day. Some day nobody at all will come and not a human beink will sit to hear my orchestra. My wife telephones me six o'clock from mountains hotel she have just been long-distanced from here that my comink season concert program it's punk. Punk. Oh, yes, punk! Must I always breathe poison? Oh, yes, and you too— you are goink to see! You all know what I mean."

Bailey Fount of course didn't know what he meant; but he perceived that the others did. They looked darkened, as if by something that shouldn't have been brought out of a background momentarily forgotten. They were like people determined to be gay for an evening but indiscreetly reminded of death and taxes. Rossbeke's face, always remotely careworn, became more vividly so; then he heaved a half-humorous sigh, threw off the shadow and called Parannik "Banquo!"

"Who is that?" Parannik asked. "Somebody from Shakespeare? If I can remember which from the operas from Shakespeare has a Banquo in it——"

"There it is!" Mr. Horne, also throwing off the shadow, was delighted. "Parannik can't remember anything unless he gets his reminder out of music. The American people can't remember anything unless they get reminders out of the movies. They know Anne Boleyn's head came off; they know it because there was a movie about that professional husband, Henry. They remember Rembrandt because there was a movie about him. How can we expect 'em to come into a museum and look at Old Crome until there's a movie about him?—and there never will be. You're a landscapist. What do you think of Old Crome, Bailey Fount?" He didn't wait for an answer. "What do you think of Theodore Rousseau? What do you think of Hercules Seghers? What do you think of Cotman and Girtin and Turner? Ah—and what do you think of John Constable?"

"I?" Bailey reddened. "What do I—— I'm only a painter, sir. I mean I'm not a critic. I like all of them—in their periods. I think they—they——"

He didn't need to struggle further; he was interrupted. Parannik, who faced the main part of the restaurant, suddenly exclaimed *"Oh! Oh!"* and sat motionless.

Helena Jyre, next to Bailey, turned her head and, like Parannik, Rossbeke and the aged Horne, stared into the restaurant. The expressions of all four were unanimous: they saw something that disturbed them; but Bailey Fount, glancing jerkily over his shoulder, found nothing in view to explain their plain perturbation.

Most of the tables were occupied by summer-clad middle-aged men—probably their wives and families were cooling by lakes or the sea—and, as it happened, only one woman was visible from the alcove. She'd just sat down, facing the other way, and was obviously young, though Bailey saw nothing of her except her back hair, her neck and the top of her bare shoulders. The hair was golden, glisteningly waved close to her head; the neck and shoulders were tanned and gracefully expressive; she seemed already to be talking animatedly. Her escort, just taking the seat opposite her, was an officer, sturdy in figure, not without agreeable good looks and, at this moment, most devoted in manner. Dimming the other diners, a superiority in worldly distinction seemed to shine about the couple. The fat sexagenarian headwaiter beamed above their "reserved" table, upon which he'd set flowers; he was in a flurry of paternal subservience.

"Call me Banquo some more!" Parannik exclaimed. "Still here! The Captain again!"

Rossbeke laughed, though perhaps with an effort. "It's only the one day's visitation. Departure to-morrow. How'd you like to write the views about museums you've just been expressing, Mr. Horne? We could use it in our September Bulletin."

The Director began to urge this, the others stopped staring into the restaurant, and tension seemed to lessen. Bailey Fount wondered what in the world these art-people had to do with an army captain and how a man so frank and friendly in countenance could have brought an oppression upon them.

Everything mystified Bailey, however. His thoughts, incurious about other people—except for his fear of his effect upon them—didn't follow the conversation but hovered among his timidities. He liked old Mr. Horne and Rossbeke and Helena Jyre and Parannik. They were much the sort he'd mostly lived with before the war, and, though he'd never cared to "talk art," he wished that he could join in their familiar chatting as once—before the war—he'd have been readily able. He couldn't now; he couldn't even eat confidently of the excellent dishes or risk a glass of wine—it might excite him. Self-consciousness was on him like the plague; indeed he knew it for a disease, and he couldn't change the posture of his feet under the table without wondering if the others noticed the movement and what they thought of it.

Miss Jyre, Mr. Horne and Rossbeke shop-talked on, mildly teasing one another, including Bailey with a reference or a question now and then but careful never to do so pressingly. Parannik had no share in this. He hadn't revived; he sat silent, eating little and frowning at what was set before him. Ices were brought; he looked indignantly at his, gave the dish a hostile push and said, "No! It makes me hotter after. I am too hot." He gazed strangely out through the alcove opening, and Bailey thought he was looking again at the mysterious captain. "I cannot stay. I cannot sit here. I must go."

Rossbeke protested. "But we're all going up to my rooms for coffee in a moment or two. Can't you——"

"No, I don't wait." Parannik rose, threw his napkin upon the table as if with violence, ran agonized supple fingers through his pale hair. "Avverythink I had to eat rolls more in a ball in me avvery second I am here! 'Punk'! I am punk musician. I create a punk program. If I stay one minute longer in this place I am goink to die."

"Sit down," Mr. Horne said commandingly. "We'll be up in

Rossbeke's apartment within a few minutes, don't you understand? Sit down!"

"No. A few minute' more it's too late; I will be det! Can *you* sit where is somebody call you punk? Me, not one second more! No! Excuse me, good-bye!"

His chair scraped the floor, he strode from the alcove, passed drivenly through the restaurant, and was gone.

VIII

We'll have to forgive Parannik," Rossbeke said ruefully. "Quite a lot of the finest artists seem to spend a good part of their lives in tragic flights. I wish he'd stayed and we could have got him to talk, because when he's interested he talks almost as well as he conducts. Too bad he's so sensitive; but you've known musicians, haven't you, Mr. Fount? No doubt you've seen how much more they feel things than the rest of us do? You understand, don't you, their emotional——"

"Of course he does; everybody does!" Bailey was relieved to hear old Mr. Horne take this up for him. "Only you're wrong, Henry Rossbeke, and so's everybody else. These music people don't feel things more; they're like actors and only express more. When trouble comes, the rest of us sit around not saying much; but they get up on their hind legs and——"

He elaborated this worn theme until his host stopped him by rising. The four passed through the restaurant and took the elevator up to Rossbeke's rooms where Miss Jyre made coffee for them; then came to sit by Bailey, bringing with her a portfolio of drawings the Director had collected for himself.

"Maybe we can't put our minds on 'em," she said, as she sat. "Not with Mr. Horne making all this noise!"

Mr. Horne was walking about the room, shouting. He'd set down his black coffee with a loud clink and jumped up—his response to something Rossbeke had said to him. "Don't repeat those moronics to me, Henry Rossbeke! Why, damn my old soul, rather than consent to the buying of a Matisse for that museum I'd——" He interrupted himself to sit down and shake a violent forefinger almost against the face of the mild Rossbeke. "There's no such thing as a revolution in art, Henry. Never let anybody talk you into believing it! Damn it, revolution ain't art; it's only trying to get noticed by being different. Different! Hell, I can be different by leaving off my pants, painting one leg blue and the other ochre! Then, if I get a 'good press,' it'll get to be the style and me called a genius!" He jumped up, paced the floor again, gesticulating. "Squawked at you we've got to be progressive, did she, had to advance, all that old parrot stuff? Threadbare! Matisse is already old hat; they've had to get different from him, too. You know that, don't you, Henry?"

"Oh, certainly! Won't you sit down and finish your coffee?"

"I won't!" Mr. Horne, however, did immediately sit down and drink the rest of his coffee—at a gulp. "Revolution, my aunt! Sheep fall for it, think it's 'Youth,' holler it's 'new' because it got made a long while ago by tired old, old men, most of 'em dead. How much of it came out of discredited Nineteenth Century *art nouveau*—yes, and even from Oscar Wilde and Beardsley? What's 'Abstractionism' except old pre-Nazi 'Symbolism' gone Frenchified for a disguise? Non-objectivity's wished on us, too, is it, meaning painting no object, meaning painting nothing, nihilism, nothingism? Stop thinking; so why not stop painting? What's the logical end of the whole non-representational eliminate-everything racket? Why not a blank canvas with an Eskimo name signed on it and a self-sacrificial dealer selling it to a millionaire's hypnotized offspring for twelve thousand dollars? Think I'm talking jargon?"

"Not at all, not at all," the patient Rossbeke replied. "Won't you have some more coffee?"

"I will not!" Mr. Horne again put his threatening forefinger to use. "You listen, Henry! Originality never tries to be original. It can't help being original. Life's a flux, never stops changing; but mere change isn't advance. Same in art as in government or the style of hats. Idiots think just changing, just turning different, is being progressive. Advance, hell! It's an advance when you take a long step forward and fall down a coal hole? Godless fools don't even know when they're in the coal hole with their addled brains bumped crazier! They flop around in the coal-dust and believe with all their might they're 'out in front,' 'daring to be themselves,' creating a bright new world!" Once more he leaped to his feet, walked and passionately gestured. "My God, what a flock of parrots!"

Rossbeke got a word in. "I was only trying to tell you——"

"Don't do it! I know the whole cockeyed argument. If I listen you'll be telling me all about 'experiments in line and form, relationships of masses'—art turned into blueprints for new types of green aluminum washing-machines!"

"Mr. Horne, I promise I won't be telling you that."

"You will, Henry, you will, and you'll be begging me to be tolerant. Tolerant? I'm too damned tired of warmed-over pre-prohibition sophistication! Whistler got funny about 'nature's looking up' trying to imitate his painting. Sheep took it up, thought they thought of it. Long before Whistler old Palomino talked about the theory that nature imitates art. Claimed nature does it frolicsomely, didn't he?"

"Yes; but he didn't mean——"

"Whoa-up!" Mr. Horne shouted. "*I* know what he meant. Twistical way of saying art helps the eye—not that art and nature have nothing to do with each other. They haven't, *she* claims! Hollers 'modern logicians' prove truly great artists throw nature plum out, nature evidently not having produced either the artists or her 'logicians'! Detach art from the works of God? Why not science, too, so nobody'll know the difference between a laboratory and any other lunatic asylum? I tell you——"

"Yes, I know, I know." Rossbeke tried to be soothing. "But after all——"

"Don't 'after all' me!" The old man turned on him vociferously. "It's wornout twaddle I knew before she was born She caught it same as 'flu when she was twenty-one. Now swallers the whole mess o' microbes, she does—all of 'em. Squeals her head off at me every meeting of that committee. 'Educate people *up* to it!' 'Can't ignore a whole great modern movement!' Same thing applied to joining the Greenback Party, Free Silver and the Ku Klux Klan when *they* were great modern movements! Damn mob contagions! All the babies ought to've joined up and died in the Children's Crusade, ought they, just to keep up with the changing times and be out in the forefront? Think every woman ignores the living present if she doesn't make her mouth a scarlet gash and a bloody crime of her fingernails? Oh, I know: I'm a fossilized old reactionary, am I? God keep me so, God keep me so!"

He continued, putting no restraint upon his gusty temper as he walked the floor, sat down, jumped up, sat down and jumped up again. Rossbeke and Miss Jyre, used to it, remained calm, and Bailey Fount, trying to look at the drawings, remembered vaguely that Mr. Horne had complained of the expressiveness of musicians. "Damblasted impudence!" he was shouting now. "Trying to shackle Degas, Seurat, Renoir, Toulouse-Lautrec, even Manet, to Matisse, Picasso and Company and to all the showmen and anarchists claimed to be spawn of poor old groping Cézanne! 'Art for art's sake'? Anarchy for anarchy's sake—and for profit? All that salesman's propaganda——"

The excitable old man's storming was little more than meaningless wind in the injured soldier's ears. With what concentration he could summon he tried to speak intelligibly of the drawings, most of which were by undeniable masters. Helena talked of them as piquantly as she could, telling him of obscure shops where Rossbeke had "found" some of them—in London, Paris, Antwerp, Bruges, Florence, Verona, Naples. By the time they'd finished the portfolio, and she said perhaps they'd better be getting back to The Cranford now, he began to feel almost at ease with her.

She made him feel more that way the next day, leading him through the routines set for an Assistant Curator of Paintings. She gave him a workshop of his own, too, a room where he could follow Colonel Bedge's instructions, change into civilian clothes in the morning before he set to work and get into his uniform again when he was ready to leave the museum in the late afternoon. The workroom was another foxhole for him; but by the end of his first week he seldom felt the impulse to bury himself in it. The galleries of the museum were cover enough.

He began to be sure that Colonel Bedge had been right: in the whole world this place, its quiet and the steadying light tasks it offered him were probably the best restoratives for a broken young soldier who'd once been a rising landscape painter but now wished to paint no more. Here, the paintings and the sculptures of other men, most of them long dead, were passive about him, seeming engaged in unintrusive meditations. He liked the long, wide galleries, neat and spacious under skylights. He liked the gleamings of gilt from picture frames; he liked the finely cracked ancient gold backgrounds of dulled red and blue primitives; and in the museum's still library, in the west wing, hours of research loosened his tensity, almost relaxed him. He liked his colleagues of the museum staff, most of them middle-aged or elderly women. He liked the janitors, old men the war had made wage-earners again; he liked the lively one-legged carpenter and packer, Arturo Meigs, who sometimes helped him with the repair of picture frames, and, as for Henry Rossbeke, Helena Jyre and Mr. John Constable Horne, the more he saw of them the less his self-consciousness plagued him in their presence.

The museum was a refuge like a series of silent great caves to which he had fled from the multitudinous explosions of the world. Even during the six days a week when the building was open to the public, not many visitors came; Mr. Horne and Mr. Rossbeke had been right about that. They'd spoken in lamentation; but Bailey was grateful for the silences—and when seeming explorers were seen, members of that populace for whom the museum had been built, they walked softly, sometimes singly, sometimes in pairs, sometimes in small family groups, not much more than whispering.

His nerves grew steadier; but one morning a crackling voice

startled him so that he jumped. He was in the gallery of Eighteenth Century British paintings, examining the surface of an Opie portrait that showed signs of deterioration. A bit of pigment half the size of a dime had flaked away from the lower border of the canvas; he thought himself alone, and, stooping double, was studying this spot when the voice spoke.

"That always did," it said from close behind him; and then, as he staggered cringingly, "Oh, excuse me! I didn't mean to scare you."

"Not at all." He stood straight, wiped his forehead. "You didn't. It's nothing—I——"

"I'm afraid I did." The intruder was the aged and over-stout Mrs. Hevlin whom he'd encountered in the Oriental collection on the morning of his arrival and hadn't since seen, except in the distance. "I was interested because I used to have trouble with that portrait, myself," she said. "I had a restorer, a Frenchman, work on it. I was in entire charge of Mr. Oaklin's collections, you see, for years and years." Then she added pettishly, "Before they had to go and put up this terrific big barn of a place and employ all these so-called experts! I'm not supposed to be in this part of the museum at all. In fact, I've had more than a hint! Probably some of the high-and-mighty'd give me fits if they knew I was talking to you." She giggled rather spitefully. "Oh, yes, nowadays I'm supposed to be just a relic they'd keep drying up out on pension if they had their way! I'm told you're quite the pet of the high-and-mighties."

"I? No—I don't think so."

"Yes, I'm told you are. Don't think *I* mind it. I'm not a jealous person and I'm sure you're nice. I just thought I'd have a word with you, though, if I don't get caught at it. They tell me you've been in the fighting and got all upset—nerves and all that sort of thing? I'm sure I can sympathize. I've been nothing but a bundle of nerves, myself, ever since I was displaced here." She came nearer him ingratiatingly. "You're new in the museum; I just thought somebody ought to put you onto the ropes a little."

"Thank you." He earnestly wished that she'd go away and stop making him sorry for her—and for himself. "You're very kind."

"Yes, I'm naturally kindhearted," Mrs. Hevlin admitted. "I wouldn't have done to anybody in the world what they did to me—first supplanting me and then putting me out altogether on pension. Now they've let me come back it's a wonder they didn't put me in as one of the scrawny old females they've got for 'guards' of the art treasures these days! What I think you ought to know—this place looks all right on the outside; but inside, it's a nest of intrigue!"

"Is it? I haven't——"

"No, of course you wouldn't see it right at first—and with them kowtowing all around you—but oh, yes!—wheels within wheels! That old Horne, he's the top muckymuck, with Rossbeke and that Jyre woman right at his heels. Horne's coldhearted; I wouldn't be back here now if he'd had his way. I've got one friend at court, though—one that's always been loyal to me. Don't you let John C. Horne set you against somebody."

"Against——" This seemed to be a distressing old hornrimmed fat woman. "I haven't heard anything against anybody."

"Oh, but you will! They're all in a league against the very founder of this institution, against the way he wanted it run." Mrs. Hevlin glanced over her shoulders, each in turn, at the two vacant entrances of the gallery. "They work night and day against the only loyal one. That's the friend of mine I mentioned and's away now; but you know who I mean."

"No, I don't."

"What? You don't? Well, I'm no trouble-maker; but I'll say this much: it's the one if they got you against would be a perfect triumph for them because you're connected with the Oaklins and it'd make a family split. It's the one that was intended to have full control of this museum, and except for this very person I wouldn't be back here now, myself. I wouldn't even be downstairs in the Oriental department. *Now* I guess you know who I mean, don't you?"

"No, I don't."

"What? I bet you do and just don't want to say! Anyhow, you look out for that old Horne and his cohorts. I thought I ought to tell you. If you're not careful——" Mrs. Hevlin suddenly whispered, "Oh, murder!" She scurried heavily to the gallery's western entrance and disappeared as Helena Jyre came through the archway opposite.

"Poor old thing," Helena said. "I hope she hasn't been bothering you with ghost stories."

"Ghost stories? No. She seemed in a flutter about something. She was a little confusing."

"Yes, with ghost stories, I'm sure." Helena laughed. "Ghosts of her past when she was Mr. Oaklin's curator. I suppose she really oughtn't to be here at all. There was some argument about taking her on for the duration, I believe; but Mr. Horne finally consented—pretty generously, too, because she was put into the Oriental department and that's his specialty. He's full of sound and fury, but's really a lamb. He let poor Mrs. Hevlin go into that department because if she got things wrong he knew he could straighten 'em out, himself. It just gives him an extra job. He's gentle with her; but of course she looks upon him as an interloper." Helena regarded Bailey solicitously. "The poor old creature just prattles. You didn't let her worry you about anything, did you?"

"No. I'm afraid she's—well, a little like me—a bit off the beam."

"You?" Helena laughed again, gave him a touch on the shoulder. "You're a better Keeper of Paintings already than I am. What's fretting you?"

"It's this flaked spot on the Opie," Bailey said, turning to it. "Will you let me see if I can fill it so nobody'll know the difference?"

Helena consented heartily. "Come ahead!" They went to his workroom, carrying the Opie portrait with them, and the fat but ghostly Mrs. Hevlin and her discontents were obscured.

IX

Mrs. hevlin's spectral hints, like other come-and-go
suggestions that something was wrong in this museum, faded
from Bailey Fount's thoughts as dust settles in the corners of a
room, still there though it lies unnoticed by a feverish occupant.
Feverish in mind he indeed yet was, after weeks of his new
work; but the work itself brought easement, and physically he
began to be more like the man he'd been. He was no longer
hollow-eyed or hollow-cheeked. "That look" was still within
his eyes, if an observer sought it; but his bad leg was seldom
painful, he limped less noticeably and he could smile, sometimes, without seeming startled and hurt by that interruption
in his melancholy. When the hot weather'd gone, more visitors
came to the museum; but this even pleased him: he was glad
to see them interested in pictures for which he'd developed a
proprietary affection. By October he'd come along so well that
he could smile all to himself—at least he did so once as he was
passing, alone, through a vacant corridor.

He stopped and listened, indulging an almost normal enjoyment—something that hadn't happened inside him for many a

month. What stirred his humor was the voice of John Constable Horne bellowing on the other side of a door somebody'd left an inch ajar. It was the door of a room wherein the committee that decided upon purchases for the museum held its sessions; one was in progress, Bailey knew, and old Mr. Horne appeared to be making things lively. Half a dozen other people were talking spiritedly but without effective competition; Mr. Horne thundered profanely above them.

"Never!" Bailey heard him shouting. "Damn my old soul, never! When this standardless tom-fool era's done and stopped its braying, John Sargent'll stand forth the greatest figure of his period. He fell down sometimes—hell, who doesn't?—but only Godforsaken jackasses——"

A feminine voice, odd because pleasant to the ear though almost screaming, contrived to be heard. "I admit Sargent's watercolors—I admit all of Winslow Homer—I admit——"

"You 'admit'!" The admitting voice was roared down. "Out of the mouths of babes and sucklings! Sucklings? No, suckers— suckers that want to pay sixteen thousand dollars for a Delacroix revived because Van Gogh said he liked him!"

"What?" the feminine voice cried. "You dare to blaspheme Van Gogh? You——"

"Blaspheme your cat's grandmother! Inside him Van Gogh's the same as Blake, and I'm more or less, mostly less, for both of 'em; but sixteen thousand dollars for a Delacroix hobbyhorse with a painted tin Turk on him rocking up and down over opera-chorus corpses! Why, damn my old——"

"You're inextricably muddled!" The feminine voice partly stopped him. "Look at what you just said about Abstractions. You don't even know that painting, like music, *should* be abstract. Painting should *be* music. Music's an abstract art. Music's always non-representational and——"

"It is?" Mr. Horne was satirical vociferously. "Music's non-representational? Did you ever go to an opera? So Verdi and Wagner ain't music any more! Who's settled all that, the C.I.O.? What damn——"

The uproar became general; the screaming sweet feminine voice, like a clarinet ascending to high place in an orchestral crisis, was again heard even over Mr. Horne, and the fascinating sound of it followed Bailey down the corridor.

Away from that committee room the museum was as placid as ever, and, after the hullabaloo session, the room stood vacant; no echoes were heard for a fortnight. Then, on a morning half through the month, Henry Rossbeke sat with the Curator of Paintings upon a massive central bench under the skylight of the Seventeenth Century Dutch Gallery. This was Monday, "cleaning day," when no visitors were admitted to the museum.

"I'm afraid our President's sulking in his tent," Rossbeke said. "He hasn't set foot in the place since that row, not even to straighten out Mrs. Hevlin's unbelievable disarrangements of Chinese sculpture. Of course, though, he always does lie up a while, licking his wounds, every autumn after the St. Lawrence respite. What's odd is that she hasn't been in again, herself. Perhaps gad-flying round poor Parannik's head instead of ours."

"No, she's not on Parannik, Henry. Her present interests are outside art and music. You never read the Sunday society columns, do you?"

"I don't read the Sunday papers at all. Sunday morning's the best chance I have for my own writing."

"Yesterday, though," Helena said, "you should have given the Globe a look."

"What was it?"

"Her captain. Captain Harold Sorgius Murties, of Middleboro, Alabama, stationed here on special duty for the last six months, the Globe explained. 'Mrs. Thomas Oaklin, Junior, announces the engagement of her daughter to Captain Harold Sorgius Murties, of Middleboro, Alabama.' "

"Of course it was to be expected," Rossbeke said. "Could we dare imagine that after the war Captain and Mrs. Murties will reside in Middleboro, Alabama?"

"Likely!" Helena jeered at the Director's innocence. "Live away from the Oaklin tradition, Oaklin Museum, Oaklin Symphony Hall? You *do* have sweet dreams! She'll install her captain in our vermiform appendix."

"Captain Murties looks rather sturdy, Helena. You don't think he'd have anything to say about——"

"Not about anything. Who ever did?" Helena said. "I'm glad the engagement's announced; but I could still worry. A new man-cousin—a picturesquely injured one—how exciting! I wish we could lock him up even where he is now if it would keep him out of the orbit of turmoil. He couldn't take it."

" 'Even where he is now'? Where's that?"

"In the cellar," Helena said grimly, and explained. "He has that old janitor, Anson, helping him get out our Pieter de Hooch, the Ter Borch, and the two Jacob Ruisdaels for this gallery. Since the bombing scare's really over, I don't see why we shouldn't put the rest of our best on show again, do you?"

"No, I'd been going to suggest it. Poor old Anson's rather a wreck, though. Do you think Bailey's hearty enough to handle such heavy pictures as the Ruisdaels?"

"It's better to let him try when he wants to," she said. "He wouldn't tackle it if he weren't getting surer of himself. That's very much to the good."

Rossbeke agreed, then added, "I notice he still seldom looks at anybody and when he talks he speaks in a voice so low it's hard to hear him. Is he that way at The Cranford, too?"

"Well, about," she answered. "When he tries to be cheerful it isn't quite so heartbreaking as it was at first. The most encouraging thing is how he's gone at his work—the new cataloguing and all the rest of it. Last week he cleaned that faded Reynolds, got every scrap of the old varnish off and not a molecule of paint. He really knows how to handle pictures."

"Yes, lucky for us! If he hadn't justified us in taking up Bedge's idea of sending him here we could have been put in a hole, Helena."

"Put to the sword!" she more than assented. "We're safe enough; but the cure's still at stake, Henry. If he didn't happen to be their cousin I'd be less uneasy about keeping him cloistered. Saturday afternoon he told me he'd noticed a middle-aged lady in a car on the driveway the other side of the Oaklin house. He said he thought it might be his Cousin Folia. He'd forgotten to leave his name with the caretaker while they were away, so now he'd have to make that call and hadn't he better get it over with? Didn't need to stay more than twenty minutes or so, did he? I told him I thought he could go on postponing it; but I——"

Bailey Fount and an aged man in overalls came through one of the entrances to the gallery, bringing four pictures. Bailey carried the two heavier ones, the aged man the two lighter. Rossbeke and Helena Jyre jumped up from their bench; Rossbeke hurried to Bailey.

"Here, young fellow!" the Director said. "Those frames and the glass over the Ruisdaels weigh a ton. You're not supposed to——"

"I took 'em away from Anson," Bailey interrupted. "Ought to save him for his janitoring as much as we can, oughtn't we? I borrowed him from his own work and——"

Rossbeke took one of the heavy pictures. "Supposed to be humoring a game leg, aren't you?"

"Not much any more. Besides, my arms aren't game. I'm not wholly decrepit."

"Here!" Miss Jyre called to them from the western end of the gallery. "All four of those pictures belong down here on this end wall. I'll help you make proper space for 'em, Bailey. We'll have to move——"

"No, let me, please," he said, as he and Rossbeke set down the two paintings, letting them lean against the wall. "I have it all figured out for a new arrangement, if you'll let Anson and me do the hanging, please." He stood, frowning, and muttered, "Too bad!"

"What's too bad?" she asked.

"The walls. Stony cold grey. Behind these old Dutch pictures, the grey ought to have a thin bluish wash over it. You'd hardly notice the difference; but it would be there and you'd feel it. I could do it easily."

"Not in one day, could you, Bailey? 'Open to the public every day except Mondays.' You could be right about your bluish tinge, though, and some time we might close off this gallery and let you experiment. Would you really rather I didn't help you arrange the placing of these pictures now?"

"Yes, I'd like to do it if——"

"Go ahead. Place 'em according to your plan for 'em, and

Mr. Rossbeke and I'll come back later and find all the fault we possibly can. Go to it!"

She and Rossbeke turned away, walking noiselessly over the cork floor toward the entrance at the opposite end of the gallery, and they had about reached the center of the big room when the Director's secretary, Mrs. Williams, came hurrying in. Her hands fluttered warnings at Rossbeke; she spoke pantingly. "Mr. Rossbeke, she's looking for you and she's got her new fiancé with her, so she's sure to be you know how. You could get out through the Flemish Room. I was afraid she'd follow me and—— Oh, Golly, she has!"

Through the archway a girl in heather sport-clothes came swiftly, a long pace in advance of the officer Bailey Fount had once vaguely thought mysterious. No one could have looked less so than did Captain Murties. Plainly a taste for art was not his; and in this museum, like a business man dragged by his wife, he had the air not of an escort but of a compelled follower. "So there you are, are you, Rossbeke?" the girl cried, with a gayety too brittle to be genuine. "How many hours have I wasted hunting you how many years!" She and her military friend joined the group of three, Rossbeke, Miss Jyre and Mrs. Williams. "Can't you ever stop giving your imitation of a lost golf ball, Rossbeke?"

He responded dryly. "Not until you make me stop wishing I were one."

"How pat!" She laughed, not cordially. "You'll have to meet Captain Murties, I suppose. You may have seen the announcement of his ill-starred fate; yes, we're betrothed." She noticeably ignored the near presence of Helena Jyre; Mrs. Williams was retiring hurriedly from the gallery. "I've been engaged to Captain Murties for almost two months, Rossbeke, so it's certainly about time he saw the inside of the Oaklin Museum, isn't it?"

Rossbeke said that indeed it was, and began to offer congratulations. He was interrupted immediately.

"Yes, it's going to be terribly darling and all that; but see here, Rossbeke, I want you to stand up to John Horne the next time he begins interfering with my poor Mrs. Hevlin. She's rearranged the Oaklin Chinese sculptures the way they ought to be. Old Horne's always insisting they should be grouped to fit the Dynasties; but that's history, not art. You'll agree there's a difference between æsthetics and documentation, won't you, Rossbeke?"

"Yes," he said, looking tired. "I'll agree to that."

"You'd better! Mrs. Hevlin's put the sculptures from the Shansi Caves next to the Afghanistan stone figures that show Hellenistic influence. Horne'll rave when he stops pouting, comes back and sees it; but I want those pieces kept precisely as they are now. The way Mrs. Hevlin's got them, their affinities of mass, form and line are correct to an æsthetically trained eye. That's the kind of eye I use, myself, as it happens, and I seldom see eye to eye with John Horne, thank heaven! You'll grant me that, too, I suppose, Rossbeke?"

"Yes, readily."

"Very well," she said. "I'll expect you to back up Mrs. Hevlin. There's another matter. Somebody's been bringing up a number of our best pictures from the basement vaults where they're safe. Nobody's asked me about that and it's rather recklessly premature, isn't it?"

"No, I don't think so."

"I suppose you wouldn't." Again she laughed, not cordially; then she used the tone of an adult amiably indulgent to absurd children. "You're delightfully the scholar of course, Rossbeke, absorbed in the lore of the ages and all that; but you *do* have to remember, don't you, that you're the Director of a modern museum? Absentminded art historians are charming in their own way; but oughtn't even they to sit up a little and begin to be aware that there's a global war on and airplanes can be injurious? They really can—or haven't you heard?"

At the end of the gallery, forty feet distant, the old janitor, Anson, half way up a stepladder he'd brought, handed down a painting to Bailey Fount and informed him privately, "That's Miss Josephine Oaklin. Her folks used to kind of own this museum; guess they still partly do or something. Pretty, ain't she?"

Bailey was anxiously examining the picture he held. "What? This canvas is blooming; I'll clean it to-morrow. Who'd you say's pretty?"

"Her, yonder. Orders me around fairly sharp sometimes; but little I care as long as she goes on payin' my married daughter's hospital expenses." The old man giggled under his breath. "Gets plenty people mad at her. Look at Miss Jyre's face!"

Bailey turned his head and looked, not at Helena Jyre, now standing aloof from the other three in the central area of the gallery, but at Josephine Oaklin.

He saw, clarified in the cool and diffused light of the gallery, a face like a fair Florentine's, as daintily modeled as Beauty's own; saw a figure light as air, all symmetry, Botticellian Aphrodite in Scotch homespun; and from this exquisite creature's every movement, from every change of her versatile lips and grey eyes, from every tone of her rich and varying voice, there radiated two informations: that she was a personage and that for men she was the most desirable of her sex. At first sight, few would not have been stirred to agree with her, women challengedly; but Bailey Fount turned back to his work untouched.

He perceived that she was what any young man would have defined as beautiful. He hadn't caught her name when Anson spoke it; but he thought maybe he'd seen her somewhere, though that was unlikely; he didn't try to remember. A recent memory, though, was vaguely stirred by the unusual voice octaving up from lower tones as suavely contralto as those of a 'cello. The voice was used over-expressively, yet had the quality of a noble instrument and among a hundred would have caught the ear. It did catch Bailey's; but he wasn't bothering about that. He wasn't interested in beautiful girls or beautiful voices. He wanted to cure his nerves and get back to the Army.

Thus far she hadn't observed him noticingly, hadn't seen his over-shoulder glance at her, and she went on talking, enjoying her own satirical instruction of the Director upon the subject of bombing, using her apparently wood-carved betrothed as audience. Wearying presently of this sport, she let her grey eyes wander and became aware of the quiet operations at the end of the room. "What the devil's going on there?" she asked, not lowering tones easily audible to Bailey Fount. "What do those two think they're doing, moving everything about? I saw to the arrangement of the pictures on that wall, myself, last spring. Who *is* all that, anyhow?"

Rossbeke's annoyance was plain. "Who's all what?"

"The officious person in the tweed jacket. What's he doing here? I never could stand the type of young men that go in for museum work. They're all delicate little supercillies hoisting their eyebrows half way up to their hair at you to cover up what they don't know. What's this one? A new janitor?"

"Not precisely," Rossbeke said. "He's the museum's Assistant Curator of Paintings."

"What?" She looked affronted. "Since when?"

"Since early in August."

"Who hired him?" she asked imperiously.

"I did—with the approval of the President of the Museum and of the Trustees' Executive Committee."

"Oh, indeed!" she said. "Are you aware that I happen to be a member of that committee?"

"Yes; but you were away."

"What if I was? Why wasn't I notified? Who's responsible for not notifying me? Just office negligence?"

"No, I'm responsible."

"Oh, you are?" she cried. "You accept the responsibility for making an appointment of that importance without consulting me, do you?"

Rossbeke looked dogged. "Yes. I've explained that you were away."

"You think that lets you out? You're virtually admitting, aren't you, that you persuaded old John and that committee to act without a word to me, Thomas Oaklin's living representative? The wishes of the Oaklin family needn't be consulted nowadays, no matter what sacrifices we made for this institution? What are that young man's qualifications for acting as an Assistant Curator of Paintings in the Thomas Oaklin Museum? What training has he had? Where does he come from?"

Rossbeke, goadedly conscious of Helena Jyre's violent gaze, lifted a protesting hand. "Be careful, please! He'll hear you."

"You're shushing *me?*" Josephine Oaklin's eyes enlarged ominously; her piquant features took on a pink that proved even outright anger becoming to her. "Why shouldn't he hear me? What's that young man doing in an art museum, anyhow?"

"Please!" Rossbeke looked panicky. "You mustn't——"

"Oh, mustn't I?" She set a gloved shapely hand patriotically upon Captain Murties's dark olive sleeve and called out the injurious words at Bailey Fount's tweed back: "Hanging pictures isn't precisely a Four-F essential occupation, is it? Will somebody kindly inform me why that young man is not in uniform?"

Bailey's back seemed to crumble inside the tweed coat. Helena Jyre took five fast steps forward and spoke in a hot low voice, face to face with Josephine. "You ask where he comes from? He comes from the Southwest Pacific. That was a rotten thing to say!"

Even upon that, Josephine Oaklin was able to continue her ignoring of Miss Jyre; but Captain Murties, though remaining stolid, spoke his mind. "Right," he said. "Nobody has any business talking like that."

The unloverlike speech brought no change in Josephine's expression; but she removed her hand from Captain Murties's sleeve, stepped aside from him and away from the angry Helena's confrontation of her. She turned to Rossbeke. "What did you say his name is?"

"Bailey Fount."

"What? Why, I've got a cousin named that. Of course this wouldn't be——"

"He is, though," Rossbeke said. "Mr. Horne especially wanted him here because his mother was Mary Oaklin. He's a nephew of the Founder."

"What? Why, really!" Josephine's displeasure seemed to vanish; she looked eager. "So that's Bailey Fount! Mother was talking about that branch of our family only the other day, wondering what had become of young Bailey Fount. She'd never seen him; I think she hadn't liked his father or somebody and neither had my grandfather. How in the world's he ever happened to turn up here?"

She didn't wait for an answer, but, evidently the creature of any contradictory impulse, ran lightly to the end of the gallery and stood beside Bailey Fount.

"Here!" she said, and caught him by the arm. "Let's see what you look like!"

X

Flaccidly obedient, Bailey let the jerk upon his sleeve turn him to face her; but after a meek upward glance kept his gaze upon the floor.

"Bailey Fount, I'm your cousin, Josephine Oaklin! Why haven't you been to see me? Wouldn't you like to know me? Anyhow, don't you think you ought to?"

"Why—why, yes."

"That all?" She let go his sleeve, flourished a hand at him, and was now of an almost dancing gayety. "You might at least look me over, mightn't you? You could be *that* daring, couldn't you?" Then, as again he glanced up and troubledly down, "Hurrah!" she cried. "That's a brave lad; but don't be so tragic at me! Haven't I seen you before somewhere? Yes, I'll swear I have! Haven't I?"

"I don't know."

"Why, yes," she said. "Yes, certainly I have! I was home one day last summer and somebody tried to come through the passage between the museum and our library. I slapped his ears down; but afterwards I kept remembering his face. Wasn't that you? Don't you remember?"

"Yes—I believe so."

"Why, of course it was you, Cousin! I'm pretty clever to remember about that, aren't I?—because then you were in a saggy uniform and all withered-up looking and now you're really quite impressive. It must have been a kind of Oaklin look about you that made me remember you. Yes, you've got it. I see it. You were just from the Pacific then, weren't you?"

"No. Hospital."

"How dreadful! I'm afraid you heard what I said just now about your not being in uniform. What a shame! How disgusting of me!" She caught his arm again and was all new-cousinly affection. "I'm going to make that up to you; you'll see! Do you know you're the only cousin I've got? Did you know that?"

"No, I doubt if I did."

"You actually are, though, Bailey Fount! Mother and I were talking about how run-out our family is on the Oaklin side, and she said we have only one Oaklin relative left. That'd be you, and think how strange it is my finding you here, right in the Oaklin Museum! You haven't answered: Why haven't you been to see me?"

"I—I'd meant to. I heard you and your mother were away."

"Well, I'm not away any more!" she cried. "You're an acquisition, and if you'll stop being so shy Mother and I'll prove it to you. First, I want you to meet my fiancé." Her fingers slid down his sleeve, took his hand tightly and she brought him irresistibly back with her to the inanimately watching group in the center of the room. "Harold!" she called, laughing excitedly as she came. "Look what I've found! This is the only new cousin I'll be able to give you, except those withered old creatures on Mother's side. Captain Murties, Mr. Fount."

Bailey's right arm moved as if with the impulse to salute; but she held that hand. He bowed and tried to smile. Captain Murties, looking inscrutable, muttered, "Very glad."

"Bailey Fount! Bailey Fount!" Josephine exclaimed. "I'm all a-flutter over you! What a discovery! Your name may be Fount; but of course you're really an Oaklin, Thomas Oaklin the Founder's own niece's son. So what do you and I care about any old split in the family on account of somebody's not liking somebody's marrying somebody? You can't imagine what a lonely little girl I was. All the children I knew had brothers and sisters and cousins—no end of cousins—and I didn't have anybody within miles of my own age. I never *have* had—until this very moment! It gives me a whole outfit of new emotions to have a cousin at last. You can't imagine! Mother told me she and I must be the only relatives *you* have living, just as you're practically the only one I have, and she said she thought you must be about twenty-six. I'm twenty-two. And only to think that you're here in the museum all day every day with only that short passageway between us! Between us—but not separating us—not any more! You like being a curator here, don't you?"

"Yes, I—I do."

"You're going to like it better, I promise you! Can't you stop looking at the floor?" She laughed, rallying him, still keeping his hand. "Don't be so shy, don't be an introvert! Look at me, can't you? It's sometimes been thought worth-while, Cousin! Stop hating me, too, can't you?"

"But I don't——"

"You do!" she cried. "Forgive me and forget it, but don't forget *me*. Ah, I'll see that you don't do that! Wasn't I a beast to say what I did about the uniform? I didn't dream you were

a veteran with a gorgeous little limp! You're lovely! Here,
I'll show you! You're my cousin and I've never even kissed
you yet."

"What?"

"I'm going to!" She dropped his hand, put an arm about
his neck and kissed him on the cheek. "There! Good-bye, but
not for long. Thank heaven I've found you!" She flitted to her
solemn Captain, poked the side of his nose with a forefinger.
"Hop, Harold; we'll be late." Then, preceding him, she half-
skipped, half-danced to the archway by which she'd entered
the gallery.

Captain Murties's broad military back seemed to express an
increased inscrutability as he followed her and both disappeared
from view. Bailey Fount went back to his rearranging of the
Dutch Masters, and Helena Jyre and Rossbeke walked slowly
away, going toward the Director's office.

"That's burnt it!" Helena said. "I knew if she once saw him
she'd grab. Actress! That farce she put on—ecstasizing over
him—for her Captain's benefit! She overdid it; but she knew
none of you men would see that and if I did, why, of course
she doesn't care a cent's worth."

"Farce?" Rossbeke was doubtful. "You think she didn't
mean it about Bailey? All that rejoicing—finding a cousin——"

"Almost touching, wasn't it?" Helena said contemptuously.
"Sweet impulsive joy in a new kinsman! Pooh! She knew she'd
made a break about the uniform, had to put herself right and
punish the Captain for sitting on her, so he had to be made
jealous. She always gets even as fast as she can for the slightest
criticism. I don't think the Captain *was* jealous, though; he
looked more like a man who's thinking a lot of thoughts."

"Yes, so he did. He might be in trouble on that account before the day's over?"

"He already is." Helena laughed angrily. "Hear her say she's twenty-two? Twenty-five's a perfectly good age; but what's mere truth ever got to do with her? To be more virginally seductive, she'd probably told the Captain she's twenty-two, so she grabbed the chance to play it up again. Spiteful of me? Yes; about some people I'm just not able to think anything but the worst. This place could be heavenly, Henry, if it weren't for her! And when I think how she treats *you*——"

"She didn't at first," he said sadly. "For a while she was amiable. When a newspaper'd rather jeered—pretty ignorantly —at the first modern exhibition I organized she was furious but sympathetically told *me* not to mind. We must remember we were above all that, she said; ignoramuses couldn't hurt us. Her kindness didn't last very long—perhaps three months. Strange girl."

"Strange nothing!" Helena exclaimed. "She changed toward you because she's one of those people who can't bear for anyone to know more than they do. They're that way about everything on earth, but most of all about art. She's convinced nobody has half her intelligence and she bristles when she suspects anyone of thinking he has. Well, she's certainly got both of us—yes, all of us here—where she wants us!"

Rossbeke's sigh was profound. "Yet we have always to remember she did make a great sacrifice when she consented to let all that money come to the museum."

"How many years has she been rubbing it in!" Helena cried. "She rubs everything in—especially her self-dramatizing. She makes life a conflict and can make it a disaster. Now that what we were afraid of's happened, what's she going to do to our

poor gentle soldier? Did you see his face as he turned back to
go at his work again?"

Bailey had done his best to keep that vulnerable face of his
from showing what he felt; but improving self-control had suffered a relapse. The tensity he'd almost shaken off came back
upon him, making its return frighteningly known by the invisible trembling he'd believed cured. In his ears there was a con-
tinual sizzling of the question that had been called at him:
"Will somebody kindly inform me why that young man is not
in uniform?"

"Hanging pictures!" he thought. "Just a quitter—hanging
pictures," and never again would he be man enough to wear
the uniform where it could get sudden holes in it.

He had no resentment. He didn't think of the girl, Josephine
Oaklin, felt no interest in her whatever; she was blurred and
lost behind the question that threw him back into the worst of
his half-shed misery. A new scald on a healing burn doesn't
make the injured person angry with the boiling water that re-
news the wound; it's the scald itself that busies him. The scald
was fresh, the trembling continued; but Bailey had well in his
head his plan for replacing and spacing the old Dutch pictures,
and he kept as steadily at the work as if nothing had happened.
It was only when his hard day was done and he walked
home to The Cranford in the concealment of smoky October
dusk that his hurt had full way with him. He limped saggingly,
and, lopsided within his uniform, his whole body seemed to
crouch.

. . . In the morning two hours of handicraft in his workroom ended when his door was rapped upon and simultaneously
opened; but he looked merely apathetic as he saw Josephine

Oaklin before him. She was hatless, dressed cheerfully in light brown and white, and, bright-eyed but preoccupied, smiled upon him perfunctorily.

"Busy, new cousin?" she asked, stepped in and closed the door. "I won't keep you long. Why all these stacks of picture frames, tools, pots, glue, cement?" She seated herself upon a wooden bench. "How industrious!"

"Am I?"

War's damage to Bailey hadn't made him observant, except of himself. Miss Jyre would have seen, perhaps gladly, that here, alone with him in his workroom, Josephine Oaklin was less enthusiastic than she'd been yesterday before an audience including Captain Murties; she could have been thought almost indifferent to the new cousin.

"Are you an expert picture-frame repairer?" she asked.

"I used to make my own frames. Some of the museum frames aren't really good; too much baroque plaster. Moving them about—especially down to the cellars and up again— gets them nicked. Not too good for the surfaces of the paintings, either. Old pictures need nursing."

"Need somebody to love 'em?" Her absentminded smile was a little mocking. "I understand you're a painter, yourself. Do you feel a special tenderness for your own pictures?"

"No. Perhaps I did for the first few weeks after I'd painted one; then I'd begin to see the blemishes and pretty soon couldn't see anything else. I'm not a painter now."

"You won't go back to it?"

"I don't want to go back to anything I did before."

"Why?"

"The thought of it makes me sick."

"Why?" she again asked, though not with much curiosity.

"I don't know. It just does."

"But you do love our pictures here in the museum?" She didn't care enough about his answer to wait for it. "Oh, yes, everybody talks about 'loving art.' Lip service! Most people haven't the faintest idea what 'loving art' means. Myself, I've not only loved it, I've lived it from my earliest childhood." Here, as she spoke, she was more interested. "I *am* this museum, these collections. Since my grandfather's death I've had to fight every inch of the way to keep the collections what they should be, to see that no unworthy object of art should enter here and that what I know to be worthy *should* find place. How many people know a genuine work of art from what isn't, how many have the right eye? Precious few, I can tell you! The harassments one suffers from people who lack the æsthetically trained eye——" She'd begun to speak with vehemence, but interrupted herself, laughed and was businesslike. "This isn't what I wanted to see you about."

"You wanted——" He showed plain apprehension of involvements.

"Yes. I had to look all over the place for you." She was amused by his half-step backward. "Don't flutter so; I never did see anybody shyer than you are! Temporary, though, isn't it? Rossbeke came in last evening and told my mother you'd had your nerves rather shot to pieces—but don't worry, I'm not going to ask anything of you that would disturb a fly. Mother wants you to come to lunch to-morrow."

"She does?"

" 'She does?' " Josephine mocked him jovially. "You sound as if she wanted to shoot you. Stop looking like a scared squirrel! Yes, lunch to-morrow; and this afternoon, if you please, you're to drop in on the only kinsfolk you've got in the world. Don't you think it's about time to stop putting it off?"

"Of course I've been meaning to come. It's just that since the museum took me on I've been getting more and more into the work and—and busier."

"Oh, terrifically busy and all that, I know!" Upon this, for a moment, she looked at him penetratingly. "By the way, the coincidence of your joining the Oaklin staff might suggest chicanery. Do you mind telling me just how it happened that you did come here to this museum?"

"Colonel Bedge did it for me. He's the Chief Medical Officer at the hospital where I was sent after—after I——"

"After you were wounded?" she asked with some impatience, as his pause proved to be a long one. "Yes, but how did it happen that he sent you precisely here?"

"He thought I needed some such work to occupy—my mind. He'd never been here, himself; but he happened to be an old friend of Mr. Rossbeke's. He knew Mr. Rossbeke was the Director here and thought he'd be kind enough to give me a—a chance. I don't see anything of what you call chicanery in that. I don't know what you mean."

"No, I see you don't. You're obviously an innocent." She rose, apparently satisfied. "No doubt it's as you say and I was mistaken in a momentary suspicion."

"Suspicion? Why suspicion?"

"We'll forget it," she said. "I'm not a suspicious person. I'm too much the other way; but there are all kinds of maneuvers here, cliques that try to rule the place, though they aren't entitled to any authority at all. I thought it just possible that you'd been imported to give strength to the opposition because you're a member of the Oaklin family. They might try to use you— claiming an Oaklin prestige as part of their own assertion of power and——"

"But my name's Fount," he said. "I don't know what you're talking about. I don't see how anybody could use me, as you say, and I don't think anybody wants to. Everybody's just been kind."

"No doubt, no doubt," she hurried to say. "I've just said we'd forget it, didn't I? I see I was mistaken and I'm only too glad you're here. You'll come to lunch to-morrow, then—and drop around this afternoon?"

"This afternoon? To-day?"

"I'd already said so. What's so alarming about it?" She laughed as she walked toward the door. "Come about five o'clock, will you?"

"Five? About five?" He went to the door and opened it for her. "This afternoon?"

"Our house isn't a courtroom where you'll be tried!" she said, as she stepped into the corridor. "What a fuss about nothing! Your mother must have worked hard on you, bringing you up. I haven't had a man hurry to open a door for me since I don't know when. I thought they didn't do that any more. Don't forget this afternoon. Make it five exactly, will you?"

"Yes, if——"

"If you must? Yes, you must!" she said. "Don't forget you've promised." She walked lightly away, and at the end of the short corridor, as she turned into a broader and longer one, she looked back, waved her hand carelessly; then disappeared from view.

He was about to close his door when a husky whisper startled him. Mrs. Hevlin stood almost at his elbow. "Isn't she sweet! Oh, my, don't jump so! I'm sorry I've scared you again."

"No." He leaned against the door-casing, recovering his breath. "Not at all."

XI

Yes, i'm afraid i did. I'm so sorry," Mrs. Hevlin said. "It's lovely, her coming here to your own room to see you because it means she has confidence in you and so you're already great friends, besides being cousins. Of course you know now she's the one I meant the other time I risked coming to talk to you. To me she's the dearest person in the world, the only loyal friend I ever had, and she didn't mind a bit how mad it made 'em, putting me back here where I used to be the whole thing. She'd face 'em all down any day; she's dauntless. She and I know more about art than the whole pack of 'em put together. It's perfect, your being on our side and——"

"My being what?"

"On our side. Of course you are or she wouldn't have been in consultation with you. You love her, don't you? I mean as a cousin, of course, because her being engaged would make any other kind improper. You know she's engaged, don't you?"

"Yes, I do."

"That's nice," Mrs. Hevlin said. "I'll tell you something. She always added to my pension out of her own pocket. You can see why I'd naturally be on her side, can't you?"

"Yes, I can."

"Always fought for me, too," Mrs. Hevlin added. "So I do the same for her. She knows she can always depend on me to tell her everything I hear 'em say about her."

"She does?"

"My! and isn't there plenty of it! You mustn't ever be off-guard." Mrs. Hevlin glanced toward one end of the corridor and then toward the other. "Watchful's the word! I just slipped up here after her and waited till she went—she gets cross with me when she knows I'm following her—because I wanted to tell you to keep a sharp lookout or they'll set you against her. A word to the wise. You know what that means, don't you?"

"Yes."

"You and I understand each other." Mrs. Hevlin uttered a whispering titter. "Maybe that's because we both have such terrific nerves. It's easy to see you have. I heard so, too. I'd better go now. Good-bye."

She went waddlingly on tiptoe; he turned back into his room and shut the door. " 'Because we both have such terrific nerves . . . It's easy to see you have . . . I heard so, too.' " He spoke the words half-aloud, much as Mrs. Hevlin had said them; then he sat down and took his head in his hands. "I've got to do something or I'll be as crazy as she is. They won't want two lunatics in this museum; nobody'd stand it. I'm slipping back. Stop talking to yourself!"

He needed help and sought it from the person with whom he could feel most at ease. Whenever she spoke to him it was in a cool unemphatic voice and often they worked together not speaking at all. Toward one o'clock he found her sitting alone in the museum's library, and, when he came in, she closed the thick book on Sienese painting she'd been studying, let it lie on the table before her. "Anything I could help you find on the shelves or in the cupboards, Bailey?"

"No, Miss Jyre." He sat down beside her. "I just wondered ———"

"Wondered if I've forgotten about that bluish tinge you wanted to put over the grey of the Dutch gallery? That it?"

"No, I wanted to—to ask you—it's rather difficult to———"

"If it's hard to say let me guess what it is. Let's see." Smilingly she seemed to consider. "You rearranged the pictures so improvingly in the Dutch room you'd like to do the same thing in one of the other galleries? If that's it, all right. Mr. Rossbeke himself's just been saying we'd better turn you loose wherever you're inclined to experiment. Something like that on your mind?"

"No, it's more—it's personal. The first day I was here you told me I'd have to get used to people again—to talking with 'em and being with 'em."

"Yes, you've pretty well done that, haven't you?"

"No. I thought I had, a little; but I see now that was only because I'd got used to being with the same few people here and at The Cranford. Any other person—any new person———"

"You get jittery again when you have to talk to any 'new person'? Even if the 'new person' is related to you, Bailey?"

"Yes. If I go to see these people I'm related to—I hardly know either of them and there might be other people there, too—I don't know how many. I ought to do it, anyhow, ought I? You still think I've got to keep on going ahead—meeting people—getting used to 'em? For instance, if I have to go there this afternoon——"

"So soon? You've seen her again? She's already——"

"That girl, my cousin, yes," he said. "She had me say I'd be there at five o'clock and her mother wants me to lunch with them to-morrow. Why do I come running to you? Well, you've braced me up before this to meet people. What I need is somebody to tell me to wash out my jitters, step up like a little man and get these things over with. That's what you'll tell me, isn't it?"

"I——" She hesitated. "I'm not sure."

"You aren't?" Bailey's head drooped. "That's too bad. You don't think I'm capable of it."

"What nonsense!" Helena Jyre showed impatience. "Of course you are! You can go anywhere and meet anybody. Don't for a moment think you can't."

"You believe so? I don't suppose—I hope——" He began again: "I was hoping it'd be just possible that if there are going to be some other people there this afternoon or at lunch to-morrow, maybe she'd asked you too. I'd feel a lot more propped up if you were there."

"I?" Helena suppressed the impulse to ask him if he hadn't seen how that girl had treated her yesterday; she said only, "No, I'm not invited."

"Perhaps—perhaps Mr. Rossbeke, then, or—or Mrs. Williams or——"

"No. Most unlikely."

"Then they'll all be strangers."

She put her hand upon his arm. "See here; you don't have to drive yourself. These Oaklins aren't such close relatives of yours; you needn't feel compelled to——"

"But I think I promised——" He broke off; then spoke thoughtfully. "My Cousin Josephine seems to be a confusing sort of girl. Wouldn't you think so?"

"Yes, I would. She made you promise you'd come to-day— and to-morrow, too?"

"It seems so. I'll have to go through with it. Maybe I can, thanks to you."

"Thanks to me? What in the world do you mean?"

"Why, for believing I'm capable of it." There was a rustle behind them as the two librarians, an elderly married couple, came in from their lunch. Bailey rose. "Since you think I can do it I'll—I'll try. Thank you, Miss Jyre; that's what I needed." He spoke almost firmly in greeting to the two librarians, as he left the room.

Helena Jyre opened her book, but didn't look for the page at which she'd closed it. Mr. and Mrs. Weil, the librarians, both felt they'd like to have a chat with her about Bailey, in whom they were warmly interested; but, after a second glance at her expression, both decided that this was not the time.

At five o'clock in the afternoon, facing the carved stone and oak-paneled grandeur of the Tudorish front door, Bailey thought, even after he'd rung the bell, "I could still get away; I could turn and hobble off without being seen. No, Miss Jyre said I could go through with it. I can, I can, I can!" The door opened and he gave himself the command, "Go in, you fool; go in!"

The colored man who greeted him was thin, tall, grey-haired, benignly dignified. "You Mr. Bailey Fount; yes, Lieutenant, sir. I'm Harvey. I used to wait on the great gentleman,

Mr. Thomas Oaklin, your uncle, sir. Yes, indeed, you one of the family! Please step in the drawing-room; yes, sir."

The drawing-room, at the right of the marble-floored wide central hall, was large and evidently altered, diverted from its original intentions. The walls, once paneled, had been made plain pale lavender plaster. The parquetry floor was covered by a rug all white; the fireplace, merely a low black opening, had above it no mantelshelf nor anything except lavender wall and an unframed oval sheet of silver so polished as to be a mirror. There were no pictures upon the walls; there was no ornament of any kind within the room, unless the silver mirror might be thought one, and the furniture, most of it upholstered in either white leather or satin of harsh blue, was severely "functional." Of these theorized surroundings Bailey was almost unaware; he found himself alone and began a muttering.

"Nobody here! Why'd I think there'd be a lot of people? What gave me such an idea? Maybe I'm too early, though. Did she say to-day? Is it even the wrong day? But that colored man seemed to——"

Clicky footsteps on marble hushed him. A slow-moving blondish woman, over-stout in a street-dress of bright coral wool, came placidly flaming through the doorway and gave him a handful of fat fingers that did nothing, then withdrew. "I'm your Cousin Folia," she said casually. "Your mother was my first-cousin-by-marriage, Bailey Fount. I'm rather surprised to see you in uniform. I understood from Josephine you were wearing civilian clothes, so I supposed you must be out of the Army."

"No! No!" He cried out this denial; then hushed his voice to explain, "I'm on medical leave. I—I change my clothes for the museum work. It's to—it's to look more like an Assistant Curator."

"I see," Mrs. Oaklin returned vaguely. "The uniform's very becoming." She sighed. "I'm a martyr to arthritis and I believe you're rather lame, yourself; so do let's sit down." With a muted grunt she followed her own suggestion; then, when she'd sunk into one of the blue satin armchairs, uttered a pettish exclamation and pushed herself up again. "These chairs! I never can remember not to sit in this one. It slides me forward, and with these short skirts one's forced to wear nowadays——" She made the plainly difficult exchange into one of the white leather chairs, pulled down the coral skirt to half-cover embarrassingly large knees, and went on with her complaint. "I hate this furniture. Even old-time horsehair'd be better. This used to be a beautiful room, the kind I like—tapestries and crystal chandeliers and French needlepoint furniture. Josephine did it over in this barbarous way before the war. Her grandfather wouldn't have liked it; but I suppose she'll do it over into something else when they get this dreadful war finished; she's so restless. Sit down, too, won't you, unless you're wearing a brace or something for your leg that makes it easier standing?"

"No, it's about well. Thank you." He took the chair she'd vacated.

"She did spare the dining-room," Mrs. Oaklin resumed. "It's Sheraton my father-in-law collected. She told me she's expecting you to lunch to-morrow; do be here by one o'clock, please—cooks are so dictatorial in wartime. She did over the music room on the other side of the hall, too; had some kind of Mexican paint such loud pictures on the walls I can't bear to go in there unless I have to. Of course she didn't touch her grandfather's Jacobean library; she wouldn't do that. She's kept it just as it was; but I don't like to go in there much, either—I always seem to see him sitting there. I suppose your mother told you a good deal about him, didn't she?"

"Yes—at times."

"You like your museum work, do you?" Mrs. Oaklin said languidly. "You look rather like your father, I think, Bailey. I scarcely knew him at all, of course. Your mother *would* marry him; nothing could stop her. He died when you were about fifteen, didn't he?"

"My father? Yes—he did."

"And your mother only about four years ago," Mrs. Oaklin went on uninterestedly. "I telegraphed flowers to her funeral. Nobody ever acknowledged them, though; so I never knew whether they got there or not. I suppose you were too busy with the arrangements and all that. She was a nice girl. I really quite liked her. My father-in-law thought a great deal of her; but he got quite upset about her engagement to your father, thought he was just a harum-scarum sort of newspaper illustrator and liked moving around from one town to another. Your father's cartooning never got him anywhere, did it? Of course that didn't matter much, since your mother'd inherited rather largely from her father, hadn't she? You three were always well enough off to get along quite comfortably, weren't you?"

"I believe so," Bailey said; but this wasn't what he had the impulse to say as he looked at the flaccid, large, self-indulgent, pink face and precisely waved greyish blonde hair before him. This call upon his relatives was grinding him harder than he'd expected. Why had he come? Because Miss Jyre said he was capable of it and he'd promised his Cousin Josephine—who wasn't here? Probably there were plenty of people who could talk to this Cousin Folia and not mind it—even if she murmured lazily about their mothers' funerals. He had a dreadful temptation to burst out at her in harebrained clamors: "You ought to be as dead as your hair and eyes are! You're just an old fat nothing, and I'm just a young broken nothing. We ought both to be dead because we're nothing, nothing!" He brought forth a handkerchief and wiped his forehead.

"Yes." Mrs. Oaklin assented to this gesture. "Josephine always has the house too hot. They don't wear anything underneath any more. A horrible fashion, I tell her; but what can I do? She never listens. You've heard her engagement to Captain Harold Murties has been announced, I suppose?"

"Yes."

"He seems a fairly nice sort of man," Cousin Folia said. "From Alabama and quite nice-looking. Overwhelmed at first sight, I believe; proposed to her the second or third time they met. She tells me she took a great fancy to you, by the way. I suppose she told you so, too; she always does."

"No. She was kind; but I'm afraid you're mistaken. Nobody could could——"

"Nobody could take a fancy to you?" Cousin Folia laughed. "I'd think it quite possible. You look more Oaklin than I thought at first—not at all unlike your great-uncle, and he was the most distinguished-looking man I ever saw. Besides that, you have an expression of having been through perfect horrors and that always impresses my sex, of course. I don't know how we all do bear this dreadful war; it's such an unending strain. I hope you won't have to be sent back into it."

"No, please!" Bailey wiped his forehead again. "Don't hope that. No! I——"

"Indeed we all shall! After she saw you this morning Josephine told me she was sure it's going to be a good thing to have another of the Oaklin family in the museum—to back her up, you see. Then of course there's this thing she wants you for and'll tell you about to-morrow. She—— Oh, dear me! They've let that dog out of the kitchen again!"

A stout brown-and-white springer spaniel, elderly but vivacious, had trotted in from the hall. He went waggingly to Bailey, confident of beginning a friendship, and was well received. "You're a fine fellow," Bailey told him, and was glad to stoop over him. "I had a springer almost exactly like you once. He lived to be fourteen years old. What's your name?"

"Roggo," Mrs. Oaklin said. "You'll never get rid of him if you go on scratching his head. He's the most awful nuisance; but Josephine keeps him around. He's ten years old and's begun to lose one of his eyes, but still behaves like a pup; he scratches hair out of himself and leaves it all over everything. There's a bell-button set in the wall by the door yonder. Will you please give it a push for me?" Bailey got to his feet, found the disk near the door and did as she desired. "Thank you. I never liked dogs much; I don't know why people have 'em, especially when they're the everlastingly hair-shedding kind like this Roggo." Then, as Harvey appeared in the doorway, she merely pointed at the spaniel and let that be her reproach.

"Yes'm," Harvey said. "I don't know who let Roggo out." He bent over the friendly old dog, gave him a surreptitious pat on the head but took him by the collar. Roggo sent Bailey an upward appeal—"Couldn't *you* do anything about this?"—and was dragged away.

"Don't let him out again, Harvey!" Cousin Folia called toward the hall.

"No'm."

Bailey, finding himself on his feet and near the doorway, thought that maybe by this time he'd finished his duty-call on the Oaklins and could respectably depart. "Thank you for letting me come in this afternoon, Cousin Folia," he began. "Perhaps some day you might be so kind again. I——"

"But you're not going?"

"Yes, I——"

"Oh, no, you can't!" she exclaimed. "I'm just filling in till Josephine gets through with her meeting. Didn't she tell you?"

"About a meeting? No."

"Why, certainly," Cousin Folia said. "She does all sorts of war work, you know. Forever flying from one thing to another, I don't know how she manages all she does. Of course you see why she couldn't be in the Waves or Wacs or any of those things, don't you?"

"She couldn't?" Bailey said—to be saying something.

"No, of course not. She has to be here when I have my attacks, naturally. Whenever I overstep my diet the slightest bit I have a terrible time; my heart goes back on me. The only doctor I have any faith in tore off to the Navy months ago and you can't get a reliable nurse for love or money. They don't care a cent what happens to the rest of us. Then of course Josephine has the museum on her hands, and the Symphony Orchestra Board. Doesn't get a breath of rest. I wish you'd try to influence her to quiet down a little sometimes."

"I? You wish I'd——"

"Why, yes, she might listen," Mrs. Oaklin said. "She'd always listen more to somebody new than she will to me. She'll have a breakdown if she isn't careful. All the people she works with are always so utterly incompetent. She decided the city

must have an Officers' Club. There's the USO downtown for
the men, of course; but until she got this idea the other day
there's never been anything for the officers, so she called this
meeting. She has 'em in the library now—eight or ten girls and
women, and Captain Murties to advise 'em how to go about
it and all that. She told me on no account was I to let you
leave until after they come out of the meeting. She's got 'em in
her grandfather's library, the Jacobean room. I'm sure they
won't be much longer. Do sit down again."

"But I'm afraid I——"

"No, no; you can't go. She wants you here, so you might as
well sit down."

XII

Bailey's right hand made a movement to bring forth his handkerchief again; but he gave that hand a look—it obeyed him, dropped to his side, and he sat down. Cousin Folia repeated the effort to shelter her knees. "Have you met many people since you've been here?" she asked. "Probably you already know some of this new committee of hers, Charlotte Parannik, Sophie Tremoille, Mrs. Francis Paylor, Josie Smith, Julia——"

"No, I haven't met them; I haven't met anybody outside of the museum except a few at The Cranford where I live."

"She doesn't think too much of any of 'em." Cousin Folia, following her own vagrant trains of thought, evidently often heard the speech of others as sounds, not words. "They seemed to be the best she could get. She got Charlotte Parannik for the name of course—her husband's the conductor of our Symphony, though he really oughtn't to be, he's so obstinate—and she didn't want Mrs. Francis Paylor but had to because she's in the Army. I don't mean a Wac; her husband's a major and they're years and years older, but he's Harold's most intimate friend. The Paylors seemed to think they practically owned

Harold until—— Oh, dear!" Cousin Folia interrupted herself
as the opening of a door at some distance within the house
made audible a clatter of women's voices, most of them sounding more argumentative than amiable. They approached
slowly, dallying with the dregs of some discussion, and Mrs.
Oaklin looked petulant. "Josephine knew she'd have a time
with some of 'em; they'd be sure to suggest ridiculous ideas.
How many of 'em'd you say you knew? Which ones?"

"None. I don't know any of them."

"Oh, dear!" Cousin Folia exclaimed again. "Then if she
hangs back with Harold—she always likes to come in last and
I wish she'd get over it!—I'll have to do the introducing of
you to all of 'em, and I always get names wrong when I introduce a lot of people."

The chattering voices drew nearer. Bailey rose as half a dozen
young women talked themselves into the room; then he found
a friend and backed to a wall with him. The friend was the
spaniel, Roggo; he'd made another escape and came in scurry-
ing search of the new acquaintance who understood what dogs
wish done to their heads. Bailey bent over him, did as desired,
and the animation of Roggo's stub of a tail proved his gratitude. Cousin Folia interrupted their affair, performed three
or four introductions flusteredly and ordered the old dog removed by Harvey, who'd wheeled in a chromium-plated
wagon stocked with little foods, tea and liquors. Roggo had to
be dragged, protestive feet forward and collar disheveling his
ears; but the new friend's loss was greater than the dog's.

What seemed a tumult made the room, for Bailey, a mere
confusion. His tricky sensations informed him that near-by
voices were screaming and that many people swept blurredly
about him. In reality, although two or three older women had

followed the younger ones, there weren't a dozen persons in the room and they were displaying no unusual animation. They were constrained, had the disingenuous cordiality of people who are where they are only because they haven't known how to avoid being there.

Josephine hadn't appeared, but neither had she lingered behind with her Harold. Captain Murties, serious, was in the room, and presently he brought an affable matron to meet Bailey.

"Fount, this is my dear friend, Mrs. Francis Paylor," Murties said. "When I met you in the museum I was stupid—I didn't get just who you were, except that you were Josephine's cousin. Last night at the Paylors' I happened to mention your name and the Major reminded me——"

"He didn't, either!" Mrs. Paylor cried. "How like a man—always giving the credit for anything to another man! Until I spoke up, neither you nor my husband realized that this Mr. Fount is precisely the Lieutenant Bailey Fount who——"

"No, no. Too much was made of that," Bailey said hurriedly, and this time he didn't check his hand when it groped for his handkerchief. Cousin Folia intervened, bringing some of the younger women to meet him. They seemed to make indistinguishable sounds at him; he hadn't an idea of what any of them said to him or of what he said in return. "Stop that! Stop that!" was the fierce command he gave himself when he discovered that he was wiping his forehead almost continuously.

Josephine Oaklin was the last by ten minutes to come into the drawing-room. She made a black and gold and ivory picture of herself in the wide doorway—gold hair, ivory face, gold clasps at throat and waist, black velvet knee-dress, ivory stockings, black patent-leather slippers. Unlike her mother, she was fashionable successfully; elegance of figure being no doubt helpful to that vanishing quality once known as an "air of elegance." Josephine possessed it intrinsically and by habit in dress; though in manner not more often than she chose. Her first shout: "My *Bailey!*" drew all eyes to the doorway. Within another swift instant, she rushed upon him, beginning her great fuss over him by kissing him.

"Oh, in uniform!" she cried. "How beautiful! You poor neglected soul, you haven't anything—no tea, no cocktail, no nothing! Here, let me bring you——"

"No—no, please." Bailey was afraid of a cocktail and couldn't trust his hands with a plate or cup and saucer. "I don't—I can't—I'd rather not——"

"How darlingly ascetic!" She put her hand on his shoulder and called out to everybody, "Wouldn't it be just my luck? Discovering I've got a cousin like *this*—and me just about to be married! Yes, it's settled. Harold thinks now he may be sent somewhere else almost any day, so I've decided on immediate nuptials. Absolutely! Two weeks from next Thursday!"

"Josephine!" Her mother made outcry. "Are you crazy? It's not possible! I couldn't be ready. We can't——"

"Can't!" Josephine laughed triumphantly. "Who ever said 'can't' to me?" She took Bailey's left hand, pulled it round her velvet waist, was archly provocative. "*You'd* never say 'can't' to me, would you, Cousin? How scandalous of me: I'd almost forgotten it's not you but Harold who'll be trying to say 'can't' to me the rest of my life! Aren't you lucky not to be in Harold's place? Bailey Fount, stay right where you are till I go and subdue Mother. I'll come back to you."

She ran to her mother and began to talk to her vehemently. Bailey, standing where she'd left him, gave himself panicky instructions: "Keep your hands down! You shan't wipe your face any more! Watch yourself!" Then he realized that one of the ladies was speaking to him. She stood close by, at his right, was young, thin, alluringly pretty, had unusually large dark eyes and the softest of voices. He caught only the end of a question put to him, but thought she'd asked him if he liked something, he didn't know what.

"I beg your pardon," he said. "Did you—did you ask me—did you——"

"Mr. Fount, I was bad enough to ask you if you like it."

"I'm afraid I—— If I like what?"

The lady was slyly amused. "I'm a spiteful person, always avenging myself, perhaps because I'm half-Spanish. From here could you hear us fighting over the new committee? Your pretty cousin made the most noise; then adjourned us, announced you were waiting, she *must* see you! She seems to love to throw you at her captain's head. I asked you if you like it. Do you?"

"Do I——" He didn't know what she meant or what anything meant. "Do I what?"

"Good!" the dark pretty lady exclaimed. "You are discretion's self! My husband has met you and he tells me he likes you but do you know who I am? No, you don't."

"No," he said desperately, "I don't."

"I'm Charlotte Parannik. You belong with the museum, I with the orchestra, being my husband's wife; so we have something in common, haven't we? That poor Mr. Rossbeke and my dearest friend, Helena Jyre! Yes, we all have the same troubles, you of the museum and we of the orchestra. Perhaps you and I could sympathize in a mutual wish: that the instant they're married Mr. and Mrs. Captain Murties will leave for a long, long honeymoon, maybe to Guatemala—maybe to Tierra del Fuego."

He still had no idea what she was talking about and heard her with difficulty, she spoke so softly and other voices were chattering close by. "Tierra del Fuego?" he repeated wonderingly. "Tierra del Fuego——"

"Yes. It's farther than Guatemala!" Mrs. Parannik smiled approvingly. "Tierra del Fuego, you're right; that would be the better. Yes, I rather thought you were a little inappreciative of the cousinly caresses—perhaps because you understood them. She's not so effusive when you're alone together? That poor Captain Murties, he must have done something very naughty to be so punished! Mr. Fount, I hope you will come to see us. My husband liked you, so you liked him, didn't you?"

"Did I?" Bailey corrected himself. "Yes—yes, of course I did."

"Everybody does—except one," Mrs. Parannik said. "I'm glad to've met you, but now I'm going—shall I say escaping? Forget my wickedness—to say such things to a cousin! Goodbye."

She turned away, joining Mrs. Paylor and Murties who were on their way to the door; but before the three reached it Josephine had run back to Bailey and linked arms with him. "Charlotte Parannik," she cried, "haven't I been sweet to give you a chance to talk to this treasure?"

"Yes—and I'm sure he is one, Josephine, particularly just now."

"Shrew!" Josephine laughed. "I hope I don't know what you were saying to him! Harold, don't come round till to-morrow night. You haven't forgotten you're lunching here to-mor-row, have you, Bailey?"

"No, I'll——"

"One o'clock," she said with less animation, releasing his arm as Murties, Mrs. Parannik and Mrs. Paylor disappeared into the hall. Bailey thought that he was now permitted to leave. "No, don't go for a minute or so," Josephine whispered. "Let those three get well away first."

He waited meekly, not wondering why she detained him; his forehead was hot again and he was trying to let it alone. Josephine turned from him, and for a few minutes was ex-clamatorily busy with her departing committee-members; then she swung back to him.

"All right now," she said. "Run along if you like. Good-bye till to-morrow."

. . . Outdoors under early starlight and passing the long stone front of the Thomas Oaklin Museum, Bailey limped only a little. "I got through it! Roggo helped; I didn't mind so much while he was there. You screwball, aren't you ever going to learn to stop talking to yourself out loud?"

At lunch next day Josephine did nine-tenths of the talking, her mother did nine-tenths of the other tenth; and all of the talk was about Josephine's wedding. Bailey sat watching him-self, instructing himself. "Eat something! This isn't bad; there's no one here except these two and they're your cousins, kin to you . . . They won't hurt you! They're trying to be kind to you or else they wouldn't have asked you . . . You're doing all right, so far; but put your fork into something and eat it! Stop breaking up bread. Eat!"

Josephine spoke to him briskly. "Bailey, do you realize what a providence it is your turning up here out of nowhere and precisely when needed? My good angel proves at last that he really exists. Think of what a gap there'd have been in the ceremony except for your happening! And how right you'll be! Harold's Best Man's to be Major Paylor of course, and with me on your uniformed arm it'll all be properly military. I hope you're flattered. Aren't you?"

"Flattered? I'm afraid I didn't hear just what——"

She laughed. "Come back to earth! Mother, I don't believe he's heard a word."

"No," Mrs. Oaklin said, "I've noticed he's a rather dreamy young man, and besides, there's what that Mr. Rossbeke seemed to be trying to impress on me—I told you, Josephine, you know, about Bailey's being all right and almost recovered from getting shot, but rather nervous and——"

"Nervous?" Josephine's laughter was continued. "Rubbish! You're not nervous, Bailey; you only think you are. You know that people aren't nervous except through thinking they are, don't you?"

"I hope so. I do hope so."

"Certainly! Here, I'm going to cure you. You listen! At any wedding who marches up the aisle with the bride?"

"What?"

"Who does?" Josephine answered herself. "Why, the bride's male next-of-kin of course. Who's the male next-of-kin of this bride you're staring at right now? Haven't I told you you're the only man left in our family, my father's own first-cousin's son? You're the male head of our dynasty! You're elected, Bailey Fount. You'll bring me up the aisle and give me away."

"Me? I? You want me to——"

"I not only want you to, you've got to! We were almost

ready to leave the giving-away out entirely, until I thought of you. The only other possibility—Mother made the brilliant suggestion!—was old John Constable Horne. Not for me! I'm hub-deep in a terrific quarrel with him right now, no novelty, and I swear I'd decline to be married at all if the only way to do it's to reach the altar on the arm of that conceited bad-tempered, opinionated old obstructionist! Praise God we don't have to be that desperate; we've got a man in the family, after all. I asked you if you don't feel flattered to be that man, Bailey. Don't you?"

"Yes—yes, I do—but——"

"Of course you do, and thank heaven you're on hand to perform!" Josephine had already taken his flattered assent as a matter of course. She prattled on. "We're going to have eight ushers, all Army or Navy, but no bridesmaids. There isn't a girl in this town I'd let be a bridesmaid of mine and I do wish I didn't have to have a Maid of Honor, either; but I've got to stand Sophie Tremoille's going through the motions. She's a gawky old thing but's been my Girl Friday ever since childhood's unhappy hour—it'd kill the poor slave if I didn't have her. You're young to be giving a bride away, Bailey, but terribly picturesque and I'm delighted with myself to've thought of it. As soon as I forgive Harold for being a snippet at me over nothing, I'll tell him you're to officiate."

Josephine and her mother thereupon renewed previous incomplete plannings concerned with florists, caterers, incidental music and invitation lists. Bailey sat panic-stricken, and, in spite of what he felt to be his vital need, no words came from his mouth. "What do I tell them?" he thought. "How *can* I tell them? Where's a decent excuse? Do I say 'No, I'm too rickety'? Do I say 'Don't count on me, I can't, I'm haywire'?

How can I tell them what I don't know how to tell them when they don't give me a chance to tell them anything at all?" Mrs. Oaklin and her daughter talked busily; they appeared to have forgotten him.

When he left the house presently Josephine went as far as the front door with him, calling back over her shoulder names she'd just thought of and wished her mother to add to the invitation list for the church. "Not for the *house*, Mother," she called. "Don't get 'em mixed up with the list for the house. Bye-bye, Bailey. Harold or I or somebody'll let you know when to meet the rest of us at the church for the rehearsal. I'll see you're notified in plenty of time."

"I——"

Josephine, already calling more names to her mother, closed the door. He whispered to the outer air the refusal he hadn't been able to utter inside the house.

Toward four o'clock Helena Jyre, seated beside him at a long table as they worked together on the museum's "Bulletin," observed him sidelong and suggested a postponement. "There's no special hurry about this, Bailey. How about laying off for to-day?"

"I'm all right. I've got to stop babying myself—ought to be ashamed of having to be bucked up to go to my cousins' house, behaving as if that were such a terrific strain!"

"It wasn't, Bailey?"

"Well—at least I don't think I made any breaks especially."

"Breaks? What nonsense! Of course you didn't. Anyhow, you've done your duty by those people, got through with it and won't have to go there again. If I were you, I'd just forget about 'em."

He seemed not to hear this suggestion. "Miss Jyre, what made you think just now that I'd better stop work?"

"Nothing—except you looked a little tired. Worried about something maybe? Until the last day or two you've seemed *so* much better—seemed so *well*——"

"You think now I'm dropping back?"

"No, not exactly. I just thought——"

"I'm perfectly all right." He withdrew into himself, though he'd been on the verge of telling Miss Jyre of his Cousin Josephine's daunting plan to make him a part of her wedding ceremony. Good Lord! Couldn't he do the simplest thing without running to a busy woman again for a bracer? He bent to his work; but a few minutes later he was whispering, apparently to the motionless fountain pen in his hand: "Maybe I could get out of it by telephone." Helena, not catching the words, thought they concerned the manuscript before him.

"Could I help, Bailey? What——"

"It's nothing. Just my disgusting habit—always blithering to myself! Will I ever get over it?"

"Wouldn't matter much if you didn't," she said. "We all do it sometimes. Me, I think absentminded people are fascinating." Then, quickly looking at the notes before her, she exclaimed, "Oh, murder!"

"What's the matter?"

"See, Bailey. Miss Bullard's spelled 'Carpaccio' without the 'i'. Isn't she unbelievable? Look!"

He looked, she pointed out other errors, and for the moment he was soothed; then nervous horror came upon him again. To face a church full of people, to parade limpingly down the aisle with Josephine Oaklin upon his shaking arm and then publicly to perform the function she'd so lightly assigned him

—"No! No! I can't! I can't!" Except for set teeth and tight lips he'd have exclaimed this aloud.

. . . That night at The Cranford he went to the telephone in the hall downstairs; but he only made gestures toward the dial. He gave up the idea for a better one, which at the moment seemed almost inspirational, and ascended to his room to write to Josephine. Why hadn't he thought of that before, he wondered, as with cheering relief he climbed the stairs. Writing his excuses would be easy, the simplest thing in the world; but at his writing-table he blackly scratched "Dear Cousin Josephine" three times on a sheet of paper and sat staring at it —"*Dear Cousin Josephine Dear Cousin Josephine Dear Cousin Josephine*"—all on one line. Send her *that* and she'd certainly understand she couldn't depend on him—and he'd come here to be cured! A fat chance he'd have now to pass an examination by Colonel Bedge!

Josephine thought he ought to feel flattered to be asked to give her away. Flattered? It was immeasurable flattery for her to think him half a man—oh, the tenth of a man! She'd been kind to him—at least she'd intended to be that—and he ought to do what she wished. He couldn't—why, he couldn't even let her know that he couldn't!

He tried again to write:

"*I am sorry, Cousin Josephine, but I must not delay any longer to let you know that I cannot take the part in your wedding you have flatteringly assigned to me. Physically since I came here I have improved beyond all hopes, but nervously (I fear I should say mentally) I find myself still in a sorry state. The simple truth is I am psychopathically a wreck and if I tried to do what you wish I do not know what would be the result.*

I cannot count on what I might do or say. I cannot cannot cannot——"

He tore the sheet of notepaper to pieces. "Poor damn nut!" he said, and sat helpless. What was he going to do—wait until the wedding rehearsal and then hide? He had no better plan and no worse one; he had no plan at all. The next day passed and the next—more than a week went by and he hadn't told Josephine he couldn't take her up the aisle of a church and give her away.

Inexplicably the mere sight of a door decided him to rush, blurt out his refusal and run. He'd find Josephine or Cousin Folia, and the instant he'd see either, he'd begin to talk. He'd not try to explain; he'd just say he was sorry but he wasn't able; they'd have to get somebody else. Then he'd get himself out and away. The door was the oaken one that led into the passageway connecting the museum with the Oaklins' house. Late afternoon of a working Sunday had gone dark outside; he'd changed into his uniform, then had gathered together some notes he'd made on the condition of the small collection of Spanish Primitives. With Miss Jyre, an hour earlier, he'd been over the suggestions he'd written and she'd told him Mr. Rossbeke ought to pass upon them as soon as possible; so now Bailey took them to the Director's office and left them upon Mrs. Williams's desk, as both she and Rossbeke had gone home. Coming out of the office he was confronted by the oaken door across the corridor, and its aged paneling became invested with sudden eloquence.

"Do it now! Pass through; it's only a step. Now or never! This is a way to get it done—a poor way, but it's a way. Get it over!"

The impulse had to move him instantly or not at all. If he went outside and round to the front door of the house, he knew he wouldn't ring the bell. He crossed the corridor sharply to the oaken door, opened it, and plungingly reached its counterpart at the other end of the passage, knocked loudly. There was no response; but he knocked till his knuckles hurt—then the door was opened by Harvey.

"No, sir." The colored man spoke into the darkness of the passage. "Sorry, sir, but nobody allowed to come this way. It the rule and——" His recognition of Bailey interrupted him. "Oh, it you, sir! Yes, Mr. Bailey, you one the family and right now's a good time you come. Yes, sir, good time any this family come! Walk right in, Lieutenant, sir, and res' your overcoat. I'll take it, sir, and your sojer cap."

"No, thank you, Harvey. I'm only going to stay a moment."

"No, sir; you'll be stayin' longer." Harvey took the cap, and, before Bailey realized it, had the overcoat too. "I'll put 'em on the front hall table for you, sir. You jes' wait here, please. Need all the family we can get at a time like this, sir. I tell 'em you come. Yes, sir; sit down, Mr. Bailey, please."

With that he was gone, taking the cap and overcoat with him and leaving Bailey alone in the shadowy big room which was but vaguely illuminated by the single bulb fitted to a tall old iron candlestick. Hurrying to answer the insistent knocking, Harvey had made only the one light; and its glow, from a side table, was impeded by a brown parchment shade.

Across the room an oblong patch of red resolved itself into the shaping of a couch covered in scarlet leather; other red patches revealed themselves as chairs. The great dark mantelpiece emerged to sight in disclosures of curved gleams faint upon the contours of its ancient carving, and from the backs of many books dim glints of gilt traversed the shadows. Bailey, already set aback by silence and continued waiting, tried to keep his mind doggedly to its one purpose; but he remembered that Cousin Folia'd said she didn't like to come to this room, she always seemed to see his great-uncle sitting here.

Bailey began to understand that. An old, old man, all grey and white, wouldn't he be?—thin, almost weightless and sitting habitually in one of these heavy chairs. Which one of them? Most likely the one nearest the fireplace. It was easy, too easy, to see him there, present though shaped of almost nothingness —perhaps quietly dying there, with last imaginings rising before him: daily crowds of people thronging gratefully through the galleries of his magnificent gift to them. Poor old man, he hadn't known how like he was to all the other noble Donors this earth has seen—planning great things to bear their more and more meaningless names until somebody drops an "atomic energy" bomb and——

Bailey started, stood open-mouthed. Shocking sounds reached him through the inner door Harvey'd left ajar—a girl's uncontrolled sobbing. Josephine Oaklin came through that door; she came stoopingly, stumbled, threw herself full length, face down, upon the scarlet leather couch without pause in her heartbroken weeping. She hadn't seen him.

XIII

Across the room Bailey stood bewildered. Of Josephine Oaklin, the person, he'd thought almost not at all; her intrusion upon his walled consciousness had been as a confusing pressure, something pushing at him to do things that frightened him. His slight visual impression of her—a nimble figure in frequent motion, a more than pretty face usually smiling, often laughing, always wholly confident—formed only the symbol of what pressed upon him. For days he'd identified her with the daunting task she'd set him, so that the thought of her was formidable; but here, flung prostrate before him by some agonizing misfortune, she came to life and was a fellow-creature.

Josephine moaned, sniffled, whimpered; she sobbed so shudderingly that she seemed to strangle and the choking contorted her whole body. She twisted herself, jerked in revoltings sourer than despair; then lay flat again, disordered in hair and dress but finally as unmoving as if the convulsion had killed her.

Into the stillness a small pattering intruded; Roggo trotted through the doorway, waggled himself loyally to the couch and began to lick the delicate hand that hung lifelessly over its edge.

That hand didn't move; but Harvey's voice was heard calling softly, "Miss Josephine, Miss Josephine?" He appeared in the doorway and for a moment Josephine was hidden from him by the high end of the couch. "I ain't found her yet, sir; but if you wait just a few minutes more I——" He saw Josephine, said "Yes'm" gently, went to the couch, lifted the heavy spaniel, held him in his arms. "Roggo, you come with me. Miss Josephine, your mamma gone to bed she feel so bad about it. It's nice you got one the family at time like this. He go' be comfort to you, yes'm."

"Go away." Josephine didn't move.

"Yes'm," Harvey said hushedly. "People in trouble got to depend on they family."

Tiptoeing, the old man went out of the room, carrying Roggo with him; but Josephine's immobility was ended. She shivered; the shiver became new shudderings. She sobbed again and, regardlessly disheveled, tossed and squirmed against the scarlet of the couch as she wept muffledly, her face pressed into a leather cushion.

Bailey Fount looked at her fixedly, said nothing and didn't move. For the first time in months he had ceased to have any consciousness of himself. During all the long period of his nervous illness, self had miserably absorbed him; but now, all at once, he was freed of that injurious preoccupation and thought concentratedly of another person. He'd seen pain and death in plenty, but grief so wildly in possession, never; and that the stricken creature on the couch was of his own kin he realized with abruptly extreme acuteness. Sympathy so sudden and so stirring can be as unrestrained as can the agony that rouses it.

"What did he mean?" Josephine muttered. She pushed herself up to sit, not upright but crumpled over and still weeping.

"Who——" She saw Bailey. "Meant you, did he?" She spoke hoarsely, not as if surprised. In this depth she didn't care who was there or who was anywhere.

Bailey crossed the room to her. He sat down beside her and his voice had no hesitancies. "I'll help you if you'll give me the chance to. What's gone wrong?"

"No. Just let me alone."

"I couldn't do that," he said. "You've told me yourself I'm one of your family, and it's true; I am. Even Harvey seems to know what's happened. Why shouldn't I?"

"Yes, Harvey knows." She spoke through catches of breath between sobs. "Of course—he knows. All the servants heard me—heard me screaming it out to Mother. What's the difference who knows? Everybody's going to know. It can't be— can't be kept from this rotten spiteful town, it can't! There'll not be a soul won't know it."

"Won't know what, Josephine?"

"What's been done to me!" she gasped. "Everybody—every soul in the place—it can't be hid, it can't! They'll all know what's been done to me!"

"By whom? Who's done anything to you?"

She turned partly toward him, staring at him haggardly through wisps of fair hair. "I've been jilted."

"You've been——"

"Jilted. Yes, me! Josephine Oaklin! With the wedding all set—the whole town waiting for it—I'm jilted, thrown over, kicked into the gutter——"

"No, you're not!" He was decisive, and for an instant he took her by the shoulders. "Stiffen up! Nobody's going to treat a nice girl like you that way. What's the straight of it?"

"Why, I've told you! Harold's gone. He's gone, I tell you!"

"What of that? You ought to know by this time that any-body in the service is subject to sudden orders—sometimes can't even say good-bye. That happens every day and you oughtn't to——"

"Harold said good-bye all right!" Josephine produced a sound of sickened laughter. "He left a note he knew wouldn't be delivered to me till he'd caught his train. Do you want to know what was in it? Everybody else is going to know what's in it, you bet, because his dear sweet old friend, Mrs. Paylor, certainly told him what to write and she'll just as certainly spread it! They needn't think I don't know that much! I know just as well as if I'd seen it and heard it, myself—that he went to her and——"

"What was in his note?"

Bitterness prevailed temporarily over the sobbing that had stopped other utterance. "It said he had orders for the coast and was leaving. He said there wasn't time for us to get mar-ried now anyhow and it would be wiser for us not to regard this as merely a postponement. He said, 'I'm afraid we've both made a great mistake in thinking we were meant for each other,' and went on he was sure I'd agree our best course was to call everything off permanently—permanently!"

"He wrote that?"

"Oh, yes—'permanently'! Then he wished me the best of luck in the world and said he hoped I could do the same for him. That's what he wrote, and he signed it 'Yours sincerely'! Sincerely! Oh, God!"

"But that——" Bailey couldn't believe it. "It's impossible!"

She didn't hear him. Her hands clutched each other about her knees and she rocked herself. "'Yours sincerely'! He's been lying to me for weeks, and I knew it. Oh, I knew he was cooling off! He and that grinning old woman—always being such a sweet dear aunt to him—they needn't think I didn't know she was working on him against me! I did everything I could to hold him. It was horrible, but I did, I did, and nothing was any good, nothing! Toward the last I even tried to make him jealous—I even tried to make him jealous of you. It was all I could do."

Bailey was only the more compassionate. "You wanted him to think you liked me because——"

"Oh, I liked you well enough," she said. "I do; but I made all that fuss over you, kissing you and everything, because I thought he needed it. He was changing and I had to try to stir him up. God knows I did everything on earth I could to keep him as crazy over me as he was at the start! He was! He was out of his head over me; but he—he just changed. There were times when I felt as if—as if he actually disliked me."

"But what happened?" Bailey said. "What made him? What——"

"Nothing! Nothing on earth! He just changed. Now he signs himself 'Yours sincerely.' 'Yours sincerely'! Oh, God! Oh, God! Oh——"

"Steady," Bailey said. "You don't need to break your heart over a heel like that. You don't need to love him that much."

"Love him?" Josephine cried. "Is that what you think? I'm in this hell of pain, am I, because I'm deprived of Harold Sorgius Murties?"

"Then what's the matter with you? If you don't care for him——"

"Care for him!" She clapped her palms to her temples. "Trying to make me hysterical? I could laugh the roof off! Think I'm suffering because I care for *him?*"

"Then what's it all about?"

"You talk like a fool!" Josephine's outcry was near a shriek. "It's what he's *done* to me! Don't you know that every girl and every old woman in this town'll be running from house to house, keeping the telephone hot, squealing it out of windows —'Josephine Oaklin's been jilted, hurrah!'"

"I don't believe it. Nobody'd do that, Josephine."

"Ah, *won't* they, though—and where does it put me? Town talk, that's what I'll be! That's where I end up, just the town joke! Took up with a fly-by-night soldier-man and got run away from! *That's* what I let myself in for. Oh, yes, I did it to myself!"

"No, you didn't. How could——"

"I got engaged to him, didn't I?" She clasped her knees, rocked herself again. "Hell, why does anybody get engaged? I thought at first I could be in love with him—sort of. Everybody else is getting married and it's time I did and he was wild about me—yes, he was, for a while! Then after that I wasn't going to let him go, not with everybody that hates me waiting to pounce! You don't know how many have always been envious and jealous of me. The more I've despised 'em, the more they've made my life a thorn thicket; I could never move an inch without getting scratched. Now they've got me down and they'll stab me to death!" Josephine struck herself over the heart as if with a knife; by no means a merely theatrical gesture—she meant it. "They'll kill me! I'm done, I'm whipped, I'm finished!"

"You're not," he said. "You don't need to be."

"You!" she cried, and in her extremity was contemptuous of him. "What am I doing, yelping to *you?* You're my cousin but I hardly know you. What are you doing here, anyhow?"

She pushed at him, shoving him, both hands on his breast. "Get out of here, will you, and let me alone!"

At that he rose but stood looking down upon her. She immediately twisted herself to lie once more at full length face down, writhing, weeping, kicking the scarlet leather of the couch, beating the cushion with her fists. To see a human being in rebellion so furious and yet so abject wrung the heart of Bailey Fount with a pity sharper than it had ever known. He spoke her name appealingly. "Josephine——"

"No!" she moaned. "Don't talk. I won't listen. Go away! I'm shamed, can't you see, I'm shamed! I don't want you here. I don't want anybody to look at me. I'm *shamed!*"

"No, you're not—but I understand." He was apologetically confidential now. "I'll tell you something. I know how it is to feel like that. The fact is I've had to feel like that for a long time. You see, I found I was all washed up. I was no good. That was what I had to face. It's what I still have to face. But you—why, you're a strong lovely girl, full of life and helpfulness. Your mother told me how many useful things you do. You're going to be all right."

"Am I?" Her voice had spent its bitterness and was thin and small, like that of a confessing child. "No, I'm smeared, Bailey. I'm smeared for good. You see this—this isn't the first time. Two years ago I—I was engaged to somebody else and—and it had to be broken off and—and people thought I wasn't the one that did it."

"Oh, poor girl!" His pity grew as his comprehension of her grew.

"Yes. So this finishes me. I'm twice-used. Nobody'd ever look at me again."

"I would," he said. To this extreme did chivalry and the

drive of an unbearable sympathy inspire him. "I'd look at you, Josephine. I've come to be such a nothing that it'd be a privilege to find I could be of use to anybody—with whatever's left of me. If it's what you need, Cousin, would you be engaged to me?"

She lifted herself, first upon her right elbow; then she straightened that arm and sat almost upright. "What did you say? Did you——"

"Yes. Wouldn't it help you to stand up to this? People ought to stand up to things if they possibly can. I haven't been able to do it, myself; but it's just struck me that maybe I could help you to. Wouldn't I do?"

"Wouldn't you do for what?"

"To be engaged to," Bailey said. "What you can't take doesn't seem to be this fellow's letting you down; it seems to be what you believe people are going to think and say about it. If you let them think I'm the reason for your not marrying him, you could maybe stand up to them, couldn't you?"

She cleared the hair from her eyes. "You're offering yourself to me as a way out?"

"Yes. I'd be glad to. You thought I had enough front to make him jealous, so maybe I'd do. We're both pretty down, aren't we? I'd feel less so if I could be used to help you up a little. It might work all right, mightn't it?"

Her stare at him, at first merely dumfounded, was altering; she seemed to grope for light. "You don't mean you're in love with me, do you?"

"No, not at all. Nothing like that. Of course not. My life isn't worth much to me or to anybody, so I just now got the idea that maybe——"

"Wait a minute!" She'd stopped weeping, and, with fists

pressed against her cheeks, concentrated upon thoughts that widely enlarged her ravaged eyes as she continued to gaze at him. "Wait," she said again. "Now just wait a minute——" and all at once was breathless. She rose and stood before him, looking up at him. "You really mean you're willing? You'd even go through with it?"

"Yes."

"Answer me straight," she said. "You're sure you'd not go back on it? You're sure you aren't a quitter?"

At that he winced, yet spoke up strongly. "I won't be one about this. No, you can depend on it."

She seemed to find herself vacant of everything but wonderment. "Why, this—it's queerer than the devil! It's *queer!*"

"Yes. I've found a lot of things that way, myself."

"See here," she said, "it couldn't be just an engagement; it can't stop at that." For the first time aware of her tousledness, she looked self-conscious and made an ineffective effort with hasty fingers to rearrange her hair. "Some day—not right now but some day—I'd have to be married—married to *you*. I mean—actually married."

"Yes," Bailey said. "We both understand that, don't we? I've just told you I'd go through with it."

"Then you'll have to!" Triumphant glintings displaced the wonder in her lovely eyes, and suddenly she was radiant. "Oh! I'll pull out; I see it, I see it! Bailey Fount, I'll adore you for this!" Looking beautiful, even more beautiful than he'd thought her, she laughed wildly, threw her arms about his neck, clung to him, kissed him upon the lips. "I'm laughing at them; they'll see! Heaven sent you, you angel of a cousin!"

She pushed herself from him. "Go along and let me get to thinking. Be in your workroom to-morrow morning at ten o'clock. I'll come there." Then she was laughing and weeping at the same time. "Take care of yourself for me—I need you, I need you!"

Bailey found his way to the front hall, picked up his cap and overcoat where Harvey'd left them, and went from the house. Exhilarated, confused, yet feeling more life in himself than for a long time past, he knew he'd done a reckless thing—a romantic and maybe theatrical thing, no doubt at all a preposterous thing—but the act was tonic. He who'd come to say he couldn't give the bride away was now to be the bridegroom!—and what did that declare of his sanity? Ah, but if he could uplift so lovely and fine a fellow-creature as this girl-cousin of his out of the black defeat in which he'd found her, wasn't he somebody again—somebody beginning to be like a man again! Life, after all, might be an experience worth having, and Captain Harold Sorgius Murties must be as crazy as he was detestable.

Something like a strange yet faintly fragrant promise seemed to float in the cold air of the street that ran before the darkened Oaklin Museum. Bailey Fount, walking that street, had no realization that for the first time since last spring he wasn't limping.

XIV

Nᴏᴛ ᴜɴᴛɪʟ he was on his way to the museum in the morning did he discover that he'd completely lost his lameness, and even then he didn't understand why he was at last fully rid of it. He perceived that although his leg had gradually ceased to be painful he must have continued out of sheer habit to limp a little, and with some cheerfulness he wondered if other habits, nervous habits, weren't retarding his cure. What he didn't yet comprehend was that his preoccupation not with himself but with another person had broken him of limping, and of more. He wasn't conscious that during the past thirteen hours he'd been thinking of Josephine Oaklin almost uninterruptedly, except while he slept—and perhaps even while he slept.

He had called her confusing; but now the confusion was all in the background from which she emerged injuriously used but gleaming. That background seemed to be a turmoil—war-like envies and jealousies ever darting at her for no better reason than that she was a shining mark, brightly and beautifully the great Thomas Oaklin's granddaughter. Life, no less than death, loves to strike at the shining mark. Bailey was aglow to think that by his privileged help this one hadn't been struck down. The dishonored Murties and his middle-aged spitefully advising friend, Mrs. Paylor—beings quite incomprehensible —had come near doing it, but only near; and now they'd disappear ignobly from Josephine's background. Clearly, a disabled veteran could operate to no inconsiderable effect—and at no perceptible cost to himself. Certainly it wasn't much of a sacrifice to be engaged to a girl as pretty as that!

Josephine was almost prompt. At twelve minutes after ten by the watch he was consulting, her knock came upon his workroom door; but when he'd opened it she didn't step in immediately. Instead, she stood still, gave him a glance, then looked down half-demurely, half-humorously, as if to say, "Well? Here's what's on your hands!"

She'd recovered her elegance, was dainty in a grey cloth suit, didn't wear a hat, and her hair denied any memory that it had ever been seen disheveled. After the moment well used in letting him look at her, she came lightly forward, he closed the door and they stood more intimately confronted.

"One reason I wanted to come," she said, with a cosily whispered laugh, "I'll have to begin to get used to you. I'll have to do that pretty fast, won't I?"

"I'm afraid I won't very soon get used to you, Josephine, or to being engaged to you."

"No, I don't mean that," she explained. "I mean I'll have to make a quick habit of behaving that way with you. You've no idea how many things I've got to do fast."

"What are the others?"

"Besides behaving that way?" She gave him a businesslike glance and sat down on the bench before his worktable. "Here, sit beside me and I'll tell you. There are details without end," she said, as he obeyed. "I've left Mother attending to one of 'em for me right now. Poor thing! I kept her up half the night. I use her as a sort of sounding-board to get my ideas straightened out; she makes all sorts of rattled objections and over-ruling 'em clears my head. Of course she set up a commotion about you. Don't be alarmed; she'll coöperate—it was mainly just flusteredness over what she thinks the impossibility of making people believe I'd flagrantly switched so suddenly. The invitations for my disbanded wedding to the gallant Harold chose this morning to arrive and I've got her attending to the burning of 'em. Next she's to call off the florists and the rest of the commercial harpies. She's too nervous to handle any of the subtle doings. For them I can trust only myself."

"What are they?"

"Oh, not too subtly subtle!" she laughed. "The only trouble is they have to be so hurried. I've diagnosed the enemy, you see; my tactics have to be counter-attacks. Don't worry, though, Bailey; your part'll be little more than acquiescence. When people are looking, give me a bit of tender gazing now and then—ardent if you can manage it—and perhaps a pat on the shoulder or a touch to the hand. Think you can?"

"Yes, without strain."

"The Paylor old woman," Josephine resumed, "won't be long starting my disgrace on its rounds from ear to ear. Of course the chivalrous Harold would have put the hush-hush on the Paylors—me to be allowed to explain things the best way I could—and the Major'll stick to it; but it'd kill darling old Aunt Jezebel if she couldn't spread it. Miss such a chance to bury Josephine Oaklin under a hundred tons of coal? Not old Gertie Paylor!"

"She's that malicious?"

"Dear boy!" Josephine gave him a compassionate smile. "I'm glad you're one of those innocent men about women; the type's rare but persists. Sweet Aunt Gertie'll be too afraid of her husband's honorableness to trot round the town openly publicizing her Dido-and-Æneas version. She'll tell just one person, first taking that person's sacred oath never to tell who told her. That'll be Charlotte Parannik—some time to-day, of course—and it'll take Charlotte just about forty-eight hours more to have it well buzzing on every breeze. You see how we'll have to rush the answer that baffles 'em?"

"The announcement of your engagement, Josephine?"

"Not instantly or we'd give our show away; they'd say that in desperation I'd seized upon a convenient cousin. The announcement'll be soon; but before it's made I'll have to set high-colored rumors on the air. It has to be spread that my unavoidable change of heart is quite a shock to me—I'm too too sorry for Harold but found myself so totally all-out for you that I had to tell him. To be plausible we go step by step, quick steps. The first one of course is to let them see for themselves that I *am* in love with you. You get that, don't you?"

Bailey thought her voice delightful as she said "that I *am* in love with you"; the seven words made a pretty sound. "But I won't be much help to you just there, will I? I wouldn't know how."

Upon this, her glance at him held an approving laughter. "You'll do," she said. "You're all the nicer for not understanding that most people who've met you'll believe it without much difficulty. It's a point I shouldn't worry over if I were you. You can leave it to me, can't you?"

"Yes, of course."

"In fact," she said, "so far as we two are concerned there

won't be anything for you to bother about if you'll just be a
little careful to follow my lead in everything when we're with
other people. You'll do that, won't you?"

"Yes, certainly."

"And you're sure you'll be willing to leave everything to
me?"

"More than willing."

"Then we're all set," she said. "The idea we convey is that
we're trying terribly hard to be decent about the whole thing
—sorry for Harold and all that—but of course can't help being
glad for ourselves. That idea has to seem just to leak out,
hurried bit by bit. It'll begin to do it after a confessional confidence session, probably tearful, I'll have with Sophie Tremoille before noon to-day; then I have a really scintillant plan
for you and me—an act we'll put on this afternoon—and to-
night or to-morrow Mother's to telephone around the invitations for the dinner she's giving for you."

Nervous habit still prevailed enough to make him look
appalled. "For me? Oh, no, I can't—I couldn't——"

"Dear me, yes!" she exclaimed. "The dinner won't be in
honor of you as a prospective bridegroom—we couldn't let 'em
think we're that brazen quite so instantly. It's to celebrate you
as a dear cousin newly come to town. Of course, though, because of what Sophie Tremoille will have been confiding
around, and because of my obvious madness over you, there'll
be revealing undercurrents. Yes, I've seen that you're the most
modest and shyest of men, but the dinner'll be this week and
you'll have to go through with it."

"I shall?"

She gave him a gay little touch on the cheek. "You certainly
shall!"

His new bravery and a pleasantly tingling cheek enabled him to say, "Then I will. What else?"

"That's for this afternoon, Bailey—the act I said we'd put on."

"Act?" He showed misgivings. "I ought to warn you—I've never been good at that."

"You don't need to be," she said cheerfully. "I'll do nine-tenths of the histrionics for us both; I like to. Here's the set-up: old John Horne's coming to the museum this afternoon for the re-hanging of the pictures in the big American Gallery. You know about it, don't you?"

"Yes, Mr. Rossbeke told me to be on hand. I'm to see to the bringing up of the rest of the most valuable American paintings from the cellars where they've been since just after the scare began. As soon as Mr. Horne arrives, Mr. Rossbeke said, we're to do the re-hanging, taking down and putting up. You'll be there?"

"Will I!" Josephine's short laughter had metal in it. "They didn't quite dare not to notify me. Indeed and indeed I'll be there, and you'll see fireworks! The fracas'll be one-sided, as usual, all of them against me. You'll have to take part, Bailey Fount."

"I'd better not." Misgivings became more evident upon his brow. "I used to be able to——" He hesitated. "I mean in the Army I used to be able to—well, you know what they mean by 'tough'—but I never was anything of an argufier, especially not about art. When I was a painter I just went out in the country and painted."

"I've heard you did landscapes. What sort were they?"

"My pictures?" He looked oppressed. "It's hard to say in words. Of course it doesn't matter because it's over. I doubt if

I was very original, though if I imitated any painter in particular I didn't know it. I thought pretty often of Constable. He was the greatest painter of clouds, I think, and there was always a lot of sky in my pictures; yet I seem to be sure I didn't just imitate him. What I was really trying to do—well, it's difficult to say——"

"Yes; but go on."

"Well—I suppose if I'd done anything of enough consequence I'd be called an Impressionist; but I think I mostly had the feeling that Constable said came to him when he looked at open country. I'm not sure of his precise phrase; but it was something like this—that the meadows and woods and streams and the skies seemed always to be saying to him, 'I am the Resurrection and the Life.' I don't suppose I make it at all clear, do I?"

She looked at him intently for a moment; then smiled. "Yes, you do. It fits in precisely, though don't think for an instant I agree with you or that your way of going at it is any way for a modern to paint pictures. It sounds sweet and you're sweet; but we aren't going to talk about that now. What's to the point is that you'll be a perfect soul-twin for that old Constable-Sargent maniac, Horne, and your attitude is perfectly dear and natural in you. It fits my idea for this afternoon like a glove."

Although he thought he'd decided that his practise of art was abandoned forever, something still sensitive within his chest seemed to shrink when she said his way of painting sounded sweet; but the feeling passed and he only asked her to be more explicit: What about fitting "like a glove"?

"Why, like this," she told him brightly. "Of course the argument'll be over what pictures are to hang where and which really ought not to be on exhibition in the Oaklin Museum at all. Every point I make, old Horne and the others'll be against; they always are. I plan for you to make it four to one; you'll side with them, not with me—and now I see from what you've just said about your painting, why, you'd do that anyhow. So you'll say only what'll be natural to you and that's all the better."

"Could you come again?" he asked, mystified. "To prove that we care for each other, I'm to side against you?"

"Yes, ponderously!" she cried, and was like a happy child planning mischief. "You're a man, you see, and even your passionate love can't cajole your artistic conscience. That's the picture *you'll* make. I'll touch a lighted match to old Horne; nothing in life is easier than to turn him into a string of exploding firecrackers. You'll join in on his side—then all at once I'll crumple up dramatically and say I must be wrong about the whole thing since *you* say I am. I'll suddenly be meek as a lamb and say all I care about is for you to have your way, because in my eyes you're right about everything. There! Don't you see?"

He was doubtful. "You think they'll believe it?"

"I'll make 'em, trust me! I'll end by running out as if I suddenly see that my madness for you's overwhelmed me and I've given myself away. You don't think I can play such a scene?"

"Yes," he said, as her inquiry suddenly brought the brilliance of her smiling face close to his eyes. "I know you can."

"Good boy!" she cried, and jumped up, laughing. "Throughout the whole show be against me in everything and stand with old Horne—even with the Jyre woman! *That* paltry creature'll be there of course. Isn't it crazy, your being her assistant? Do you have to see much of her? I'm afraid you do, you poor boy!"

This disposal of his kindest friend—"Jyre woman," "paltry

creature"—dismayed Bailey. "Why, but—but she isn't," he said. "I can't let you say that, Josephine. You're altogether mistaken about Miss Jyre. She's——"

"Balderdash!" Josephine exclaimed. "Don't you like that nice old-fashioned word, 'balderdash'? Better than just 'Oh, bugs!' don't you think? The Jyre is almost my pet black beast, Bailey. Been trying to marry poor Henry Rossbeke ever since she cluck-clucked her way into the museum. It's a terrific jest: Rossbeke's too musty and lost in his books even to see what she's up to. Besides, she wouldn't know the Portland vase from a Navajo jug; she's a complete dud. What she doesn't know about art——"

"But you're mistaken, Josephine. Miss Jyre——"

"Oh, see here!" With gayety only increased, Josephine overruled him. "We haven't time to begin discussing everybody's unimportant character, have we? At any rate, *I* haven't! There's just one more thing I ought to bring up before I fly. Do you think you can stand its being pointedly personal?"

Bailey remembered that he'd never understood the mysterious feuds of women, even the best of women. He abandoned the defense of Helena Jyre. "What's the 'personal' thing, Josephine?"

"It's this," she began briskly, then paused and, highly amused, shifted to a question. "Oughtn't you to have thought of it, yourself? Really, isn't it yet in your mind at all?"

"How can I say when I don't know what you mean?"

"What a man!" she cried, and half-mockingly gave him an exhibition of sheer coquetry. Smiling uncertainly, she looked up at him, then down, let her eyelashes flutter, put a tremulousness into her sweet voice as if of shyness. "Of course I know that my—my looks are against me, Bailey. For anybody who'd like to have somebody—somebody some time—interested in her for her mind alone, it's a handicap to be—to be so rhythmically but obviously pretty as I am. I was always afraid I'd grow up to find myself helplessly looking like a Nineteenth Century candy-box cover girl. With you I'd—I'd have to overcome that, so you'd begin—begin to think of *me* instead of just my outwards, wouldn't I? You see what I'm coming to?"

"No, I don't."

"It's a thought I'll leave with you till we meet this afternoon," she said, and, abruptly becoming businesslike again, turned to the door. There she waited until he'd opened it for her. "We might both be thinking it over, Bailey. Our peculiar present circumstances compel some consideration of the idea, don't they?"

He was good-humoredly exasperated. "*What* idea, Josephine?"

"Only this," she said. "Do you think we might eventually need to fall rather in love with each other? Do you imagine it's at all possible? Don't answer." Instantly she turned her back upon him and walked away.

As he stood looking after her, a faint rustling accompanied the advent of Mrs. Hevlin, who came half-shuffling, half-tiptoeing in humble pursuit. Not even glancing at Bailey, she passed him, her broad face timidly aglow with the single devotion of a poor old dog who trots after the master, source of all goodness.

That pleased Bailey Fount. He went back into the room and closed the door. Josephine still seemed to be there.

XV

AFTER LUNCH he was busy in the museum's massively walled basement under the eastern wing. With old Anson and the brisk, one-legged carpenter, Arturo Meigs, to help him, he carefully removed framed canvases of price from the racks that had held them since a month after Pearl Harbor. Then in the freight elevator he and Meigs ascended to the second-floor corridor, bringing the larger pictures one or two at a time, carried them to the American Gallery, set them against the wall, and returned to the basement for more. A part of the Assistant Curator's mind was necessarily upon the work, but most of it dwelt upon pictures newer than those he carried. He found himself in possession of a whole collection of freshly vivid sketches in color of Josephine Oaklin, her gestures, quick-shifting expressions, poses of the head—profile, full-face, three-quarters, swift foreshortenings. All were charming, so he was charmed—but he had itchings from a scratch or two. His own way of painting, Helena Jyre and Constable plainly weren't among the enthusiasms of his betrothed, whose taste seemed controlled by crystallized antagonisms mistaken for the voice of God.

He couldn't recall which Eighteenth Century Frenchman it was who'd said something now pertinent about the convictions of women: that those of women were rooted in emotion but those of men in reason, and so the convictions of men could sometimes be changed by reasonable argument but those of women, never. Bailey hoped that this was only some Abbé's or Marquis's bit of twitting of the Pompadour and not the shrewd truth, since if it were that there wouldn't be much chance of straightening out Josephine upon matters he thought she ought to see differently. However, all this wasn't of present high consequence, and she was—she was being delightful to him!

He and Arturo Meigs had brought half a dozen pictures into the gallery before anyone else appeared there; then he found Helena Jyre and Mr. John C. Horne upon one of the central benches, talking, and when he came the next time Henry Rossbeke had joined them. The opening of the elevator door, when he came up again, admitted the musically cadenced sound of the voice of Josephine. He and the carpenter were carrying a large portrait of Thomas Oaklin by John Singer Sargent, and, as they entered the gallery, he saw that Miss Jyre and Mr. Horne had risen and stood beside the museum's Director while Josephine, a little apart, regarded them with a chiding amusement. Her back was toward Bailey; nobody paid any attention to him.

"Don't tell me," he heard her say, "don't tell me, Rossbeke, that you're joining our horse-and-buggy Chairman in his backwoods obsolescence." It seemed clear that she was ignoring Helena Jyre. "Why don't either of you ever deign to glance at any work on the philosophy of art criticism that wasn't written before Noah?"

"Read 'em all!" Mr. Horne's retort was vehement. "That's

the trouble with you six-year-olds. You think nobody except you's ever read anything or thought anything. By Cripes, you think nothing was ever done right in this billions-years-old world till you got born into it a few minutes ago! Because you've read some twist-word rhapsodies printed last week, you're the élite of the universe! You think you're the only souls alive that understand the latest pseudo-art pseudo-scientific dialects. Why, *you* think——"

"Mind reading again?" Josephine laughed jubilantly. "Dear Mr. Horne, for years and years I've known everything that you think; but *I* never think what you think I think. For instance, you think——"

Mr. Horne began to shout. Josephine, not stopped, accompanied him with derisive refutations; and Bailey, having set the Sargent portrait against a wall, heard both of them indistinguishably all the way down the corridor.

"Goes fer 'em, don't she?" Arturo Meigs said in the elevator, and chuckled. "Always did. Got her own notions about art. Nobody's going to tell *her!* She's a case all right; gets 'em *all* mad. Fight an elephant any day. It'll be hotter still amongst 'em next time we come up."

He prophesied well. When the two entered the American Gallery again, Helena Jyre, red-faced, had moved away from the disputants as if struggling to control herself; Rossbeke, pale, sat upon a bench, looking at the skylight; Mr. Horne was gesticulating with a forefinger, which Josephine was pushing away. The debate was so loud, so rapid and so simultaneous that Bailey caught only bits of it: "You couldn't understand Braque or Leger or Miro or Harry Pilker if you tried a thousand years!" from Josephine, and "Homer-Eakins-Ryder, Homer-Eakins-Ryder, Homer-Eakins-Ryder!" from Mr.

Horne, who seemed to be chanting the three names. "Homer-Eakins-Ryder; that's all you know, Josephine Oaklin! For the whole of American art, you just echo that eternal parroting—Homer-Eakins-Ryder!"

To Bailey the disputants seemed to be at cross-purposes, each having long since stopped listening to the other; but, when he and Meigs came again—this time with the last of the paintings the Assistant Curator had been told to bring—attention had centered upon a particular picture.

It hung conspicuously at about the middle of the northern wall, and he'd often wondered whose taste had added it to the collection. It was an upright oblong, five feet by about three, and upon a tablet attached to the slight pine frame it bore the title, "Arrangement: Illinois Toilers." Three yellowish paper-doll-like figures with flat lavender hands and faces appeared to be doing something with pitchforks to an orange dome, presumably a haystack; figures and haystack being based upon a saffron area symbolic, perhaps, of grass. Over the figures was the square red façade of a house enlivened by six intentionally lopsided green windows. Above the house a wobbling turquoise band might be guessed to indicate a river, and, above the river, more saffron, denoting the farther shore, rose to unbroken cobalt blue, a firmly cloudless sky. The workmanship was that of a hand experienced in placing pigment neatly upon canvas.

Josephine, Mr. Horne, Helena Jyre and Rossbeke stood confronting the picture in a momentary silence—a loaded one, Bailey thought, as he and Arturo Meigs set down their paintings and let them lean against the wall. Helena heard the slight noise they made, looked over her shoulder and spoke. "All right, Bailey; if that's the last of the lot, we can get to work making wall space. I'll help you and Arturo. Fourteen of these substitutes we've had up are to go to the cellar. You and Arturo can begin by taking down our celebrated 'Illinois Toilers' by the famed Harry Pilker. It's not so heavy as it looks."

Josephine took two steps forward and turned half round. Thus, with her back defensively against the frame of the condemned picture, she faced everybody present and challenged a hostile world to move her; but she spoke quietly. "Bailey, you and Arturo can get to work on something else. The 'Illinois Toilers' stays where it is. That's settled."

"Settled?" Mr. Horne's voice seemed to burst into flame. "The hell's whiskers it is!" Inconsistently he added, "You bet your bottom dollar it's settled! It goes to the cellar—ought to go to the trash pile!"

"You feel so?" Josephine's tone was one of sympathetic inquiry. "Dear Mr. Horne, oughtn't your concept of art to go there with it?"

"Damn it!" the old man cried. "This Pilker monstrosity never had any right to be here. You hornswoggled the Committee into buying it while I was sick abed. It's a sweet thing, ain't it? It's a child's daub, I tell you! It's a moron's——"

"We've heard all that, Mr. Horne." Josephine's interrupting voice became sharper. "Do you know how many museums have been buying Pilkers lately?"

"Yes, I do—blast their parrot souls! *Let* 'em fall for the wornout bunk if they want to, God help 'em! It's a children's disease, epidemic among mental adolescents ever since it got started in Paris before you were born. You've just caught it; you're all broke out in spots with it and you think it makes you look stylish!" The immoderate old man had his scolding forefinger up again, and again Josephine pushed it away; but it came back elastically. "If somebody didn't stop you, Josephine

Oaklin, you'd have this museum sell your grandfather's Barbizons out of the French room, on my soul you would! You'd sell Theodore Rousseau to buy Rousseau le Douanier! 'Folk Painting'! Stick it in an ethnological museum or a Hoopole County Fair; but for God's sake don't———"

"When you're through raving———" Josephine began; but he shouted her down.

" 'Illinois Toilers'! Look at the perspective; there ain't any! Nothing goes back, it just goes up. There's no distance, no———"

"Perspective? Of course there isn't! Why don't you stick to K'ang Hsi porcelains, Mr. Horne? You *know* a little about *them*. Pilker boldly states the fact that painting is a two-dimensional art. Has a canvas surface more than two dimensions?"

"No!" he answered, bellowing. "Neither has the retina of the human eye! This picture's kindergarten painting! Farmhand painting!" He calmed himself somewhat. "Have you the faintest idea, Josephine Oaklin, how your unspeakable Harry Pilker got going?"

"Somewhat, Mr. Horne! Carol Kernig saw Pilker's work, went wild over it and got a one-man exhibition in New York for him. It had tremendous notices. The appreciation of Harry Pilker's been an excitement everywhere in the country ever since. Just the other day Kernig announced that Pilker's exciting new———"

"You bet Kernig did!" Mr. Horne said. "He's announced something 'exciting' about Pilker every month since he began to clean up with him. Started by claiming Pilker's exciting 'Folk Painting' was 'like the Persian miniatures.' Next he claimed Pilker's 'Folk Painting' was symbolic of America at Peace, excitingly kind of isolationist; then Kernig saw the tide turning and Pilker was 'excitingly significant' of America at War. Pretty soon 'exciting' won't be exciting enough. Carol Kernig'll go all-out Hollywood and Pilker'll be 'terrific.' We'll be hearing everywhere that this greatest, most significant of all 'Folk Painters,' Harry Pilker——"

"You goose!" Josephine stamped her foot. "What's this twaddle you keep on babbling about 'Folk Painting'? You don't even know the difference between one modern school and another."

"I know *all* about 'em! I know——"

"You poor old silly!" Josephine cried. "Pilker's no more a 'folk' painter than Picasso is—or than Proust's a 'folk' writer Pilker studied in Paris. Matisse himself accepted him as a pupil."

"He did?" Mr. Horne, briefly discomfited, recovered himself. "Matisse did? Got anything *worse* on Pilker, Josephine?"

She scorned this. "Pilker came home and changed his style. He suited it to the expressionist concept of the plain goodness and dignity of the American common man. But look at *design* in this picture—look at its linear pattern, form, the relationship of its planes. Look at its pure color! Look——"

" 'Pure'? You mean raw! You mean——"

Josephine wasn't stopped. "Look at its subjective lyricism; it's *there*—in those rhythms and correspondences. Drop your pre-conditioned reflexes for once, can't you, and just *look* at this painting! Look at it objectively or look at it subjectively, but at least *look* at it!"

"That's my trouble." Mr. Horne made an unsightly grimace. "I *am* looking at it. I'm looking at it objectively, I'm looking at it subjectively, and each is worse. It's like Prince George of

Denmark. King Charles said, 'I've tried him sober, I've tried him drunk, and there's nothing in him either way.' This non-representational layer-cake painter, Pilker——"

"Oh-ho!" Josephine exclaimed exultantly. "So you *admit* you were wrong when you called him a Folk Painter! Any schoolchild ought to know that the early Pilkers stemmed from Matisse and that now he stems——"

"You bet he stems! That's the lingo, Josephine; but don't forget his 'articulation.' He's got some of that besides his stems, hasn't he? Aren't you going to spring 'statics,' 'dynamics,' 'architectonic' and 'organization' on us to-day? And isn't it about time you called me photographic?"

"That's the least of what I'd call you, Mr. Horne!"

"Call me what you like," he said, "but, damn it, be serious one minute. On the south wall opposite this space John Sargent's portrait of your grandfather, Thomas Oaklin, is going back to-day to where it always hung. What used to balance it on this wall here is one of the finest Inness landscapes in the country. Tell me honestly: Do you want to see that magnificent Sargent of your grandfather balanced by this hideosity of a Harry Pilker?"

"As an honor to Sargent!"

"Now damn my old soul——"

"I agree!" Josephine's chin was up. She seemed to address a multitude. "It's exactly what's happening to your dogmatic old soul! Art's liberated from the old slaveries, freed of the ancient Greek curse; art is the 'imitation of nature' no longer. It flies on its own wings, not chained to nature—dares to become music! It dares tell of the very essence of thought; dares to be pure emotion. It explores the abstruse and the irrational, fears no dissonance. It laughs at all your middle-class genteel twitters, at your worship of the sweet, the pretty and the 'real'! It——"

"Wait a minute!" Mr. Horne was shouting again. "Wait a minute, can't you?"

She wouldn't. "Call it decadence, call it insanity, call it all the names you can, they prove only your own stodginess. They prove——"

Mr. Horne laughed loudly. "I was waiting for that. How about 'academic'? Don't you want to get in 'stodgily academic'? Why, damn my old——" Surprisingly, he quieted himself, put his hands in his pockets and spoke in a reasonable tone. "No use your mounting the rostrum any longer, Josephine; you're voted down—we're three to one against you, so the Pilker goes to the cellar."

"It does not!" Josephine, dangerously alert, still stood with her back against the frame of the picture.

Horne made a gesture toward Helena Jyre. "You're our curator, Miss Jyre. You'll see that this thing's replaced by our great Inness."

"I will," she said. "Bailey, you and Meigs take down the Pilker at once, if you please."

"Yes, certainly." Bailey came forward.

"You keep away from me!" For the first time Josephine appeared to see Bailey. "You keep away from me, both of you!" Arturo Meigs halted; but Bailey still advanced. "This picture stays where it is; you'll not touch it!"

"Sorry," Bailey said, and, close before her, thought her superb in the rôle she'd that morning assigned herself for this scene. She had grown pale and the rapidity of her breathing was visible. "Sorry," he repeated. "Miss Jyre's my superior officer; I'm her assistant and I'll have to obey orders."

"You'll obey mine! Keep away from this picture!"

"It goes to the cellar," Bailey said, and, jostling her shoulder as slightly as he could, lifted the picture from its fastening, lowered it to the floor.

"*You!*" Josephine cried. A sweeping red replaced her pallor, her right hand flashed upward to his cheek. No one could have said whether that cheek was slapped or merely pushed; but essentially a blow was struck.

Helena Jyre took a fierce step forward; Rossbeke uttered an anxious exclamation; old Horne said "For God's sake!" and Josephine, hand to mouth, ran toward the wide doorway to the corridor. She'd almost reached it when she stopped herself suddenly, wheeled about and faced them. "What *am* I doing?" she asked bewilderedly. Then she returned, crossing the floor trancedly, walking toward Bailey and staring at him as if he were the strangest sight she'd ever seen. "Did I do that to you? What was it?" she asked in a childlike voice. As she reached him, she bent a knee, sank as if unconsciously about to kneel before him, but came up straight and put forth appealing hands. "Tell me truly, did I strike you?"

"I don't know." He spoke the truth. Dumfounded, he knew neither that nor what she now wished him to do.

"I couldn't have," she said. "The one most impossible thing in all this world is that I should have done anything—anything!—that might hurt you or make you think less of me. You know that, don't you? *Say* you know it!"

"Why—yes." He was trying to "follow her lead" as he'd promised.

"Of *course* you know it, Bailey! We both do and we ought to—by *this* time—oughtn't we? Rather!" She laughed half-happily, half-hysterically, put one hand upon Bailey's arm and with the other pointed at the disputed painting. "You don't like that picture much, yourself, do you, Bailey?"

"No, I can't say I do."

"Then neither do I!" she said. "Take it away! *Throw* it on the trash pile if *you* want to. I don't care what you do with it or with anything in the whole museum. I'll make myself stop liking that Pilker; I'll hate it if you want me to. What's all the art in the world to me now? What am I saying before these people? Oh, Bailey, I——" Again she clapped her hand over her face and ran toward the corridor doorway. This time she went all the way, sped onward and was gone.

XVI

BY THE END of the afternoon the rearrangement of the American Gallery had been completed; Bailey changed into his uniform but decided upon a final glance at the surfaces of the rehung paintings before going home to The Cranford. In the corridor he paused to switch on the lights, then saw that the gallery's wide doorway was already bright, and went forward. Alone in the great lighted space where Sargent's half-reverent, half-satirical interpretation of her grandfather looked across to George Inness's deep-colored "Showery Evening," Josephine Oaklin was waiting. Seated upon the central bench, she faced the doorway.

"Come here and sit down," she said, and, to make place for him, pushed away a fur jacket she'd dropped from her shoulders. "I watched from a window of our house for you to come out of the museum—I meant to run after you—but when you didn't come and didn't come I thought probably you'd do what you've just done, trot back to look at the paintings again, and anyhow I knew you'd have to pass through the corridor yonder on your way from your workroom. What happened?"

"Nothing," he said, as he sat. "Nothing at all."

"You don't understand. I mean what happened after I put on my act and ran out?"

"I know. Nothing at all, Josephine. Miss Jyre and Arturo Meigs and I just went to work. Mr. Horne and Mr. Rossbeke looked on for a while—until they were satisfied the gallery'd be about as it was before it was changed—and then they went away."

"I see. Leaving you with your Jyre."

"She's not my Jyre, Josephine."

"No, of course not. Rossbeke's, if she can ever wake him up enough!" Josephine made a petulant gesture. "Talk, can't you? I want to know what they said and did after I made my romantic running exit. You don't mean to tell me none of 'em referred to it or there wasn't even any embarrassment?"

"Well——" He considered the matter. "Nobody made any comment. Nobody said anything at all—at least, not for a while after you'd gone, and then they didn't mention you. I suppose there may have been some embarrassment. I started right in to work, myself, and kept my back to them; but perhaps I had a feeling that they were all looking at me—for some moments, at least. I kept myself busy, so I'm not sure whether you got the effect you wanted or not."

She uttered a low-voiced laugh of commiseration for his little alertness. "Don't you worry, young son, I *did* all right! Felt 'em looking at your back, did you? That tells it! I knew anyhow I'd pulled it off, but that looking at your back puts the stopper on the bottle; everything's bubbling inside beautifully. I almost ruined it, though."

"How? When did you almost?"

"When I smote you. That was real. Golly! I never made a worse break. That infernal old Horne got me frenetic; I was so off the ball I didn't know what I was doing, and on top o' that when you walked up and told me to go to hell, you had orders from the Jyre, and pushed me——"

"Oh, very little! I was careful not to——"

"Never mind! You virtually laid hands on me at her command and——"

"But you'd virtually told me to, Josephine. I was to be against you, to side with them in everything."

"Yes, I know," Josephine said; "but when you actually did it—and besides I saw you *really* didn't like the Pilker. Of course I'd already perceived that in art you're back in the Dark Ages with old Horne. You know you are, don't you?"

"No." He was troubled. "I never could talk much about art, Josephine. I'm a painter. I mean I was one. It's all over; but, inside me, much talk about art makes me want to get away. I couldn't possibly bear to argue about it. I mean all this tumult about what art really is and what it ought to be and what it oughtn't. Of course I can listen, and sometimes try to talk, too, about ancient art or painters who died a long while ago—long enough for me to feel they wouldn't much mind art talk, themselves—but all these excited new kinds of controversy, ninety-nine percent of it on the part of outsiders——"

"Why, you little brute!" Josephine's eyes widened. "So you're an artist and I'm only an outsider! Unless I'm a painter, myself, I don't know anything, haven't a right to say anything? That your posture?"

"No, no; I mean only—only——"

"Only that if I say anything about art you don't want to hear it?"

"Well, I——"

" 'Outsider'!" she cried. "You prig, do you suppose I've

never done any drawing or painting, myself; never studied in an art school? That's the least of my training. I had Latin and French and Italian and Spanish and after that I learned German for the books I wanted to read. Try me, not on painting and sculpture alone but on every technique of etching, engraving, lithography you please. I've lived art! You're just a boy who's done some brushwork on canvas and you tell me I'm to hold my tongue on the subject I've given my life to!"

"No, no; I don't say that."

"You did! You called me an 'outsider'! Me! I've had to fight old Horne and his stooges over almost every modern addition to these collections since my grandfather died; but you'd make a quitter of me, would you? Yes, you've told me I haven't any right to speak of art at all, not even when I absolutely know those people are wrong!"

"I didn't say you hadn't a right, Josephine. Of course anybody's got a right to talk all the art or anything else he cares to."

"I see." She let him hear a sigh of exasperation. "You mean I can talk art all I wish to other people; but you wouldn't listen, couldn't bear to hear it—because you're a painter! Creators of art can't stand its being talked about—unless the talk's all purest admiration?"

"Maybe not even then," Bailey said. "If we listen to the admiration long enough we usually find it's for the wrong reason."

"So the rest of us—we 'outsiders'—are inevitable boobs! What a modest, pleasant connubial companion I've chosen— well, maybe not precisely chosen!" Josephine's mood changed; she looked at him whimsically. "You're rather surprising; I hadn't suspected it. For the time being, suppose we drop the subject. Perhaps later you'll permit me to return to the discussion of whether or not I'm ever to be allowed to speak of art in your presence. It needn't matter much just now, need it?"

"No, of course not."

"No," she said, and gave him a sidelong look unmistakably gentle. "We have all the rest of our lives to discuss it in, haven't we?"

"All the rest of our lives?" He seemed not to have thought of this.

"Why, yes—so it appears." For several moments they looked at each other wonderingly; then she jumped up. "Come along. I knew, without asking, how those fussed buzzards must have taken my performance. What I really came for's to walk home with you."

"You're going to?"

"I told you I'd have to get used to you pretty fast, didn't I?"

In the corridor they met a stooping greybeard who scuffled slowly toward the light-switch that governed the gallery. "I'll turn it off if you don't want it lit any more, Mr. Fount," he said.

"Thank you. Goodnight, Mr. Morrison."

"Goodnight, Mr. Fount."

Josephine frowned, seemed to look far before her as they went toward the great stairway. "Can't get away from the war for long, can we? How much of a fight could poor old Morrison or any of our decrepit night watchmen put up against a prowler who'd break into the museum? I don't know how many pathetic wrecks the staff's had to take on since Pearl Harbor."

"I do," Bailey said. "I know how many. Seventeen all told, including the sixty-eight-year-old gardener Mr. Rossbeke hired yesterday. Of the seventeen, I'm the fourteenth."

"You? Fantastic!" She gave him a humorous push with her shoulder. "Where in the world did you pick up this whimsy of always talking about yourself as a wreck? I suppose you think ruins are picturesque; but you'll have to give up trying to be one, my Bailey! Come, though; just for now let's forget the war."

"All right. Just for now."

When they'd let themselves out of the building and in the dark were upon the broad stones of the entrance path, she took his arm and spoke softly. "How many hundreds of times— maybe thousands—do you suppose we'll be walking arm-in-arm, Bailey?"

"There's a thought!" he said. "It's not easy to realize."

"No; so it isn't." When they reached the sidewalk and turned westward toward The Cranford she held his arm more closely. "Do you know you feel quite strong, Bailey? You've begun to seem pretty soldierly again. What a change since the first time I saw you! Had you had malaria or something besides being wounded?"

"No, I hadn't."

"That all? Just no, you hadn't?" She laughed indulgently. "By the way, the late discarded Harold told me something about you. It was an evening or two after that day at the museum when he kindly helped to put me on a spot for asking why you weren't in uniform. A tremendous lot's happened since then, so it seems quite long ago; but you recall that vile outburst of mine, don't you?"

"Yes, I do."

"Hateful of me," Josephine admitted lightly, then resumed: "I've been trying to think what he told me about you. He told me you—no, I can't remember it; but it was about some exploit or something. He was indignant with me and I was furious with him; and of course I wasn't really interested in you, Bailey—not then. To goad him, I pretended to be terribly excited over whatever it was he said you'd done; but I was so angry with him—he was only telling it to make me seem more degraded for having been fresh with a veteran—I really didn't take in the details of what he said about you. Now I wish I could remember. You distinguished yourself pretty brilliantly, didn't you?"

"No, I did not."

"But I know you did."

"No!"

"Oh, well——" she said. "Your ribbons don't say no; they say yes. You'll tell me all about it some day—or somebody else will, I'll see to that! I've begun to believe you're quite a fellow. It isn't bad at all to be walking along with you like this, in the dark. Do you mind it?"

"No."

"Couldn't you say, 'No, dear'?"

"Yes," Bailey said. "No, dear."

"That sounded almost right, Bailey. We'll have to get used to dearing each other, won't we?"

The question asked for no response. They walked on, not speaking; and when they came within view of the brick house that was The Cranford, now with the trees bare in its side yard, she once more clung closely to his arm as if this short stroll in the night together had tightened the tie that oddly bound them and she sought to know it as reality before she parted from him. At a little distance from the street-lamp nearest The Cranford, she stopped but didn't release him.

"So this——" she said. "It's been our first walk together, hasn't it? It wasn't too unbearable, was it—or was it?"

"Not for me. We haven't come to the end of it, though, Josephine. Of course I'm going back with you. You can't go home alone. I'll take you——"

"No." She stepped away from him. "This is the end of our first walk together. I feel just the way I was trying to. It'd be an anti-climax if you came back with me."

"Why, no, I can't let you——"

"Yes, you can. This is my own neighborhood where I grew up, Bailey; you needn't fear——"

"Yes, I know, but——"

"No. If you come after me, I'll run. I almost always run wherever I go, anyhow, and I'd love to have you think of me as forever running away from you. That's how it should be. Goodnight!"

She turned and did run, flitting swiftly into thicker darkness. Her sweet voice came back to him in another "Goodnight!" from a distance, and, as she passed the next street-lamp, he saw that without looking back she waved an extended hand, white in the electric light, to show that she knew he must still be standing watching her until she disappeared completely from his sight.

He sighed suddenly, was surprised to hear that wistful sound from himself, and went into The Cranford smiling.

XVII

"Yes, like Lourdes," Mrs. Williams agreed. She sat at her desk in the Director's outer office, where she was chatting with Miss Bullard, an assistant secretary who also looked after local "publicity" for the museum. "We ought to set up a tablet commemorating such a cure. Comparing him now with how he looked last August, you're right it's a miracle."

"It's exciting!" Miss Bullard said, falling back on the professional word. "For instance, his lameness—it's gone altogether. He stands straightened up, too, almost with his chest out. I've even heard him laugh—I mean comfortably, you know, like anybody else."

Upon this, both ladies themselves laughed in the pleasure they had of Bailey Fount's laughing. "And what you think?" Mrs. Williams added; "I was outside his workroom half an hour ago. He and Arturo Meigs are in there repairing and regilding frames, and I heard somebody whistling 'Oh, Susanna, don't you cry for me'! Arturo can't whistle on account of his teeth, so it had to be Our Darling."

The squeak of a swivel-chair was heard from the inner room; then Henry Rossbeke came to the threshold. "You'd better not let 'Our Darling' discover that's the name his female colleagues have taken to calling him—not unless you want the poor fellow to make a premature dive back into the Army!"

"It's a perfect name for him," Mrs. Williams insisted. "He's exactly the self-effacing, all-good, always-considerate kind of young man all older women always call darling. Don't worry, though; we won't let him hear it. He's just about the most sensitive person I ever saw. Don't you think so, Mr. Rossbeke?"

"I do."

"I mean he was," Mrs. Williams said, after a moment's reflection. "Of course he still is; but yet, if you know what I mean, I think he's lost a little of that. Seems to me he's been gaining just a shade of wholesome hardness. No, 'hardness' isn't quite the word. I mean his expression seems to me to've taken on a hint of ruggedness—not even that exactly, but as if, well, as if he's begun to know where he's at and could jolly well handle his own affairs and look out for himself, thank you! Don't you agree, Mr. Rossbeke?"

"Take care," he warned her. "See much more of that in him and he won't be eligible to be called Our Darling."

Helena Jyre came in from the corridor, just then. "Miss Bullard, Mrs. Hevlin's been telling me—with a curious air of triumph—that you've been 'collecting material' for Josephine Oaklin. She told me it was 'very, very interesting' but wouldn't say more and evidently thought I'd mind not knowing what it is."

"Oh, Mrs. Hevlin!" Miss Bullard laughed. "Yes, Miss Oaklin was talking to me about it yesterday afternoon in the Oriental Gallery and that creepy old gal kept standing around with her spectacles glittering. It's her pet mania to make secrets out of everything, isn't it? This wasn't one, of course."

"Then what was it?" Helena spoke crisply. "Do you mind telling us what type of 'material' you collected for Miss Oaklin?"

"Not at all," Miss Bullard said. "You know she's always assumed that the museum's publicity department is at her personal disposal. I had a note from her Tuesday—I think it was Tuesday; yes, it must have been because it was the day after you were busy rearranging the American Gallery. Her note said she'd heard Bailey Fount did something spectacular in the Pacific fighting; she wished me to go down to the Globe office, look over its files of about six to eight or nine months ago and copy every mention of Lieutenant Bailey Fount I could find."

Rossbeke came all the way into the room. "Did you do what she asked?"

"Yes. Yesterday morning. The Globe didn't have anything; but I went to the City Library and looked over files of New York papers and found several accounts."

"I'd like to see 'em, myself," Mrs. Williams said. "What did they say?"

"Rather meager, Mrs. Williams; they just told about his holding that advanced position and the others all dying and he was to have decorations. Everything in the papers was practically the same as what Mr. Rossbeke told us was in Dr. Bedge's letters when we were expecting Bailey here and weren't supposed to mention to him, and none of us did."

"I did, though," Rossbeke admitted. "The day he came I just touched on the honor of having a war hero with us and it gave him a miserable jolt. Nobody's been that stupid since, I believe. You turned over the items to Miss Oaklin, did you?"

"Yes, I copied 'em for her and she was thanking me in the Oriental Gallery when Mrs. Hevlin tiptoed up to dust ceramics as near as she could get. Fat as she is, she seems to think she's invisible when she wants to be and——"

Rossbeke interrupted. "Did Miss Oaklin say what she intends to do with the items you gave her?"

"She only said she wanted to know because he was too modest and she'd never get it out of him."

"Did you tell her we've all made it a practise not to speak to Mr. Fount on the subject?"

"No; I think she understands that. I had the impression that what she wants is to do a little bragging to people about having a cousin who——"

"Wants to brag, does she?" Helena Jyre said. "Raking up everything she can? I dare say! I can't tell you now; but I think before long you'll all understand why Miss Josephine Oaklin is pretty desperate for something to brag about. In fact, one might expect to find her just now rather thoroughly crushed."

"Josephine Oaklin?" Mrs. Williams made her disbelief evident. "Crushed? Could such a thing ever be hoped for?"

"Listen!" Miss Bullard held up a finger. "What's that?"

A soprano voice, facetiously lugubrious—Josephine Oaklin's voice—was heard singing in the corridor. The words came clearly as she approached the half-glass door of the Director's office:

> *"Oh dig my grave both wide and deep,*
> *Lay tombstones at my head and feet,*
> *And on my breast then carve a dove,*
> *To show the world I died of love!"*

She flung open the door and came in skipping, waving her arms, all sun and smiles. "Hello, hello, hello!" she cried. "Where's Our Darling?"

Rossbeke stared at her. "How did you know they call him that?"

"Spies!" Josephine laughed. "In the House of Oaklin our old Harvey's an atrocious gossip. He knows everything that goes on at this end of the passage almost as well as my poor dear Mrs. Hevlin does. They both told me. 'Our Darling'? Very nice. The only thing I'd question would be the pronoun. Maybe I'd better say '*My* Darling.' Where is he, Rossbeke?"

She laughed again as this produced a silence until Rossbeke spoke. "I believe Mr. Fount is repairing picture frames."

"Where?" Josephine asked; but, not waiting for the delayed reply, she ran back, still laughing, to the door. "Skip it! I've never had any trouble finding what's mine, you know."

She left them gazing dumbly at one another. The look that passed between the Director and the Curator of Paintings was the most significantly grim, and, when it ended, Helena went abruptly from the room.

She was gone half an hour, and then, darkly flushed, returned, swept by Mrs. Williams's desk and into Rossbeke's inner office. She shut the door. "I have the answer, Henry," she said.

"To what?"

"To everything! In particular to last Monday afternoon when she did that Duse over the 'Illinois Toilers' to swindle us into discovering she'd lost her head over Bailey Fount. Wanting to give up her soul's art convictions—oh, anything on earth! —make herself over and be whatever *he* wants her to be! I told you it was phony, didn't I?"

"I've found that rather hard to accept, Helena. Look where it put her—engaged to another man and making such an exhibition of herself. Would she intentionally give herself away like that when she's on the very point of being married?"

"Oh, no, she isn't, Henry Rossbeke! Not to Captain Harold Sorgius Murties!"

"She's broken it off?" Rossbeke showed more disquiet. "If she's done it because of Bailey——"

"To make us all *believe* that," Helena said, "she's begun the wrecking of Dr. Bedge's cure. I've just called up Charlotte Parannik and she says I can tell you, 'in confidence,' what I meant a while ago about Josephine's being 'crushed.' She *ought* to've been! Murties has jilted her."

"What?"

"Jilted her," Helena said. "He was ordered away, but everybody's expecting of course he'll be back for the wedding. Well, he won't."

"How do you know?"

"Out of the horse's mouth, Henry. Captain Murties's old comrade and best friend is that quiet, middle-aged Major Paylor. Mrs. Paylor was a maternal sort of confidante of Captain Murties's long before any of 'em came here. From the first she opposed his engagement to Josephine Oaklin. Anybody could see why, couldn't they?"

"I suppose so. Anybody who got to know Josephine at all well."

Helena Jyre's laughter was sharp. "It didn't take *me* very long after I joined this staff, did it? Murties finally told Mrs. Paylor he was so desperate he'd do whatever she advised him to. He said it'd got so he simply couldn't stand Josephine. Charlotte Parannik told me those were his actual words—he just couldn't *stand* her! You saw Murties. He's a broad-shouldered, steady, sensible, healthy man; but the prospect of a life with Josephine Oaklin—well, you can see why he had to go to Mrs. Paylor for help, can't you?"

"It's pretty awful," Rossbeke said. "Yes."

"There he was," Helena went on. "He was on the very edge of being tied up to spend his life with that girl. He couldn't expect to be freed by a bullet, he said, because he's not in combat service; so for God's sake tell him what to do! Of course there was only one thing on earth *to* be done. Gertrude Paylor told him he'd have to do it, and he did."

Rossbeke shivered. "I can't see how any man could go through such a scene as that, telling a girl—and such a girl!—that he'd found he couldn't——"

"No, he wasn't up to it, Henry. Mrs. Paylor helped him with a note—the decentest they could write between 'em. Then he left for his train, and she had the note sent to Josephine for him. That was last Sunday afternoon; but the only person Mrs. Paylor's let it all out to is Charlotte Parannik. Charlotte told me last night—'in strictest confidence'—but I'm not the only intimate friend Charlotte has, you know; she's got a lot of 'em. How many besides me do you imagine already know—or will pretty soon?"

"It *is* awful," Rossbeke said, and his gloom grew heavier in the repetition.

"Worse than you've so far perceived," Helena assured him. "You needn't think Josephine's been fooled for a minute. She's smart! She'd instantly have doped it out he'd been to Mrs. Paylor and that the jilting wasn't going to be kept any deadly secret! She didn't take long to make up her mind to be ready for it when it comes out. Ready what with, Henry? With Bailey Fount."

"But she couldn't——"

"Couldn't? She *has!* You saw it with your own eyes, Henry Rossbeke. By the end of that row over the 'Illinois Toilers' she

had you half-believing she'd passionately love to drop Murties
for Bailey. She means to have everybody thinking that; then
she'll spring it she's the one did the jilting because she'd *already*
dropped Murties—had to tell the poor broken-hearted man
she'd fallen in love with Bailey at first sight! You don't see it?
Good Lord! Not even when you've just heard her jeering at
us that Bailey ought to be called '*My* Darling'—and she could
always find what was hers?"

"But there's Bailey himself," Rossbeke objected. "He'd have
some say, wouldn't he?"

"Not a whisper! Was there ever a more helpless boy than
he's been since he came here—ever anybody more meekly wandering in a trance? *Now* look at this sudden difference in him—
all brightened up!—and think of the beautiful, flashing thing
that Josephine Oaklin is physically. She dazzles everybody—till
everybody knows her! He's falling for her, I tell you! Damn it,
he *has* fallen for her!"

"He hasn't had time, Helena."

" 'Time'! Hasn't Josephine Oaklin *yet* proved to you that
when she wants anything she's the fastest worker in the world?
She wants Bailey Fount and, what's more, she'll make him go
through with it. She won't take a chance of his being the *third*
man to turn her down!"

"Third?" Rossbeke had forgotten; then he remembered.
"Yes, there was that young Englishman here with the asphalt
company quite a while and then——"

"Then he left!" Helena said. "That girl's always held to the
pose of living far up in the unreachable heights. Aspersions are
mere low envy of her remote sublimity! That's her front, and
what it means is she can't bear the faintest flicker of a glance
that doesn't look up to her with unmitigated admiration. In

other words, she's so far above criticism that the slightest hint of it sets her wild."

Rossbeke was ruefully perplexed. "Maybe you overlook a point. There's something very appealing about Bailey Fount. It's just possible that she may have——"

"Genuinely fallen in love with him?" Helena's contempt for this idea was complete. "Other women might, but not the concentrated essence of self called Josephine Oaklin. Look at what she's been having Miss Bullard do—digging up those newspaper accounts. Isn't that a purely cold-blooded plan to go about bragging, making Bailey more important? She drops a desk-job officer to take a hero! Isn't that why she wanted those items?"

"Not certainly, Helena. All of us like to know what our kinsfolk have done in the war; it's natural. Evidently, though, she'd already tried to speak of it to him. Probably got a stagger of pain out of him and just brushed that aside. I do hope she won't tell too many people——"

"She'll tell dozens; she'll make him as 'distinguished' as she can! She means to use him to the limit. She'll actually make him her husband because he fits in to save her from the tongues she despises—and dreads."

Rossbeke made a final remonstrance. "After all, why should she? People don't look upon jiltings, or divorces either, as they used to."

"No; but Josephine Oaklin's not going to have jiltings happen to her three-in-a-row—not in this intimate old town! Bailey wouldn't, though; he'd never do it. The poor boy's too damned booby sweet and old-fashioned good! The others ran away when they found her out. He won't. He'll stick to his word and end in a worse collapse than had him before he came here. It won't take long."

"Could anybody talk to him about it?" Rossbeke asked, and answered himself. "No. I couldn't. Nobody could."

"Then what's to be done? Just pray?"

"It'll have to be stopped, Helena."

"By whom?" she cried. "Your friend Bedge trusted him to *you,* didn't he?"

Henry Rossbeke dropped into a chair, his chin on his collar.

"Yes, you're a man," she said. "I'll do what I can."

XVIII

In bailey's distant workroom Josephine had just added another entertainment to a singing trio. Arturo Meigs was instructed to continue his bass Oom-pah while Bailey carried the air—"Oh, what a beautiful morning—" and Josephine, whipping off the paint-spotted denim coat they'd lent her, sprang up from the bench by the worktable and began to dance. She sang, too, chiming her voice above Bailey's and quickening the time of the over-used song to give her a faster movement.

The dance was improvisation, yet had moments coquettishly satirical of the professional gyrations, tappings and revealings seen on the stages and screens of the day. Incessantly plastic, she practised a dozen differing beguilements in as many instants, bewitched Bailey's eyes with twinkling, over-shoulder glances that seemed mockingly to ask, "Do you like that? How's *this?*" Gracefulness wasn't lost in any shortest segment of swiftest gesture; gold lights rippled upon her fair hair, and the impulses that successively remodeled her quicksilver figure were seen, too, in the changing expressions of her face. "Are you mine? Am I yours?" she seemed to ask mysteriously and then to answer, "Yes, yes, *yes!* No, no, *no!* Do you love me? Do I love you? Now? Shall I ever? Will you never? No—but perhaps!"

Bailey forgot to sing. He still thought he'd never paint again —but some day, if he did, he'd paint a portrait of Josephine. He saw before him fifty compositions for such a picture and every flying, symmetrical posture of hers was a new canvas in the air. He couldn't have been more entranced had she used her total energy and every guile she had, instinctive and acquired, to charm him. This of course was what Josephine, not ungenerously, was doing.

"Well, doggone!" Arturo Meigs said, as she stopped and, neither flushed nor breathless, skipped laughing to sit upon the bench again. "I'm certainly glad they turned me down for war work at the Bewley Engine plant. Yippee! What I'd 'a' missed!"

"We've heard from Arturo!" Josephine's swept glance from the enthusiastic carpenter to Bailey was merrily provocative. "How about the Lieutenant? I know what you're thinking, Mister: when you paint again it may not be landscape; you've remembered how Sargent did 'Carmencita' and you'd like to do somebody much the same way. No, no, my boy! You'll have to lift out of your Sargent-Constable-Millet-Chase-Whistler low-keyed delusions before I'll let you paint me."

Bailey laughed. "Anything, just so you'll let me." He couldn't have imagined, just then, that two friends of his in another part of that consecrated building were worrying about him. He couldn't have imagined anybody's worrying about him. He was elate. Josephine's flashing up into her dance in unscarred light-heartedness brought to him, as an extremity of contrast, the picture she'd made when despair had flung her upon a dimly

lit scarlet couch. Except for him, that despair would still have
her down; and, thinking this, his cheerfulness grew so complete
that he wasn't even aware that he was cheerful. He felt for
Josephine the delighted fondness of a doctor or a nurse for a
patient brought from black disease into strong life again.

Self-congratulation enhancingly accompanies such an emotion and this enhances the admiring tenderness for the patient,
thus forming not a vicious but a loving circle. Bailey had gratitude, too. Being Josephine's rescuer was what began to make
him believe that before long he could go back to Colonel Bedge
and pass an examination that would once more make of him a
soldier. He wanted to do everything on earth for Josephine
Oaklin. She'd said "You'll go through with it?" The question,
tragic when she'd asked it, had become fascinating.

"Half-past twelve," said Arturo Meigs. "My feed time.
Think you can get along a while without a chaperone?" At
the door he looked back over his shoulder, winked as a companion sharing agreeable private knowledge, giggled and took
himself off.

"He likes me," Josephine said detachedly. "In this institution I have at least the halt, the deaf and the superannuated
to back me up. It's only my supposed equals who abhor me.
How about you, Cousin Bailey? Do you?"

"No."

She gave him a moment of scrutiny. "You wonder about me,
though. You're wondering right now how the devil I could
have been just a few days ago on the point of marrying one
man and in the twinkling of an eye take up so gayly with another. After such an exchange you wonder how I can dance
like a madman. Makes you think I'm a strange girl, doesn't it?"

"No, and I haven't been wondering about it at all."

"Yes you have and I want you to think out the explanation. I'll give you an hour to ponder over it, and then if you haven't got it I'll slip you a tip. That'll be after lunch." She jumped up, took his hand and retained it as he rose. "Come along. I want to tell Mother something before I forget it."

"But I had lunch with you yesterday, Josephine."

"Can't stand it two days in succession? That's bad. Think of the lifetime of meals ahead of you!" She let go his hand to take his arm instead; they left the workroom and went toward the great stairway. "You see, Bailey, I had Mother telephone the invitations for the dinner in honor of the new cousin to-morrow night and——"

"To-morrow night?" Bailey's voice could still betray a qualm.

"I told you. Everything's had to be pushed. Mother did the telephoning yesterday evening, but I hadn't thought of putting Rossbeke on the list. I want to tell her to ask him, so the Jyre can get her fill of our show. She'll get it from the women, too; but she'll be waiting on Rossbeke's doorstep to put him through a questionnaire, and a man's he-view'll be all to the good for us."

Bailey had another qualm. He wished she wouldn't always refer to the museum's Director as "Rossbeke" or address him so, and that she'd stop always speaking of Miss Jyre as "the Jyre" or "your Jyre." He also wished that Helena herself could like Josephine; he had the impression that she didn't. It was pleasant, however, to have Josephine again clasping his arm possessively close to her, as on the night when she'd walked home with him. She began to prattle of some of the people who'd be at the dinner, only names to him; but her voice was like a harp and a flute made one, he thought; and in content he thus went with her down the stairway and through the long gallery that took them to the eastern corridor and the oaken door of the passageway.

Josephine didn't release his arm until they'd passed into the Jacobean library and Roggo came bouncing in greeting to them both. She stooped to pat the effusive old dog and so did Bailey.

"Roggo wouldn't mind how many meals he'd have to face me across the table," Josephine said. "That prospect wouldn't frighten *you,* would it, Roggo?" She straightened out of the stoop; but the spaniel still jumped up at her skirt. "Down!" she said. "Don't dirty me; you've been digging in the garden. You're a bad old nuisance and I wonder I don't get rid of you. Bailey, don't forget you're supposed to be working on the puzzle about why I'm so gay. Come along, though, now, while I find Mother and tell her about Rossbeke."

With the fat spaniel at their heels, they passed together through the Jacobean doorway and were in the Oaklins' "music room." Here Josephine paused as they were crossing before the long piano, sat down and began to play. "Just to show you," she said, lifting her voice to be heard above the magnificent chords she was sounding. "Accomplishments, what? Dance, sing, play, a fair hand at tennis, too, and I can ride, sail, swim—three silver cups for diving. Maybe not such a bad bargain for you, young fellow-my-lad, after all?" Then she was on her feet and confronting him with a kind of sternness. "What do you say to it?"

He only smiled, and, apparently pleased by that, she smiled too, said "Wait here," and left him.

Roggo ran after her devotedly, and Bailey, alone with his thoughts, had an odd one. It was that since the night of her agony and his lifting of it she hadn't kissed him again. He hadn't minded her earlier kissings of him but now he felt strangely enriched because she hadn't repeated them. He couldn't think why it was that his realization of this made him happily breathless.

Josephine wouldn't let him go back to his work immediately after lunch, though he said Arturo Meigs would be waiting for him. "No, you can't," she reminded him. "You have that puzzle about me to work out and the hour I gave you isn't up yet. You'll have to stay for at least two cigarettes." They'd come into the living-room she'd remodeled in streamline, and Mrs. Oaklin, accompanying them, again sat down in a wrong chair and murmured her complaints of it. "Be reasonable, Mother. It's your structure that's wrong, not the chair's."

Mrs. Oaklin removed herself to a sofa. "This is almost as bad," she complained. "I hate 'em. They all slide me forward and I can't keep my dress down; everything's so indecent, these days. Do put the dog out, Josephine, or else have Harvey or Lorinda or somebody take him away. His paws are dirty and his bad eye is so white and watery I can't bear to look at it. When I was a girl we didn't let dogs come in the house; they were supposed to live outdoors. Of course I'll do what you say about to-morrow night, but I don't see what you want Rossbeke for, anyhow. He's so frostbitten he never adds anything."

"Never mind, Mother. You're not expected to follow all my threads."

"Good thing I'm not," Mrs. Oaklin muttered, was digestively silent for a time, and then, glancing at Bailey, became reminiscent, though without much interest. "My memory's getting queer. I don't remember things well any more, especially after meals. Let's see, though, Bailey. One day not long ago I was figuring out your age. I'm pretty sure your mother wrote us about it when you were born and I think I recall it was the year after she and your father moved from Atlanta to Wilmington. That would make you twenty-six now, wouldn't it?"

"No. Twenty-seven, Cousin Folia."

"Yes. Twenty-seven, so it would," she said. "I was wrong, Josephine, when I told you he must be twenty-six; I've got it straight now. You were born just two years after he was, Josephine; so of course Bailey'd be twenty-seven now, not twenty-six."

Josephine was carelessly a little amused. "Isn't that a symptom of dotage, Mother?"

"What is? Bailey's being twenty-seven?"

"No. When people begin to think it's important to be accurate about every detail of obsolete family history."

Bailey's attention was oddly caught and arrested by this slightest of conversational trifles. A little plaintively, yet examiningly, he looked at Josephine as she began to talk to her mother about the placing of the guests at the dinner. The daughter's expression was carefree and he saw that he had a choice: either to believe she had forgotten she'd told him she was twenty-two or to conclude that she didn't care whether he remembered or not.

. . . Among the Italian pictures in the museum was a Mainardi Annunciation that Bailey thought a radiantly perfect painting of its type; but it was done on wood, and, although the old panel had been "cradled" to protect it from warping, there had lately appeared a bad crack that threatened to cross the Madonna's face. Of course there were remedies, the harm needn't be serious; yet it already affected Bailey's enjoyment of the picture. He couldn't bring up the lovely imagining of it and not see the endangering crack, and so in his mind's eye this Mainardi was now a beautiful thing a little damaged—that is, not quite a beautiful thing. A similar slight defect was happening to the picture his mind had been holding of Josephine Oaklin. Of course women weren't supposed to be realistic about their ages, and why need they be?—and what could be less sensible than to be even infinitesimally disturbed by a misstatement that skipped only two or three years? It meant nothing at all; Bailey felt foolish to think of it for a moment—yet he did, and for more than a moment.

He finished the second cigarette absentmindedly and remained somewhat in that condition as Josephine went with him across the hall, through the "music room" and into the library. At the door of the passageway to the museum she caught his arm, detaining him. "Arturo can wait a minute longer, Bailey. You've not been listening to a word I've said."

"Yes, I have. You were telling me you wouldn't see me again until to-morrow night because you have to do a turn at the Red Cross this afternoon, dance at the Officers' Club to-night to show how lighthearted you are, and to-morrow you'll be twice as busy as to-day."

"Ah, you've proved it!" She was affectionately petulant. "I told you all that as we were crossing the hall and the 'music room' back yonder. You don't know a word I've been saying to you since. What's worse, you've completely forgotten what I gave you to think out. I was telling you that the hour had passed and it's time for you to give me the answer."

"The answer to what, Josephine?"

"Good grief! The answer to what I knew you were wondering about—how I could be so strickenly off with the old love and immediately so merrily on with the new. You don't yet see?"

"Why, yes, I suppose I do." Bailey Fount was blunderingly honest. "It's just relief, isn't it? You feel pretty sure we're putting it over and people are going to believe you dropped him for me. Naturally you'd——"

"Naturally your grandmother!" There was the edge of a flash from her eyes. "No! You can call it relief if you want to, but while you weren't listening I was telling you that you haven't understood about Harold Murties at all. That's the tip I promised I'd slip you if you couldn't think the answer out for yourself."

"I don't get it, Josephine," he said. "For that matter, I don't see any use thinking about Murties or of what he did. There's no way to explain it or him, so why not just let him go as an inexplicable defective?"

"But he wasn't, Bailey. Anything but! He was just a man. I didn't see it, myself, in that first hour—really because the explanation of him was too simple; then, after you'd gone that night and I got calm enough to think, I saw the whole thing. In reality you and I haven't been putting over an act at all; we're just letting people see the truth."

"What? I don't——"

She put her hands upon his shoulders, affected to shake him. "Bailey! He *was* jealous. Wake up! He was in a fury of jealousy —jealousy of you. That's why he tore away. It was because he couldn't bear it any longer."

"What?" Bailey said again. "Why, no. That couldn't be, because——"

"Because you're blind as a bat! Bailey, he was crazy with sheer jealousy. I made him so, I know; it was my fault. I didn't see how far it would drive him; but now I'm glad it did." She laughed excitedly. "Don't you see how much more picturesque it makes everything for *us?* I suppose you think it's too utterly frivolous of me; but you see my knowing that Harold broke away out of jealousy restores my *amour propre.* Then there's another thing, the best of all." She took her hands from his shoulders, stepped away from him, danced back, lifting her face to him. "You see what it does for me about you, don't you?"

He didn't. "About me?"

"Why, yes! You *had* to propose to me of course, didn't you? Since you and I got my fiancé so jealous of you that he resigned, what else could you do? Couldn't we even say what else did you *want* to do? Wouldn't that make me pretty happy, Bailey?"

He remained serious. "I still don't see——"

"You do, too!" She jovially pushed his shoulder. "Don't be such a prig. This isn't encyclopædic. It's simply A,B,C. I know I told you he'd begun to be different with me; but *you* were the reason. We thought we had to pretend that; but it was true, so now there's no pretense about it. Wouldn't any girl be overjoyed to get out of an engagement with as fussy an old Othello as Harold Murties? Yes, and to have as darling a hero cousin as you be the real reason!"

" 'Hero'?" he said, and drew back from her. "Won't you please never use that word about me?"

"Bye-bye!" She gave him another jocular push, really a

caress. "Run off to your old Arturo, but don't forget you know now why I'm on top o' the world. You do begin to think of me a little sometimes when I'm not with you?"

"Yes—I do."

"Righto! I'll reciprocate! Good-bye till to-morrow night."

He liked her saying "I'll reciprocate!" In fact, he more than liked it—something treasurable seemed to go with it—but it didn't disperse the uneasy absentmindedness that had come upon him and now, by tenuous connection, made him go and look at the Mainardi Annunciation before he returned to his workroom.

Already frowning, he stopped close to the rich, warm-colored old picture and stared calculatingly at the threat to the Madonna's beauty. It wasn't merely a crack; he found additionally a series of incipient blisters in the early Sixteenth Century paint, or perhaps where some of that paint had suffered an old restoration. There'd be serious damage soon unless the surface had expert treatment. "Ah, too bad!" Bailey murmured, while across his inner gaze slid the face and figure of Josephine Oaklin, taking the place of the Renaissance Madonna. About Josephine there was something wrong. She hadn't been straight with him.

That gabbling of Murties and jealousy was all off-key; had even sounded so. Too many things were contradictory—most of them things Josephine herself had said. Now, in the mid-action of a useful conspiracy, harmful to nobody, she asked her fellow-conspirator to believe that no conspiracy existed—that the play they were acting wasn't one. He was expected to be gullible, supinely so; but his deeper suspicion was of Josephine Oaklin's own gullibility—about herself. Was she one of those people who so determinedly gild themselves that they see themselves shining, *all* gold? Was she one of those who make fact plastic to their needs, distort it adorningly, always save face at any cost, and so have never true vision of themselves or of their kinship with their unperfected fellow-creatures? Such a one is not a beautiful sight—no, the rather ghastly—a deaf and blinded hermit walking abroad through crowded life and unaware of what's all round him.

Josephine had been put in a spot, a bad one; now she denied this, even to him she'd called an angel for helping her out of it. Women don't find humiliation more unendurable than men do, Bailey thought; but to wriggle themselves above it women are readier to build up appearances and swear masquerades to be realities. Would Josephine next maintain, gayly eye to eye with him, that he'd in some sort made love to her before her engagement was broken? Next? Why, no, she'd just said virtually that very thing! Of how much truth from her would one ever be sure—about anything?

The paint-blisters that could ruin the old Florentine's daintily sad blonde Madonna became all at once too threatening a defacement; he refused longer to look at them, turned away to fill his eyes with beauty more secure.

About him there was plenty of it, for he stood in an alcove just off the main Italian Gallery and here, close to him and warmly to his taste, hung six samples of Thomas Oaklin's shrewdest looting—a Botticelli head, undeniable; a Pietà if not by Giovanni Bellini himself then certainly a work by the best of his great bottega; a Crivelli Madonna and Child; an Enthronement by Mainardi's brother-in-law, Ghirlandaio; and two deep-colored portraits of fierce Quattrocento youths by Alvise Vivarini. Lately, since he'd helped Miss Jyre to reestablish the alcove, dismantled during the "scare," this had become Bailey's favorite spot in the museum; but now he tried in vain to lose himself in contemplation of the pictures. Renaissance art didn't serve him to-day.

"The Jyre," "Your Jyre," "Rossbeke" . . . He heard the sweet jeering voice of Josephine Oaklin—whom he was to marry. He heard that voice, genially superior, half-mocking his way of painting as old hat; he heard her voice, oracular though never an ugly sound, proclaiming the greatness of Harry Pilker. He heard it interject the misinformation that she was twenty-two; but most repeatedly he heard its exquisite cajoleries insist that jealousy of him had scourged Murties into despairing flight. A man who drives away a woman's lover owes her another—himself. Bailey was to be the debtor, not she.

People seldom remember accurately the words they utter in moments of anguished crisis. Josephine had forgotten her outcries from the scarlet couch. Bailey hadn't. "Oh, I knew he was cooling off . . . There were times when I felt as if he actually disliked me . . . He just changed!"

Those solicitous fond new friends who called Bailey Fount "Our Darling," partly because the loving tenderness of women is most of all roused by wounded soldiers and helpless children, didn't know him; they had knowledge of him in only his injured condition. A reticent, absorbed yet by no means passive young landscape painter, he'd begun to be remodeled by the Army before Pearl Harbor, and often for such natures the Army is an injection of iron. Later, when he'd had his commission, the metal had bent perilously in the Pacific crucible; but bent isn't destroyed. He was still sensitive and ever would be so, as his museum friends perceived; and Helena Jyre was fearfully sure that he still could crash—as who can't? Nevertheless he'd of late quickly returned a long way toward stiff-backed soldierliness.

His expression, as he left the alcove, might have been described by a former comrade-in-arms as dead-pan.

XIX

AT THE DINNER in honor of the "new cousin," but understood by the sixteen subterraneanly excited guests as otherwise,
mementoes of Thomas Oaklin's grandeurs were handsomely
upon display. Eighteenth Century silver, Royal Worcester porcelains, old English glass and a long field of Venetian lace
richly attended Lowestoft bowls of Spun Gold roses in the wax
light of four ducal but chaste candelabra. This illumination
gently sculptured the features of the guests with a becoming
chiaroscuro, and, so mellowly revealed, even the apoplectic
contours of John Constable Horne were wrought into a har-
mony, as by coats of golden varnish over a cantankerous old
portrait. Moreover, if ladies were rouged or lipsticked or both,
those carnations attractively appeared indigenous.

Mr. Horne's presence was a surprise to Bailey Fount. So was
Mrs. Parannik's. So was that of the hostile Mrs. Paylor.
Plainly, Josephine believed in riding straight at the heart of the
enemy. Bailey had a detached thought that if need be he could
like Mrs. Paylor; her expression, matronly and thoughtful, was
that of a good woman.

He sat at Mrs. Oaklin's right and between her and Jose-

phine's all-time adherent, Miss Sophie Tremoille, whose looks
were something close upon misfortune. Eyes so protuberant,
outlined by sparse pink lashes, he'd seldom seen, or more chin-
lessness beneath a wider fluctuant mouth. He feared to look at
her more than fleetingly, lest she detect that it was a trial to do
so; but Cousin Folia had come to the table to eat, and Miss
Tremoille applied herself to him with a confidential eagerness.

"Isn't she gorgeous to-night?" Sophie said, in this tone.
"Those Delft blue brocade patterns on silver, with all that
definitely perfect bareness above! Somebody's pretty lucky, I
think; don't you?" The unctuous, half-whispering voice became arch. "They're all doing a tingling lot of guessing, Mr.
Fount."

He was laconic. " 'They'?" he asked. " 'Tingling'?"

"Yes, extremely tingling! Every one of these people here to-
night. It's terrific! I said 'they,' Bailey, because of course *I*
practically know. I'll have to begin calling you Bailey. I'm her
lifelong most intimate friend, you see. How's it feel to be so
raved over?"

"I don't know."

"Oh, no, you don't!" Sophie's elbow poked him surreptitiously in the side and she muffled a giggle. "I suppose, for
instance, you don't know what she says about your eyes. Want
to hear? I can give you her very words. She says your eyes are
so startled by the tragedies they must have seen, and yet so
magically gentle whenever you look up and let her look into
them for a darling instant, she just doesn't know what to do
about it! She's told me that at least three times! You must feel
like young Lochinvar. Don't you?"

"No; I'm afraid I don't feel very young or see where the
Lochinvar comes in."

"Oh, but very!" Sophie said. "Dashing in like that, sweeping her up, snatching her out of the very clutches of her affianced! I'm sure you know, yourself, you're a most dangerous person, with nobody safe from you—and you did it all so quietly, too! She's really a glorious sight to-night, isn't she? I do wonder how a man feels to think he owns something like that. I mustn't keep you talking when I know you want to look at her, so do. Look all you want."

Bailey did look, and the devoted serf's phrase "glorious sight" didn't appear to be over-statement. Josephine sat at the other end of the table and in the adorning candlelight might have been the realization of a sentimental youth's picturings of the yet unknown perfection he'd surely some day find, adore and wed. Bailey remembered that she'd deplored her looks: "It's a handicap to be so rhythmically but obviously pretty as I am. I was always afraid I'd grow up to find myself helplessly looking like a Nineteenth Century candy-box cover girl." Bailey'd never seen any Nineteenth Century candy-boxes but supposed their "cover girls" might have been remotely derived from Greuze and Nattier. If so, those decorations certainly weren't up to a Josephine Oaklin, and "pretty" came nowhere near her. She'd intimated that she'd like him to be in love with her for her mind's sake, and to-night she looked entitled to some confidence about that.

For a girl, twenty-five is one of the critical ages, but is often of all the most enhancing. The shapings of character begin to be heralded by hints of what will supplant mere bud-bloom, that young-animal beauty commonly snatched up, for permanent better or worse, by recklessly self-swindled dwellers in the evanescent instant. Twenty-five's facial portents can prophesy the best heaven that comes to earth, and when modelings begin a tale of inner enrichments, twenty-five is unmistakably lovelier than twenty. The face of Josephine, as Bailey stared down the long table, refuted the dark doubts he'd had of her. The rhythmic obvious beauty she'd decried was sparklingly all there; but so were the enriching promises. In spite of the frivolous animation and multiplied movement with which she was talking to Henry Rossbeke and a chilling girl beside him, Josephine could be seen as the lustrous foreshadowing of the woman she might possibly become—a delightful, rare, fine being, learnedly intelligent yet generous in kind human understanding and in humor. What might be, could be, and if——

All at once Josephine realized that Bailey was looking at her. Abruptly she broke off her talk with Rossbeke and the inimical girl; she leaned forward and conspicuously responded to Bailey's gaze—responded with a velvet look, long and so profoundly caressive that to save him he could not but half-believe what she sent him real.

"Oh, Golly!" Sophie Tremoille muffled another giggle as she whispered, "No wonder you blush! Sensation! Everybody's gandering; but you don't care, do you? *She* certainly doesn't! How *does* it feel to have her do that?"

Bailey was startled by the violence of his wish that the message from Josephine's eyes had been truthful. She'd ended the look with a little jerk, as if startled, herself; then with a confessing shyness she spoke to her next neighbors but made her words audible to everybody: "What *were* we talking about? I've completely lost the thread! I'm afraid I always do when I find 'Our Darling' looking at me. Rossbeke'll tell you that's what we call him in the museum, Rosalie. All the staff are off their heads about him, so why blame *me!*"

At Cousin Folia's left sat Mr. Horne and next him, darkly

handsome in black and green silk, was Mrs. Parannik. She leaned a little forward to glance expressively at Mrs. Paylor, who returned the ocular communication with so much knowing significance that she might as well have nodded. What the silent dialogue conveyed between the two was, from Mrs. Parannik, "You get what she's up to? You see Helena Jyre was right, don't you?" and from Mrs. Paylor, "I certainly do!" Josephine didn't miss a word of it.

She knew who her enemies were and had already guessed what they must have been doing. "Seeing much of Helena Jyre lately, Charlotte?" She spoke down the length of the table and the inquiring lift of her voice was cordial. "You and our dear Gertie Paylor ought to do something about that poor woman—if you're still fond of her."

"I am," Mrs. Paylor said incautiously. "What ought we to do about her?"

"You ought to keep Rossbeke, here, from running her to death trying to carry out his slightest whim. He never even notices how exhausted she gets, pleasing him. Don't you both think he ought to be ashamed, the way he treats her and doesn't even know it?"

"I?" Rossbeke said uncomfortably. "I can't imagine——"

Josephine ignored him. "Don't you think it's a crime, you girls? Oughtn't you to tell him? Isn't it time for him to begin to take at least a humane interest?"

Rossbeke frowned, sorely wishing Helena hadn't made him come; Mrs. Paylor looked annoyed and Mrs. Parannik, reddening, said "Oh, nonsense!" as she turned to talk to John Constable Horne.

Bailey felt that something under the surface had just been going on, he didn't know what—except that there'd been another belittling of Helena Jyre for no reason and out of a clear sky. Was there even spite in it, for where was the gain? Josephine hadn't finished with Mrs. Parannik.

"Charlotte," she said, "you're wasting your time if you're trying to talk music to Mr. Horne. The dear man doesn't know anything except art and even there his mind's been a blank ever since the Davies Armory Show in New York in Nineteen-thirteen. I did you an enormous favor, Charlotte—putting you near enough to my priceless cousin to talk to *him*. I wouldn't have done it if I'd realized why your precious old Parannik wriggled out of coming to-night. I've just got it. He was afraid."

Charlotte Parannik's dark prettiness was brightened by an amiable smile. "Of you, Josephine?" she asked. "More than usual?"

The girl Rosalie, next to Rossbeke, laughed applausively. So did one or two others; but Josephine apparently overlooked this demonstration. "Yes, I think so," she said judicially. "In fact, I fear he ought to be more afraid of everybody, just now, than usual."

"Parannik ought?" Parannik's wife still smiled. "But isn't 'everybody' just you, Josephine—as usual?"

"In a way," Josephine replied. "It happens, you see, that I know what music everybody'd like to hear. Of course I'm personally too modest to remind you, besides, of certain historical facts that——"

"I'll do the reminding for you, dear," Charlotte Parannik said affably. "We're to remember your grandfather. There wouldn't be any orchestra otherwise—no Parannik, no me, no nothing!"

Josephine kissed a hand to her. "And no museum either,

dear. Mr. Horne and Rossbeke wouldn't like your forgetting to mention that."

"No, they'd be prostrated," Charlotte said. "Aren't we to remember, too, how at the age of seven you chose this life of squalor in which you're still grubbing and let your grandpapa spend his own money the way he wanted to? So now you're on all the Boards or something, aren't you? That makes it really naughty of Parannik ever not to be in a state of fright about you. Dear child, it's a duty he never neglects."

"That's wise of him, Charlotte. It's I that have been the neglectful one lately, though. I've been so busy in the museum. these days"—Josephine's flagrantly tender glance pointed out Bailey as the reason—"I haven't been thinking about the orchestra at all. In fact, I haven't been able to put my mind on a lot of things I should have." She glanced toward Bailey again as she made the hurried admission. "I couldn't help that, you see; these things will happen! Some of 'em distress me—in particular *one* pretty harrowing thing I couldn't help having to do. To-night I'm sure you all see why that just *had* to be, so you'll give me a break and make allowances for me." Once more a winsome glance designated Bailey. "After all, there's a pretty good excuse for me, isn't there?"

"Isn't she a genius!" the rapturous Sophie whispered to Bailey. "I wondered how she was going to let it out she sent poor Harold skidding. Cute, oh, cute!"

Josephine was continuing: "So you see, Charlotte, I even neglected to find out beforehand precisely what program your Parannik has shifted to for his next concert, and here we have it actually upon us—and is it a mess!"

"You feel so?" Charlotte made her tone brightly hopeful. "Then perhaps I could tell my husband he won't have the— the pleasure—of seeing you in his audience to-morrow night?"

"No, he won't. I've promised to begin duty at the station canteen Saturday nights; but I might make an effort to sit through the Sunday afternoon concert. Sorry to say the whole program strikes me as deplorable, and the prime feature of it is really atrocious. Rossbeke's just told me Parannik's brought Borfsky here again to play that tiresome old Brahms Concerto in B-flat Major."

" 'Tiresome'?" Rossbeke said. "I didn't say that. In fact, there isn't anything I'd rather——"

Josephine was prompt to cut him off. "So you all of you see what we're in for and Parannik understands perfectly well what I think of it. He knew that if he came to-night he'd have to pretend he didn't remember what Mother and I distinctly told him the last time he had Borfsky and that everlasting old concerto. We told him frankly the whole town's sick of it. You were there, Charlotte. You heard us telling him, didn't you, dear?"

" 'Us'?" Mrs. Parannik asked. "Did your mother say anything at all, Josephine? Did she—ever?"

"Ever? Oh, several times—in my infancy!" Josephine's sunny look was that of a girl too overwhelmingly happy to be anything but good-natured. "Sometimes she still does. I'll prove it. Mother, say something. Speak!"

Mrs. Oaklin looked up from a quail she was plastering with sauce and browned crumbs. "What?" she said.

"Sunk!" her daughter admitted, doing most of the laughing. "I'd better hurry back to Brahms and Parannik and Borfsky. Everybody knows Parannik lets you put in your oar when he plans his programs, Charlotte. I'm afraid I'll have to think the guilt for the Brahms Concerto largely yours. I suppose they're all busy as beavers rehearsing it to-night?"

"No, dear. I got them to rehearse this afternoon so I could be there and not miss coming to-night. I was bound not to skip this dinner, and so was Gertie. We both simply *had* to see how you'd do it."

The recipient of this stab didn't reel; she was a gallant hand at double-talk and ladies' in-fighting. "Yes, it's remarkable to have a cook still; we've always known how to treat ours, you see. Of course I might have known you'd arrange not to miss a Borfsky rehearsal. Adroit of you, Charlotte, sliding him back here for another concert so soon. Of course Parannik doesn't mind; I'm sure he doesn't. It's all just music—or *do* I seem to recall your acting as a charmingly amorous sort of convoy round Borfsky, last time he was here?"

"Yes, I had to," Mrs. Parannik said. "He begged me to defend him."

"From me?" Josephine's bantering seemed only gossamer. "Is that how you explained things to Parannik?" Knowing well how to conclude such warlike episodes with the air of victory, she turned at once to the people at her end of the table and began to talk rapidly of the Mediterranean campaign.

Mrs. Parannik, after a quick-drawn breath, spoke in an undertone to Mr. Horne; but Bailey heard her. "Parannik wouldn't come to dine here to escape a firing squad."

"Good food, though," the old man returned. "Tradition of the house. I can always eat—anyhow as long as she can be kept off of art."

"That splits it," the lady added. "You can eat when it isn't art and I can when it isn't music." She looked across Mr. Horne and the disregarded Mrs. Oaklin at Bailey, saw that he was listening. "How about you, Mr. Fount? We're expected to understand, are we, that everything's delightful for you?"

Bailey contrived to make his responding smile a little fatuous. "More than delightful, Mrs. Parannik. I'm not sure what you mean by 'everything'; but if you include my experience in the museum along with other matters I'm not supposed to mention quite yet I——"

She interrupted him quickly. "Other matters? Oh, those are much the most interesting. They seem very, very different from what they did the first time I met you. Couldn't you tell us at least a little about those 'other matters,' if only a word? Everybody'd be simply——"

"I'm afraid not yet," he interrupted in turn, and, determinedly performing his part, sent a consciously smiling glance toward Josephine. "I'm free to talk of the agreeableness of my experience in the museum, though, if you like, and I could go on about that at great length."

"Then do," Charlotte Parannik said, perforce swallowing her curiosity. "I think I told you I'm part Spanish. Perhaps you'd shed me a little light upon the Spanish primitives in the museum. I've been several times to look at them; but I don't understand them at all."

"For me, too," Bailey returned, "they're mainly gorgeous enigmas. Mr. Horne, though, holds a real title to talk about them. I haven't the presumption—not in his presence."

"Modest feller, ain't he?" Horne said. "Like his mother. Quiet woman. You'd 'a' thought you could get her to do anything you wanted her to; but try her out and you couldn't budge her. Museum's Spanish primitives? Fifteenth Century Catalan and Aragonese. Got one we claim's a Huguet and two we'll swear are Martin de Sorias—beautiful embossing, typical, with the right peaked visages and painted backgrounds, not gold. If you wanted to you could do a neat bit of research, Bailey Fount, investigating the recent effect of Catalonian altar backs. For instance, who brought that Fifteenth Century Spanish influence into modern art? Know the answer, don't you, Mrs. Parannik?"

"I? Good heavens, no!"

"John Singer Sargent!" Mr. Horne announced, speaking the name sonorously. "John Sargent came up from Spain with——"

"Hurrah!" This cry came from Josephine, who apparently couldn't keep her attention upon her end of the table—because of Bailey. "He's off! Upon my soul, I thought I heard him use the word 'modern'! Mr. Horne, do you really think you're telling somebody something about modern art? Hasn't your psychiatrist *yet* told you to stop trying?"

"No," the old man retorted. "He only told me to stop short of murder, just barely short of it."

"What a mind!" Josephine exclaimed. "Begins a lecture on Spanish primitives and skips straight to John Singer Sargent and murder. Bailey, ask him if he still claims he's talking about modern art."

"I am," Mr. Horne said. "Pointed out how Catalonian altar backs came into it. Only a whiff of 'em, of course. The great Spanish stream toward the moderns flowed through Velasquez, Mrs. Parannik. Opposite it, on the other big Mediterranean peninsula, Italy, you get the stream from Titian that split into the two separate flows down through Rembrandt and Rubens to become elements of genuine modern art along with that from Velasquez; but Velasquez is the fundamental under the last great types of modern painting. You'll find him behind Raeburn, behind Sargent, behind——"

"Behind Picasso?" Josephine suggested winningly. "Stimulating, how blandly you omit Tintoretto, El Greco, Hieronymus Bosch, Matthias Grünewald, Goya and Blake as leads to the genuine modern. Charlotte, you haven't the remotest idea what he's talking about, I know; but do anyhow sweetly ask him if he finds Sargent and Velasquez behind the one supreme masterpiece of this age."

" 'The one supreme'——" Mr. Horne paused, then conspicuously shuddered. "Whenever she talks like that she's going to mention something hideous. What's the supreme masterpiece you have in mind, child—'Illinois Toilers' by Harry Pilker?"

"No. Bailey didn't like it. I mean 'Guernica.' "

" 'Guernica'!" Mr. Horne set down his fork with a clink. "Why was I such an ass as to come to this dinner? 'Guernica,' the 'one supreme'——" His voice, suddenly hoarse, uttered a profane sob, and failed him.

"You art people!" Mrs. Parannik exclaimed, pleased. "You're worse than we music people are. Of course I know there's some sort of furious split among you over modernism, and you and Josephine are eternally clashing about it, Mr. Horne; but doesn't the difference go deeper than that? Isn't it really because you arties are two different types of beings— you and Josephine, for instance? Isn't it because you're a steadfast sort of man but she's always doomed to keep changing and changing, so she has to go wild over any new thing that comes along? Isn't that it?"

"Almost," Josephine said, and beamed upon her. "You're almost right, Charlotte. I go wild over every new thing until the right one comes along; but I *stay* wild over that—forever!"

"You do, Josephine? Even if *it* gets a little tired of all the excitement and——"

"And runs away?" Josephine supplied this joyously. "It won't, Charlotte. Look for yourself and see if you think it's the sort to behave like a hunted pianist."

In spite of herself, Charlotte Parannik sent a glance of chagrin at Bailey, who sat smiling, looking tall and solid in his uniform. Josephine's air of triumph was not to be dispersed by anything Charlotte could say or do. Bailey heard Sophie Tremoille murmuring happily at his ear, "She *does* rub it in on 'em, doesn't she?" but he didn't answer. He felt a gentle pressure on his knee—the head of his friend Roggo, whose better eye glistened up at him wistfully from beneath a fold of Venetian lace. Bailey'd have hiddenly given him something he asked for; but the old dog's presence was discovered.

"Oh, my! That animal's got in here somewhere!" Mrs. Oaklin looked up to say. "I know it because he rolled in a fish this afternoon and nobody's had time to wash him. Harvey!"

"Yes'm." Harvey knew where Roggo was; removed him.

The ladies' war, anything but abandoned, reached a lull that lasted until the party had returned to the drawing-room. There a re-grouping took place as most of the women, like scouts summoned to headquarters, hurriedly clustered upon a center formed by Mrs. Paylor and Mrs. Parannik. Across the room from this suppressedly vociferous knot, Josephine stood beside Bailey, her arm through his with an air of already customary possessiveness while she chatted carelessly with Rossbeke and Sophie Tremoille. Mr. Horne joined Mrs. Oaklin, not only upon a sofa but in objecting to the furniture, all of which he cursed; and then, after an almost scandalously brief saving of appearances, the Oaklins' guests began to make for home—or for gathering places where they could speak out frankly.

The group about Mrs. Paylor and Mrs. Parannik broke up;

Mrs. Paylor came somewhat brusquely to say goodnight—she'd
promised to help her husband with his reports, she said—and
Bailey heard the girl, Rosalie, just behind Mrs. Paylor, titter
to Charlotte Parannik, "The sooner we go, the less we're damaged, what?"

Josephine stopped saying, "Oh, must you," left this duty
entirely to her mother, and, not relinquishing Bailey's arm,
drew him across the hall and into the "music room." Mr. Horne
called after them: "It's raining again, Bailey; but I've got a
taxi and I'll wait for you." Out of sight of the departing guests
Josephine withdrew her arm, touched keys of the piano mood-
ily.

"You did everything well, Bailey—followed my lead as you
promised—but I'm sensitive to emanations. You didn't approve. I did things you dislike."

"No. I felt you were doing only what you thought you had
to. It was all part of the——"

"You sound evasive," she said. "You loathe women's squab-
bling, I suppose. Men always do—when they comprehend
that it's going on. Mine was pretty plain. You rather hate me
for it, don't you?"

"Certainly not. Maybe I didn't take it all in; but under the
circumstances I supposed you thought you——"

She stopped him. "You really don't like me to-night, do
you?"

"Why, yes, of course I——"

"No," she said. "I see you don't." She had been standing
with her back to him, her fingers not sounding the piano keys
they successively touched; now she turned to look at him with
a penetration so grave, an inquiry so searching, that a strange
and new experience was evoked within him—he seemed to be

telling her something that he didn't know, himself. Wishing her different, he couldn't have said whether he "liked" her or not; yet all at once he felt near to the mystic very self of her.

She knew this. "Why, yes!" she said. "Isn't it strange—this moment right now? You haven't answered me. You needn't. It's like a thicket that's suddenly opened into a vista and we've just caught a glimpse of each other through it. Isn't it so?"

"Yes."

She sighed, smiled, patted his sleeve, and they turned back toward the hallway. "You'll go on following my lead? Don't too much mind some other things I've had to do. I'll let you run along now; Mr. Horne's waiting. You mustn't get wet and catch cold."

"I'll try not to."

They'd come into the hall; Mr. Horne stood waiting, and the last of the other guests were moving toward the side entrance that led to the porte-cochère. Josephine laughed. "Think of my telling a war hero who's been through what you have 'not to catch cold'!"

Bailey spoke under his breath. "I asked you not to call me that."

"I won't again. Don't be angry—dearest."

Suddenly enraptured, touched to the heart by her tremulous speaking of that last word, Bailey said, "Never!" then blindly and deafly thanked Cousin Folia; bade her goodnight. In the cab with Mr. Horne, he had Josephine's face before him as he'd seen it in his last backward glance at her from the door. He was mystified by the impression that she looked frightened.

XX

On SUNDAY MORNING Henry Rossbeke, slippered and wearing an old dressing-gown of Chinese-red silk, sat before the book-strewn writing-table in his apartment, working intently upon a letter of remonstrance he was writing to the editor of a magazine of art and archaeology. On Sundays the museum didn't open until two o'clock in the afternoon; the Director had until lunchtime to devote himself to this letter, which he intended to make about three thousand words long when it should be completed, perhaps a month hence. The editor had asked for the letter, desiring it to obliterate a critic who'd superiorly objected to both the magazine and a scrupulous article, Rossbeke's, printed some months earlier, on the subject of North Italian Wood Sculptures of the Late Twelfth Century.

Rossbeke worked with a delicate concentration, probing his mind not merely for phrases of precision but for those that would sprinkle intellectual venom and at the same time maintain for him the amusedly satiric mien of a philosophic commentator. There must be no appearance of heat, so the style takes time; but he hoped to finish the first draft of a paragraph, a column's length, by noon. He wasn't pleased when he heard the bell of his outer door ringing.

He rose, moaning patiently, went to the door and found Helena Jyre dourly facing him, a folded newspaper in her hand. "I wouldn't disturb you for anything ordinary," she said, as they came through the short hallway and into his living-room. "You're at the letter, aren't you? I know I oughtn't——"

"No, no; it's all right." He returned to his table, cast an absent, wistful look at his manuscript. "I'm always glad; but you know that. I'd meant to call you up presently, anyhow. I wanted to tell you on no account to miss the orchestra this afternoon. Parannik gave a fine show last night, a really beautiful program, and Borfsky was surpassing. You'll be going, won't you?"

"I don't know." She spread the newspaper upon the table, and with her right forefinger touched a subordinate headline half-way down the front page. "Please read this."

"I must?" he said plaintively, resumed his chair and began to read, half-aloud, " 'Hero in city for months . . . too modest to make himself known . . . Lt. Bailey Fount, recovered from wounds . . . an Oaklin curator . . .' " Rossbeke looked up. "What's this? How the devil——"

"Read on," Helena said.

He showed agitation. "But see here! I told Miss Bullard, myself, she wasn't to allow any publicity whatever about him to——"

"It's not her fault, Henry. You haven't forgot who set her to rooting it out, have you? We needn't waste any time blaming Miss Bullard. You'd better read it all and try to get some idea of the damage——"

"It's pretty bad?"

"Just read it."

Rossbeke's expression showed his deepening apprehension as he read the spectacular story built upon a few despatches and exhumed bits of narrative by war correspondents.

Lieutenant Bailey Fount, with seventeen men, a remnant, had held a jungle river ford after orders to fall back failed to reach them. They had clung to their position for eleven days; and when their ammunition was gone and not a man of them left unwounded, the last of the tragic defense had been with the bayonet and hurled rocks. Then an American advance cleared out the Japanese and found only Lieutenant Fount and a Corporal alive. Lieutenant Fount's leg had been broken by a sniper's bullet on the third day of the fighting; he'd received five bayonet wounds after that. The Corporal had been shot through the chest and succumbed in a field hospital; but Lieutenant Fount, though his injuries and exhaustion made his recovery unlikely, had undergone remedial surgery with success. He was the sole survivor.

The Globe expanded the event, was elaborate with embellishing stencils, applauded the rewarding citation and medals, brushed brilliantine all over Lieutenant Bailey Fount. His modesty was a special theme: he had chosen to make himself inconspicuous in a patriotic city that would have rejoiced to do him public honor; but, avoiding all fanfare, he had self-effacingly allowed himself to be installed as Assistant Curator of Painting in the Thomas Oaklin Museum of Art. Such action on his part, however, was peculiarly appropriate since this outstanding war hero was a member of the very family who were the founders of that institution. It was a privilege to learn from another source that "Lieutenant Fount is a grand-nephew of Thomas Oaklin and therefore a kinsman of Mrs. Thomas Oaklin, Jr., and her daughter, Miss Josephine Oaklin, whose lives are devoted to the maintenance and development of Thomas Oaklin's munificent endowments and gifts to the city."

The Globe added finally that a reporter and a photographer had found Lieutenant Fount absorbed in his work at the museum late on the preceding afternoon. With genuine embarrassment he had insisted that there could be no possible public interest in himself. He had shrunk from the photographer and resisted every temptation to be glamorized. He could not be brought to talk of his exploit, made nothing of it but in a few halting words attributed everything to the valor of the men who'd fought beside him. The reporter was disappointed, yet could not help admiring the abnegation that gave the glory of a gallant action to others. That was the spirit of the Army.

Rossbeke read through to the finish. "You say Miss Bullard's not responsible? She furnished the material."

"Don't accuse her of knowing how it would be used, Henry. I've had her call up the Globe. Josephine's responsible entirely. Don't forget about a third of the stock in that paper was a part of the Oaklin estate that didn't go to the museum or the orchestra. When she wants to, she orders the editor around much as she does the rest of us. She talked over the telephone to him a day or so ago and again yesterday after lunch, a girl in the office told Miss Bullard. This is the result. You see why she did it, don't you?"

"She *couldn't* have understood what effect——"

"Do you suppose she'd care!" Helena cried. "All she wants is to make him more important so it'll be that much more plausible she threw Murties over for him. People are to say, 'Who wouldn't—for such a hero!' If it knocks Bailey Fount flat in his tracks, what's the difference?"

Rossbeke began a dubious protest. "But I told you how she looked at him at that dinner and how she——"

"If you fell for that," Helena jeered, "the rest of 'em certainly didn't. Charlotte told me they all——"

"Yes, I know; but she *did* seem to show something like a genuine——"

"Henry Rossbeke, it isn't in her to care what happens to anybody except herself."

His doubt persisted. "She wouldn't mind a newspaper's trumpeting about herself; I think she'd rather like it. So she'd hardly understand how acutely painful this will be to him."

"You think 'acutely painful' covers it, Henry? Nobody knows how that boy's struggled to get back on his feet! Old Mackailie, the all-work man at The Cranford, says Bailey's been doing setting-up exercises in his room till you'd cry to see him at it. Says he's been doing 'em ever since he came here. Besides that, every morning before breakfast he'd go out for a walk—better call it a limp!—making it longer and longer, plodding along as hard as he could. Lately, since he got rid of his lameness, he gets up before six o'clock, exercises himself to pieces, then walks and walks and walks. This'll knock out every bit of good he's done himself!"

"He's seen the thing?"

"I don't know. I think so, because he wasn't at breakfast. He didn't come back from his walk. That looks like it, doesn't it?"

Rossbeke gave his manuscript a rueful glance and got to his feet. "I'd better go out and find him. I don't want him to suspect for an instant that this publicity came from the museum. I can explain that much to him, anyhow."

"No," Helena said. "You'd hesitate over explaining where

it *did* come from, and it's precisely what he needs to know. I told you I'd do what I could; this is an opening at last. Women have to do this sort of dirty work about other women when it's right to do it."

"You'll tell him——"

"I'll tell him," Helena said, with deep-breathing anger, "I'll tell him what she *is*—if I possibly can! It's time somebody dared, isn't it? You agree, don't you?"

"I'm afraid so."

"That's all I came to hear you say." Helena Jyre took up the newspaper, crumpled it to shapelessness, threw it into the wastebasket beside the table. "I'll do it now."

Bailey hadn't returned to The Cranford. She went to the closed museum, entered by a rear door, explored the silent galleries, tried his workroom; then descended to the Director's office where Mrs. Williams sat alone in the outer room. "Do you know where——" Helena began; but obeyed a gesture that instructed her to wait.

Mrs. Williams, looking angry, was speaking placidly into her desk telephone. "No, I don't think he's been here this morning. No, I haven't an idea where he is . . . No, I can't leave the office to look for anybody just now. There's no one else to answer calls on Sunday . . . I'm sorry, Miss Oaklin; I positively can't . . . No, ordinarily he's not on duty on Sunday . . . Yes, certainly you could leave a message for him, either here or at The Cranford where he lives . . . You've tried The Cranford? . . . I'm sorry but—— Yes, of course I'll give him your message if he . . . You want him to what? Please don't speak so rapidly . . . Yes, I asked you not to speak so rap—— Miss Oaklin, there's no reason for you to be irritated with me . . .

I can't understand a word you're—— Will you please repeat what you asked me to tell him? . . . Hello, hello——"

The instrument, having delivered itself of a flurry of indistinguishable sound, had become silent. Mrs. Williams, returning it to its prongs, explained to Helena: "That was the Pest. Insisted that I instantly put him on the wire, and when I couldn't, why, of course she took it as an insult. I should think she *would* want to see him—after what she's done to him in the Globe this morning! You've seen it, haven't you?"

"Yes. What did she——"

"Ended by shouting she's somewhere and wants him to come there immediately or join her somewhere else before three o'clock."

"Three? Are you sure she said three o'clock, Mrs. Williams?"

"I think so. That's when the symphony concerts begin, isn't it? Maybe she wants him for that, I don't know. She was in such a hurry and so annoyed with me for not producing him, she might as well have been talking Cherokee. When I tried to tell her I didn't get it she was ringing off in my face."

"I'm trying to find him, myself," Helena said. "I don't know where else to look. All I can do's go back to The Cranford and just sit there."

At The Cranford she was waiting in a small "reception room" off the entrance hall when Bailey came. As he closed the front door she stepped forward to detain him. "Will you —— May I see you in here for a few minutes?"

He stalked into the room, and, without any comprehensible expression upon his face or in his voice, stood passive. "What is it?"

"Bailey, Mr. Rossbeke wants you to know—all of us at the

museum want you to know—we'd never do anything that might distress you. If something is doing that, it hasn't come from any of us."

His attitude altered as she spoke. He looked away from her and stood stooping lopsidedly, an old posture of his she'd hoped never to see again. "You're talking about that newspaper, aren't you?"

"Bailey, Mr. Rossbeke and all of us understood from the first you didn't want to be treated as a 'war hero.' We knew you wished it not even mentioned. We knew how you dreaded ever having to speak of it."

"Yes, I—I should think anybody'd have known how I'd feel about the sort of thing that was in the paper this morning."

"Anybody?" Helena spoke quickly. "Anybody with the slightest consideration for you would have known. Any human being with the least regard for you would know that every time it's spoken of you'd have to live through the whole tragedy again and——"

"That's not—that's not——" His voice was low and uncertain. "I mean living through it again isn't—isn't the worst of it. It's not the wrongness of it. I don't like the word but there are heroes. I'm not one of them."

"Oh, but you are!" Helena's impulse was too strong for her. "You don't want to be *called* one, but if anybody in this war deserves——"

"No, that's wrong," he said muffledly, but with eloquence heart-rending enough for Helena Jyre. "I just happened to be the only one that didn't die."

She began to cry, got at her handkerchief, used it without being seen. "Bailey dear, I didn't mean for you to talk about it."

"Yes. I've started," he said. "Those men who died were friends of mine. I was all washed up, myself, after the third day, mostly just makeshift splints and bandages. All I did was flop around in the way, a burden on everybody. It was they who stuck it out, not I; I was useless. Well, they're dead and can't take the credit for what they did. Do you think I——"

"Bailey, you don't need to tell me!"

He changed again, stood erect, turned upon her angrily. "My God! Publicity and molasses for just being still *alive?* What half-way decent man could stand for it? My 'heroism'! My 'modesty'! That unspeakable hooey about my 'modesty'! Modest about having been an encumbrance? I tell you I don't see how anybody on earth could have been so damned callous as to dig it all up again and plaster it over the face of a newspaper!"

Helena Jyre cried out, "Oh, you poor boy!" but in her heart she was fiercely glad, for now indeed she had her chance. "Do you want to know where that plastering came from? Straight from the house that's shackled on all of us—the house that nine-tenths of any trouble in the museum always does come from!"

"The house?" He didn't understand at once. "The house that——"

"Your Cousin Josephine!"

"What of her? What did she do?"

"Josephine Oaklin virtually dictated the whole thing to that newspaper."

"Josephine?" He spoke the name slowly. "You say she——"

"She did it. We know she did it. Do you suppose I'd tell you so if I didn't know?"

"What did she do it for?"

"You really want me to——" Helena faltered, hung fire for a moment; then spoke out. "She did it to glorify herself, not you."

"But it couldn't."

"Oh, yes, it could! For one thing, you're her cousin. Blazoning you as a hero is a credit to the Oaklin family. That's pointed out in the paper pretty blaringly, isn't it? She'd have done it for that alone; but it's only the lesser part of it."

"What's the rest of it?"

"I'm afraid I've got to tell you." Helena took thought within herself. "You've come to know me pretty well, haven't you? Mr. Rossbeke, too? You've seen the kind of man he is. His goodness is written pretty plainly in his face, isn't it? You wouldn't think either of us spiteful or underhanded, would you?"

"Never."

"Very well," she said. "I can go ahead. During all the years that Mr. Rossbeke's been the Director of the Museum and the whole time I've had my position there, his life and mine have been absorbed in the work and there'd never have been any trouble—except for one person. There are people in this world who bring hurt and discord to everything they touch. She's done that and she'll do it to every life that has to be associated with hers. All of us in the museum have thought a great deal about you, Bailey. You know we're as true friends of yours as you're willing to let us be, don't you?"

"I hope so."

"I count on your being sure of it, Bailey." Helena turned half away from him, spoke without looking at him. "She put this in the paper not caring what it would do to you. She did it because she thinks she owns you and you'll have to take it.

She did it because she thinks it will help to make people believe that she threw Captain Murties over for you."

She heard him say "Oh," and, after a pause, add expressionlessly, "I see." At that, she turned to find him sitting stiffly upon the reception room's green denim-covered sofa.

"Does it already hurt you so much to hear the truth of her, Bailey?"

"No." He spoke as stiffly as he sat. "Not exactly."

"I'm afraid it does!" None the less Helena Jyre was determined to finish her task. "Bailey, it may seem to you I've said too much. To all of us who'd like to be useful to you I give you my word it would seem infinitely too little. My excuse for speaking at all is that some day you'd—— Good heaven! You have eyes and ears; you couldn't *help* finding her out and it might come too late. This newspaper—— You do begin to see what she is, don't you? You understand why Mr. Rossbeke felt that either he or I *must* speak out to you, don't you?"

"Yes, I do." The rigidity of his posture, back straight, neck straight, hands flat on his knees, and the blankness of his stare, frightened Helena for him.

"This won't do!" she cried. "That *damned* newspaper! Can't you just forget it—and forget your Cousin Josephine with it? You can't sit here like that and——"

"No." He rose abruptly. "I'll be moving on. I'll get out of here."

"Yes, but I'm going with you," she said, as a summoning gong was sounded in the rear of the hall. "You didn't have any breakfast, I think; but I don't care to listen to the chatter of our table-mates just now any more than you do. You and I'll go out to lunch and then you'll come with me to the symphony concert. Music's an antidote for almost anything. Parannik's

built up a fine orchestra and you haven't heard it yet. I promise
you that from this instant on I'll never speak to you again of—
of any unpleasant people. At lunch I won't say a single word
about anything but music. All right?"

"Thank you," he said stolidly. "All right."

XXI

In the matter of possessing, so to say, a public, Parannik had an advantage over his friend Rossbeke: three or four times as many people attended a single concert as usually visited the museum in a month. That afternoon, as Borfsky was to play, the comparison was harder on the museum than ordinarily; a quarter of an hour before the concert began, the great slanted balcony showed not a vacant space, and a voluminous rustle increased as more and more people were distributed to their fixed brown chairs on the floor below. When the benevolent Helena Jyre and her still inexpressive companion had settled themselves into the pair of forward seats she held for the season, she cast a sweeping backward glance over her shoulder and spoke enviously.

"I'm never here but I wonder why it is that this one of the arts has so much wider an appeal than the others. We poor lonely souls wandering about in our big galleries try to make things attractive; but really we don't compete at all. I doubt if more than a fifth of this audience have ever visited the museum even once; yet in general they seem to be rather interesting peo-

ple and certainly they're all looking forward delightedly to
what they know's coming to them here to-day. Why don't they
know what they could have from us?" She gave him a solicitous
side-glance. "Bailey, do you mind all this prattling I've been
doing? Does it make you more nervous?"

"I'm all right."

"Bailey——" She was timid. "It sounds ridiculous, but
could you tell me: Are you beginning to feel just a little bit
better?"

"Don't worry. I'm all right."

"You will be," she said. "I mean I think the music'll do a
good deal—perhaps for both of us." Her tone apologized for
the hint that doing what she'd felt she ought to do put emotional strain upon her, too. "I always find easement when I
need it if I can have music then."

He made no response; nevertheless, she felt that she was
doing pretty well with Bailey Fount, and for him, too. It was
true that she'd been under some strain, and still was; but she
didn't need much of the easement she'd mentioned; her emotion came near partaking of triumphancy. She'd have said and
believed that it hadn't been easy to bring herself to undermine
a fellow-woman, even conscientiously; yet the accomplishing
of this duty didn't preclude some warmish satisfactions. To
Helena it seemed that she was defending the helpless from a
dragon and doing it for Rossbeke, who couldn't. Of course it
was also for the saving of Bailey, who from the first had roused
in her a maternal championage—and finally, though Helena
Jyre didn't elaborate this to herself, a part of the gratifying
warmth in her bosom glowed upon her own account. Too long
protracted ranklings can't be altogether denied that recom-
pense when the chance comes.

She began to talk again, soothingly, in an undertone. "I always like this pause before a concert, don't you?—musicians beginning to come out upon the stage, the auditorium filling up, people finding their places and murmuring, looking over their programs—and then pretty soon a conglomerate tuning-up, and finally, before Parannik makes his dashing entrance, the concertmeister sounding the pitch on his violin; then more tuning and—yes, I like it all. There's a kind of hushed pomp about the preliminaries before a great orchestra——"

"How *nice!*" She was interrupted by a pleased voice from directly behind her, and Bailey, feeling soft fingers upon his shoulder, turned to see a pretty face between his head and Helena's. Charlotte Parannik, just seated, was surprised and delighted. "Lieutenant Fount, what an honor for such a celebrity to come to our concert to-day! Now, now, don't get so red! What a triumph for you, Helena, to be the one to bring him! So lovely to see you two here together. Things do work out well sometimes, after all. I hope——" She was never to speak further of this hope; she exclaimed in a whisper, "Oh, look!" and gasped out a brief giggle as her two listeners perceived what so stirred her.

Their seats were a few yards to the right of the large stage box at the left of the proscenium arch. The box had been empty; but now Josephine Oaklin came into it, looking casually imperial and attended self-deprecatorily by a lady-in-waiting, Sophie Tremoille. The two had the whole of the box; they sank into brown velvet armchairs, and Josephine, throwing a mink coat back from her shoulders, began to chat negligently to Sophie, but without looking at her. Josephine took much of the attention of about two thousand people and somehow imparted to many of them the realization that upon the façade of the building in which they sat were the words inscribed in stone:

SYMPHONY HALL
DEDICATED TO THE CULTURAL LIFE
OF THIS CITY
BY
THOMAS OAKLIN

Thomas Oaklin's granddaughter, conspicuously that in her appropriately conspicuous place, examined the audience with a slowly circling impersonal gaze. It was the look of a dignitary, one who sat in remote grace above the people; but it was not an impervious look. As Josephine's eyes, having encompassed the varicolored width of the balcony and the farther rows of filled seats below, shortened radius to observe what was nearer her box, there came a change in her expression. Bailey Fount and Helena Jyre didn't see it—both were now looking steadily at the stage—but the attentive Sophie Tremoille whispered hurriedly, "What's the matter? Why the flinch? Something wrong?"

"Be still," Josephine said. "What's the first number on the program? I've forgotten."

"Corelli. Two by Corelli. Then comes———" Sophie interrupted herself. "Josephine, what *was* the matter? You almost jumped. You looked———"

"I did not!"

"Dearie, you did. Something you saw, wasn't it? I wonder———" Sophie, too, saw. *"Oh!"*

"God, how I hate women!" Josephine said behind her teeth. "They're mean."

"What, hon?"

"Nothing. Be still!"

The multitudinous tunings of the instruments thinned and ceased. Parannik came forth dramatically, the audience rose, he led them in The Star Spangled Banner, they sat again, and the concert opened gayly, fountaining out a modern silvery trifling with Corelli. Parannik projected his first brief offerings exquisitely yet with nonchalance; but when applause after the second had been sufficient for him to bring the orchestra to its feet in acknowledgment, he left the stage and returned with a changed manner, suggesting that he approached something serious. The orchestra sat, tuning surreptitiously here and there until was heard the preliminary click of a baton upon a music stand, and the torpedo-shaped, long black back of the Conductor on his podium assumed a tense immobility. The hundred musicians seemed poised, the baton rose, dead silence fell— then into this great hush a sweetly disgusted voice penetrated.

It came from the stage box on the left, made a pretense of being decorously suppressed but was heard throughout perhaps a fourth of the auditorium. "Oh, now really!" the voice said, and there was the noisy rattling of a program. "That squirrel-in-the-cage old Brahms Second again! How *can* they do it?"

Parannik's baton quivered, people said *"Sh!"* and Josephine Oaklin sank back upon her fur coat with a loud despondent sigh, having somewhat marred the opening of Brahms' Second Symphony. Conductor and orchestra recovered themselves, however; and, a few yards from the disturbing box, a searching side-glance of Helena Jyre's seemed to reveal that her escort was occupied solely with music. He was intent upon it, in fact; absorbed in messages it had for him.

His appreciation of the symphony was what a musician would call naïve; thus he had the experience of hearing angels' voices chanting for him a transcendant sermon. With a swelling heart he seemed to hear the voices calling to him, to the Bailey Fount he once had been and must be again: "Hold a strong faith, now more than ever. The thing is almost done. You are your old self again. You're not a dozen shattered selves but one and indivisible. In mind and body you're what you used to be, and again you shall be a soldier."

. . . Throughout the repeated applaudings that followed the symphony he was raptly motionless, and Helena Jyre, discovering and respecting his feeling, didn't speak to him even after the intermission had begun and people were rustling up the aisles to smoke and chatter in the lobbies. The lady seated just behind them, however, leaned forward and addressed them both.

"I can't get over it, Mr. Fount, how nice it is you could come, and above all with our dear Helena! I do hope that nuisance from the box didn't disturb your enjoyment too much. Of course we could all see they heard it on the stage as well as we did. My poor Parannik!" Bailey felt soft fingers again upon his shoulder, this time placatively. "I beg your pardon, Mr. Fount; I'm always forgetting she's your cousin."

He didn't speak; but Helena said quickly, "In spite of what happened Parannik got them all going marvelously, Charlotte. Of course anybody'd know how taut his nerves must have been; but he always covers that up so well that——"

" 'Always'?" Mrs. Parannik repeated skeptically. "You think so? I hope he'll be able to control himself for the rest of the afternoon. He——" Her tone changed. "Look! She's going. If she'll only stay out!"

"No." Helena's slight inclination of her head toward the stage box was understood.

"No hope of it," Charlotte said. "Left her mink in the chair. Gone to smoke in the Trustees' Room. She and Sophie always leave cigarette stubs everywhere in that room where smoking's forbidden because of the insurance. Oh, dear, there I go, once more forgetting about cousins!" She leaned back, feigning a sigh for her stupidity.

Helena gave her an over-shoulder glance. "We're looking forward to a great treat from Borfsky."

"Yes, enormous!" Charlotte leaned forward again; but this time not with her head between Bailey's and Helena's. She spoke to Helena from the other side, affecting the most confidential of tones, as if Bailey were not to hear though it was certain that he did. "Enormous only if everything is right. I'm sure Parannik has Borfsky now in the Conductor's Room talking to him quietingly. He always does, just before; but this time, you see, we made a change in the program at the last moment, so Borfsky's unusually nervous."

"Then why'd you make the change?"

"For a bad good reason," Charlotte Parannik said. "Weeks ago Parannik and I planned for Borfsky to play the Brahms Concerto in B-flat Major; but after the last time Borfsky played it here a certain disturber, I wouldn't say who, set up such a clamor against it that Parannik began to get frightened about doing it again. So, when the programs had actually begun to be printed—we had to stop them—the poor terrified man got Borfsky on the long distance and they substituted Tschaikowsky's Concerto Number One in B-flat Minor. Will that satisfy the disturber?"

"Will anything?" Helena whispered.

"Yes, what she dictates, herself! Unfortunately Borfsky's a great pianist but has certain limitations. The other night at that dinner she made another uproar against the Brahms; but I didn't tell her we'd changed, because whatever we'd changed *to* I knew she'd insist was horrible. I warned Parannik he might be jumping from the frying-pan into the fire; but she keeps him in such a panic my voice was weak." Charlotte's confidential tone was allowed to express the heat of a long indignation. "*Now* will she prove her superiority by injuring the work of an artist like Borfsky and a high-strung conductor like my Parannik? You've heard her already to-day; we'll have more of her. You'll see!"

When Josephine Oaklin, followed by her attendant, returned to her box, she did not repeat that previous wide glance over the auditorium but sat staring fixedly at the stage where the musicians had already taken their places. Parannik appeared, self-effacingly; the imposing Borfsky made a slow magnetic entrance, bowed three times to the correct ovation, then seemed to compose himself, seated before the noble black piano. The members of the orchestra poised again for important effort; Parannik, pallid, faced them—then again there was the shock-producing crackling of a program in the leftward stage box and uttered words sounded through the preluding silence.

Josephine's skill in the use of her voice for a pseudo-whisper was astonishing. So was the amount of scorn conveyed by her lamenting titter. "Tschaikowsky! Always more Tschaikowsky! Can we *live* through it?"

Borfsky's remarkable hands, preparing to rise above the keys, jerked in his lap; his large body screwed half round, his head turned farther, and he stared full at the too-vocal box. So did the pale Parannik, chest heaving, stare at it; and again was heard from the audience the protestive *"Sh! Sh!"* Though the devoted Sophie shrank like a scorched worm, Josephine Oaklin only looked as if she distantly observed children who were trying to be naughty. The shushing grew louder and a woman near the box said huskily, "Insufferable!" Abruptly, Borfsky returned to the contemplation of his piano, and, after a few additional fraught moments in that attitude, nodded to Parannik. The Concerto began.

Indomitable, Josephine crackled her program at intervals during the first movement, at the end of which she rose and drew her fur coat about her shoulders. "Haven't we had about enough of it, Sophie? Good Lord!"

The two left the box, and Josephine was heard complaining fatiguedly from the outside aisle as they departed.

The second movement of the Concerto had begun; but Helena Jyre was aware of a "Thank heaven!" just breathed into her right ear from behind. After that, Charlotte Parannik gave no further sign of her feelings until the final offering of the program had been played and her husband had made the last of his three returns to the stage to bow to the consequent applause. The audience, risen, began to shuffle toward the open doorways, and Helena and Bailey, waiting for the people before them to move on, saw that Charlotte was smiling.

"Even that rumpus couldn't ruin it," she said. "Parannik won't believe so; I'll take him home and go through his despairs with him. He'll drink pints of tea and shout at me that twice to-day she made him bungle a passage of great music. He'll swear that either he becomes her abject slave or she kills him, so we've got to quit and go to Portugal! Mr. Fount, you'll never forgive me; it seems impossible for me not to forget she's your cousin."

Bailey smiled wanly. "Never mind that," was all he said.

Outdoors, where the crowd was dispersing in the early twi-light, Helena took her leave of him. He'd surely had enough of her for one day, she said; she had an errand that didn't take her in the direction of The Cranford and she wouldn't be there for dinner. "I need a last word of reassurance if—if you can," she added timorously, though an inwardness of full satisfaction now underlay that manner. "I shouldn't like to think I—I mean I really didn't say too much, did I? If I've over-step-ped——"

"Nonsense!" he said with a heartiness that pleasantly aston-ished her. Then he thanked her for the concert and set out for home.

He'd walked two blocks when a green-black coupé drew to the curb just ahead of him, and the driver, Josephine Oaklin, called to him.

"Come here!" she said in an angry voice, as he halted on the sidewalk. "Get in!"

XXII

H<small>E</small> OBEYED WITHOUT A WORD, she set the car in motion, drove slowly. "What the devil do you mean?"

"By what?" he asked calmly.

" 'By what?' " She mocked him. "You saw me leave the concert, why didn't you get up and come out to join me? You swore you'd follow my lead. I've been dabbing round in the car ever since, waiting for it to be over so I could pick you up. Now you wonder why I'm slightly irritated by your——"

"Slightly?" he asked, and added thoughtfully, "You sound 'slightly' more than that."

"Why shouldn't I? Am I supposed to enjoy discovering that you're trotting all about, going places with a woman who hates me and that I despise—especially places to which I've previously asked you to go with me?"

"With you?" he said. "I don't recall your asking me to——"

"So that's to be your excuse!" she cried. "You're going to claim you didn't get any message from me?"

"Certainly. That's my claim."

"You think it lets you out?" She jabbed the car into speed.

"How much effort do you suppose I wasted on the telephone trying to get you at The Cranford at lunchtime? Where were you? Out lunching with Helena Jyre?"

"Yes."

"Delightful!" she said. "When I'd spent hours trying to get you to meet me at the Jefferson for lunch and go with me to the Symphony! I told that dumb secretary of Rossbeke's, Mrs. Williams, to find where you were and get that message to you; but of course she didn't. All those people try to infuriate me because I've had to show them what they don't know about the conduct of an art museum. They've certainly had a march of triumph over me to-day—thanks to you!"

The bitterness of her three concluding words brought only the laconic inquiry, "To me?"

"What!" she cried. "You pretend you don't know what you've done? I wasn't going to their silly Borfsky concert at all; then I saw the chance to show us together in public, you in the box with me and everybody guessing you're the Lieutenant Fount who's my cousin and telling one another we're probably engaged. To-night they're telling one another you're engaged to Helena Jyre!"

"No, I think not."

"Pleasant for me, wasn't it, when I came in," Josephine said, "to find you sitting there with her? Everybody seeing that I had to trail in virtually alone and with you in tender escort of the worst enemy I've got—and another of 'em buzzing you with her hand on your shoulder! How could you more conspicuously have displayed yourself as their possession? What'd you do it *for?* Just to injure me?"

"No. Just to hear a concert."

"I don't believe it!" She made this an outcry. "You're not

that stupid. You deliberately lent yourself to a nasty female plot."

"That bad, was it?"

"A rottenly vindictive one!" Josephine said. "I left word all over town that you were to come to lunch at the Jefferson or at least meet me before three o'clock. Whether you got any message from me or not, *she* certainly did."

"You're wrong. She didn't."

"She *proved* she did!" Josephine cried. "She knew I was going and meant you to be with me. She proved she knew it by displaying you there with *her!*"

"You think so? Do, if you like."

"So you *have* gone sour!" Her voice became more uncertain. "I've been wondering—I've had a suspicion—possibly you were angry about that newspaper this morning and, like a man, had to take it out on somebody. All right, if you want to hate me for it, go ahead; it was I who had it done. But you ought to've liked it. It helped in what you promised you'd help me to do and it certainly couldn't injure you with anybody. Well, what about it?"

He looked steadily at the street before them, and made no answer.

"So that's it," she said. "How was I to know you'd object?"

"You did know. That's why you looked frightened the other night as I left your house."

"I didn't. Nothing of the sort! Why should I when it was the right thing to do?—but Helena Jyre found out I'd had some connection with it—she could easily—so she told you, and you decided you didn't like it and gladly took your annoyance out on me by showing yourself to everybody at the Symphony with her!"

"No, I don't do things like that."

"No? Could you realize that sometimes you're in danger of sounding just a bit too damn smug?" Josephine jerked the wheel, headed for the curbstone dangerously and stopped the car with noisy brakes.

He asked quietly, "You want me to get out and go home?"

"And leave me sitting here alone?" she cried. "That'd be like you; but I didn't know till to-day that it *would* be like you! I suppose at lunch you enjoyed Miss Jyre's sympathetic twaddle so much you forgot that her life really belongs to your sponsor, Rossbeke? I've no doubt you even think she's rather good-looking, since you prefer her to me for your concert-going. Your whole show to-day's most cheering for me, isn't it?—when our engagement's just going to be announced."

"Is it? When?"

"To-morrow!" she said fiercely. "In the papers and everywhere. Have you forgotten you said you'd go through with it?"

"No, I haven't forgotten."

"Then why, the very day before the announcement, did you humiliate me by leaving me to face that audience alone—with everybody staring at you and Helena Jyre linked in divine music together? You, God save the mark! you who said you'd follow my lead!"

"Yes, I expect to do so."

"Then do so now!" she said, opened the door beside her and jumped down from the car. "Come on!"

"Come on where?"

"Here! Good heavens!" she shouted at him, and, as he descended deliberately, her furious gesture apprised him that their destination was the brick apartment building before which she'd halted the car. "Think you can live through a cocktail party in Sophie Tremoille's flat without your Jyre?"

She turned her back, swept away from him. He stood reluctant, but only for a moment; then followed her into the building, up a flight of stairs and into Miss Tremoille's apartment. Josephine entered it plungingly without ringing the bell. Sophie's crowded living-room, festooned with slowly undulant smoke and scented with chrysanthemums and rum, was already a vocal commotion. Josephine instantly doubled that. She set her voice into rapid-fire, seized upon people and pushed them at Bailey, shouting their names and his. Then, without warning, she uttered a rapturous shriek, rushed to the center of the room and strong-armed through a group surrounding a jaunty dark gentleman in the uniform of an officer of the United States Navy. She seemed about to fling herself adoringly upon him.

"My first and only!" she whooped. "Why didn't anybody tell me *you'd* be here? My own long-lost Commander Iffington!"

Sophie Tremoille deplored this admiringly. "Josephine, aren't you dreadful!" she screamed, made gestures burlesquing horror, and retired scuttlingly from the group.

Josephine but emphasized her devotion to the smiling officer. "Angel of my heart!" she cried. "How was I to know you'd ever come back? Here I've been getting myself engaged to heaven knows how many in the lower ranks—Army heroes and all sorts of people—and never dreaming my sailor'd turn up again! Don't I have the devil's own luck?"

Faithful Sophie, maneuvering toward the wall and Bailey, uttered the flattering squeal: "Josephine, you're *too* wicked!"

Josephine was heard above everything. "Don't tell me it's too late! Swear to me *you* haven't any awful entanglements! Tell me, oh, tell me——" She continued to produce an amatory uproar over the pleased Iffington.

"Of course you don't really mind?" Sophie Tremoille, laughing, had reached the solemn Bailey. "Nobody ever knows what she's going to do and you were pretty naughty this afternoon, yourself, you know!" She leaned to him, whispering. "I had a terrible time with her at the concert after she saw you; I was afraid she'd do even worse than she did. Of course you knew it was all your fault, didn't you?"

"No."

"Of course you did! She's marvelous; not like anybody else. It's all frightfully flattering to you. You surely see by this time that the wilder she is about you, the less she can bear your not seeming as much so about her. She can't stand the slightest thing. You must study her."

"Must I?"

"Yes, hard, or you'll never know her. Don't think it's simple. You're just a man; but she's got a woman's hundred angles. More than that, she's Josephine Oaklin."

"Yes, I think I've grasped that."

"It's a great thing for you," Sophie said hurriedly. "She told me it's to be announced to-morrow. Warmest official congratulations!"

"Thank you," he responded unsmilingly, and, as Sophie sidled away to greet a newcomer, he stepped behind her, edged his way along the wall until he reached the door.

Josephine was preoccupied with the caressive ado she was still making over the gallant Iffington, who'd now begun to show a rosily fatuous tint above his widening smile. She was so busy that she didn't see the departing figure. The rest of her work on the Navy was thrown away; though she was late in realizing this. By the time she discovered Bailey Fount's defection he had walked, at a soldierly stride, all the way to The Cranford.

XXIII

"Mrs. THOMAS OAKLIN, JR., announces the engagement of her daughter, Miss Josephine Oaklin, to Lt. Bailey Fount, U.S. Army. Lieutenant Fount is well known to this city, not only by reason of the fame he won in the Pacific, but also because for some time past, while recuperating from wounds incurred during his heroic exploit, he has been acting as Assistant Curator of Paintings in the Thomas Oaklin Museum of the Fine Arts and is a great-nephew of the founder of that nationally acclaimed institution. The date of the wedding has not yet been fixed but will be announced in due course."

Lieutenant Bailey Fount, earliest to breakfast and alone in the dining-room of The Cranford, looked for the proclamation in the paper the waitress had brought him; he had no trouble in finding it—at the top of the column.

He was gone before Miss Jyre came downstairs, and she didn't see him until about ten o'clock, when she and Rossbeke came into the museum's Seventeenth Century Dutch Gallery. They halted just inside the entrance; gravely remained there. Old Anson and two house-painters he'd somewhere found were

235

at work with Bailey, spreading his bluish wash: they had the pictures down and an end wall finished. Bailey, in overalls and stirring more color into a big bucket, was aware of the two spectators but didn't look at them directly until after the mixture in his bucket had completely satisfied him. Then he crossed the gallery to them.

"You're doubtful of it?" he asked. "I'm afraid you look that way. I understood from Miss Jyre last week, Mr. Rossbeke, that you and she had decided I was to go ahead with my bluing on cleaning day. I can stop it right now if you've changed your minds."

"No, no," Rossbeke said. "That's not what——" He didn't finish.

"Of course," Bailey continued reasonably, "you can't tell how the pictures are going to look against this tint until we get them replaced; then if you don't like it I can either take the wash off or put the original grey over it so everything'll be as it was; but if you'd rather I stopped now——"

"No, indeed." Rossbeke shook his head. "I think the idea may be a good one. Do go on with it. I—ah——" Too plainly uncomfortable, he walked away to speak to old Anson.

Bailey remained beside Helena Jyre, whose expression was carvenly tragic as if to stay so forever. "I'm sorry you don't approve," he said. "I can get the blue off in an hour or two if you can't wait to see how the paintings'll look against it. There's no reason for you to feel quite so appalled."

"If I look appalled," she said in a thin voice, "that color isn't the cause."

"Not the color?" he asked; but the somberness of her full-eyed gaze at him permitted no further evasion. "I see. It's that announcement."

"Naturally. After what I told you yesterday—and my knowing what you felt—because I *did* know——"

"Just a moment," he said. "I want to say something as rightly as I can, but it's—well, intricate." He looked down at her gently. "You and Mr. Rossbeke have done so many things to help me get back on my feet I'll be thanking you all the rest of my life. I——"

"You needn't," she interrupted stiffly. "The one thing we most should have done for you, we couldn't. It outweighs the rest. Since we haven't been able to prevent——" She broke off; then spoke with emotion less suppressed. "Since we've failed in that and it would be better if you'd never come here, I don't know what you have to thank us for."

"Don't say that!" Impulsively he caught her hand and held it. "There's no other place in the world where I could have got back on my feet as I have here. Look at the difference in me since I came! If you won't let me tell you how grateful I am for everything you——"

Brusque interruption stopped him.

Unheard within the gallery, an angry girl and a busybody follower had approached through the broad corridor outside. Rossbeke caught but a glimpse of the follower, Mrs. Hevlin, flitting in retreat, as Josephine came purposefully through the entrance in the newly tinted wall near which he stood with old Anson. "What *is* this nonsense?" she was already imperiously asking. "I've been informed that somebody's putting blue all over——" She saw Bailey releasing Helena Jyre's hand. "Hold it, hold it!" Josephine cried at him. "Tableau! Don't change the pose. Hand in hand among the old Dutch Masters. Idyllic! My fiancés *do* seem to go their own sweet ways, don't they!"

Bailey, at the other end of the gallery, began to walk slowly toward her. She ignored him, whirled upon Rossbeke. "Who's responsible for the hideous blue on this wall? You, Rossbeke?"

"Certainly I'm responsible. It's an experiment."

"What for?" she cried. "To prove you're insane or just to finish ruining this museum? I'll get that repulsive color off that wall if I have to bring every trustee here to do it!" She swung round, met Bailey half-way, in the center of the gallery, and didn't care who heard her. "What the devil did you mean running out on me yesterday afternoon at Sophie's? I spent half of last night trying to telephone you at that boarding-house of yours. Where were you?"

"Out for a walk."

"A damned long one!" she said. "With whom? Don't answer; I don't care to hear the name. I've been looking for you all over the museum this last half hour. Found you when you least expected me, apparently. Anything to say for yourself?"

"Yes. Plenty!" Bailey's tone made Rossbeke stare at him.

"Then keep—keep it to yourself!" Josephine said; and that break in her voice turned the Director's astonishment upon her. Her twitching lips were beyond control; she sobbed aloud and ran out of the gallery.

Bailey spoke to Anson. "Get ahead with the other walls; I'll be back as soon as I can." He made the gesture of an open hand extended first toward Helena, then toward Rossbeke, and, as if they needed no further explanation, strode through the archway and followed Josephine.

He saw her far ahead of him, still running, her hair and jade-green wool dress alternately catching color and losing it as she passed by the successive sunlit windows of the corridor. When he had descended the stairway and entered the collection of mediæval art, she whom he pursued had already crossed the easternmost corridor beyond. He heard the oaken door to the stone passage slam resoundingly and the iron bolt clang home.

Thereupon he left the museum by a side way; a moment more and he was at the Oaklins' front door. Harvey came presently to stop the ringing, lifted his eyebrows in plaintive inquiry at sight of Bailey's overalls, but was too well mannered, and also too melancholy, to refer to them. "Yes, sir," he said, as he stood aside for the frowning caller. "No Roggo. No Roggo come jump on you, Lieutenant, sir."

"What?"

The old man made a sorrowful gesture. "Always look to me like Roggo got the habit run jump up on you, make fuss over you, right away from the first time he saw you. Look like right away he knew you one the family. Nice little dog. Too bad."

"What's too bad?" Bailey paused. "What's happened to Roggo? An automobile?"

"No, sir. Vet'nary. Roggo gettin' old. One eye gone; vet'-nary say he go' lose his other one some day maybe; leave hairs all over the house. She say Roggo too much of a nuisance, too old. Had vet'nary take him away, put Roggo to sleep."

"She did?" Bailey's face reddened with a violent suddenness. "Why, he was a happy dog and he'd have lived for years! He's dead, is he? She had him killed?"

"Roggo gone, sir. Vet'nary took him, put Roggo to sleep yest'd'y."

"Where is she?"

"Sir?" Harvey looked puzzled.

"Where is Miss Josephine?"

"Think I heard her in the liberry just now, sir. I go see——"

"No." Bailey strode by him. "I know the way."

Josephine was sitting in her grandfather's favorite scarlet chair by the great fireplace. She didn't move and gave him but a negligent glance as he came in. After a silence she said indifferently, "That's a nice way to stand looking at anybody. You're quite a strange person, after all. You've fooled everybody, me with the rest."

"That all?" he asked.

"Well—nearly. I just wondered if you knew, yourself, how you're looking at me. People think you're such a dear, retiring, apologetic sort of person. These old women in the museum who call you 'Our Darling' might be surprised to see you now. They think you're just sweet and kind. So did I—once."

"Yes," he said. "You had that impression of me because I was sick so long—scared to death of everything on earth. A patient in the hospital's likely to be pretty different from his real self. When he gets back to that he's liable to shock the nurses."

"You look upon me as one of the nurses, do you?"

"You? Hell, no!" His burst of laughter, harsh and brief, brought a gasping breath from her. "I've come to tell you," he said, "I see Murties was right. If he were here I'd apologize to him. I'd take back all I've said about him to you. A desperate man's got a right to use his only means of escape."

She was contemptuous again. "You talk like a tough sergeant."

"I was one for quite a time," he said. "Getting to know you has put a lot of that back into me, thank God!"

She jumped up. "You're explaining that this is your natural self and you're not a gentleman except when you're sick?"

"Right!" There was a flash in Bailey Fount's eyes, too. "I'm not sick any more and I'll be no gentleman in my dealings with you!"

"You assume that you're *going* to have 'dealings' with me?"

"Yes. Right now."

"So? Did Helena Jyre suggest your taking this tone with me? It won't work, bully boy! Misconceived popular vulgarities—masterful terse men browbeating headstrong females into mush—all that sort of thing doesn't entertain me." With a hand that shook, she pointed to the passageway door. "I'm forced to ask you to return to the museum. You can come back when you're in your senses again. That way out, if you please. It's shorter."

"No," he said. "I'm going, all right; but it's not time yet. You're twenty-five. The first time I met you—to know you— you said you were twenty-two. Plenty of women lie like that. I'm not blaming 'em, it's nobody's business; but you didn't have to. Nobody'd asked you. Thinking it over, I see it shows you've got the habit of never even wondering whether a thing's true or not. You're one of those people who just naturally man-handle any fact into whatever shape they think's to their advantage."

"Oh, wise young judge!" She laughed at him. "All because I changed my age to please Harold!"

"I'm not judging you," he informed her. "I'm only giving you my observation of you. Here's more. You're so ingrowing you don't see anything outside of you. The rest of us have no existence except in relation to you. So anybody's an outcast villain if he doesn't look up to you. Anybody you even suspect of not admiring you, you despise. To make people understand your intellectual superiority you treat 'em as inferiors, the best mechanism to get yourself exactly what you don't want. Why don't you stop annoying everybody?"

"Lessons for the backward young?" Her scorn of him was fiery bright. "Did you hear me when I asked you to leave this house till you come back to your senses?"

"Easily," he said. "Your voice is always distinct but's even more so when you say something insulting. That's another clue to you. When good-hearted people find they're compelled to say something insulting they muffle it."

"As you're doing now?"

"I'm not insulting you," he said. "An insult's meant to injure; I'm just explaining. You don't understand that. You don't because when anybody hasn't your own view of yourself you take it as an insult and hate him. It's one of the reasons you spend half your life fighting. More than that——"

"There's *still* more, is there?"

"More and worse," he said. "It's not only your view of yourself you fight people if they differ from. You despise and fight 'em if they differ from any view of yours at all. Whenever you see anybody doing anything—anything whatever—you're always likely to think of some other way to do it and you never doubt that your way's the better. That isn't because your way *is* better; it's only because it's yours. I got Mr. Rossbeke to let me put that bluish tint on the Dutch Gallery walls and I——"

"*You* did?" she cried. Surprise and instant fresh resentment made her sweet voice for once almost harsh. "So even *you* set up to alter the Oaklin Museum as you please without authority. You presume to smear its walls as only an utterly color-blind——"

"Don't you ever hear yourself?" he asked. "Don't you even hear yourself now when you're proving what I'm explaining to you about yourself? You tore into that gallery in a rage because somebody'd told you something was going on there that hadn't been *your* idea. You made up your mind to get my color off—even before you saw it. If you'd been the one who thought of it you'd have fought for it. 'Color-blind'? For any color not first inside your own fancies your eyes are dead."

"They're seeing *you* pretty well," she told him huskily, "for the first time!"

"Glad to hear it," he said casually and continued that manner as if his subject were impersonal, thus of small concern to either of them. "Do you ever call Mr. Rossbeke anything but 'Rossbeke'? Have you ever said a decent word to Miss Jyre? You appear to be one of those thousands of descendant geese who feel it's a family perquisite to be rude. Top o' that, your bright little head's convinced it holds a hereditary right to interfere with everything more intelligent people try to do. I've seen enough in the museum to conclude you've been making yourself obnoxious there for years—because your grandfather built the place. Offhand, I can't say what else you've mussed up, positive you're the Law and the Prophets; but only yesterday I happened to be present when you——"

"Take care," Josephine said. "When I what?"

"When you made yourself objectionable to a whole audience, interfering with their pleasure and getting hundreds of people to despise you because you——"

"Because I what?"

"Because the orchestra played what it thought best, not what *you*——"

She struck him upon the breast so hard that she sent herself backward against the chair from which she'd risen. She toppled, came down upon it sitting.

"Another act!" He stood, contemptuous. "How much of your life do you spend putting on acts? You put on several with poor Murties, trying to make him jealous of me. Later, you put on another to make me believe he really *had* been jealous. You thought I was as dumb as I was sick, so I'd believe I was responsible for his walking out on you. Yesterday you tried to make me jealous of that Navy man—same sixteen-year-old highschool-girl rudimentary technique as your throwing me at Murties. This time it was a double act, though—part to make me think you were jealous of Miss Jyre. You pull off these transparent shows believing yourself the only creature in the universe fitted with even slightly perceptive eyes and ears. You think you get away with——"

"No." Josephine sat, bent over, looking at the floor; her voice was faint. "It wasn't an act."

"Not an act—pretending you were jealous?"

"No."

"Trying it again?"

"No." Her fury had disappeared; but there was a returning flicker of it. "*She's* what you like. You let her take you to the concert——"

"Wasn't that detestable of me?—just when you wanted to show me off as preface to advertising the engagement! Bad! —it interfered with the use you were making of me. Oh, yes, I expected you to make that use of me, certainly; but not to try to put a lot of hooey over on me. On my soul I don't believe you're capable of a real jealousy!" There was a sound within her throat, and he paused, thinking that she spoke. "What?"

She sat now with her head farther forward, face down, so that he didn't see it, and her hands flaccid upon the arms of the chair. Her voice made the least of audible murmurs. "I—I didn't say anything."

"Good enough!" he said, but no longer spoke with any coolness. "Sit and listen. You claimed to be grateful for what I offered to do for you. Then you got a newspaper to print truck about me that would sicken any decent-minded man half to death. If I hadn't got my nerve again it would have thrown me back to what I was when I first came here. I'd stood for the rest of the game we'd agreed upon; but your plastering me all over the place as a 'hero'——"

"I told you I didn't know you'd mind." She muttered this interruption hurriedly. "I didn't suppose you would—so much. I didn't see——"

"You took damned good care not to let me know about it beforehand! Why lie?"

"I—I only——"

"You only thought I'd be maybe a little cross about it," he finished for her. "You're explaining that you didn't even suspect what any human being with one spark of sensitiveness for another would have known. Good God! don't you see how you're giving yourself away?"

"No."

"You've just told me you were so absorbed in yourself that you didn't *care* what such an exploitation would do to a man who'd seen his best friends die one by one around him while he —while he couldn't——" Bailey's voice had begun to shake and break; he stopped that, walked away from her; then turned again. "What's the use trying to talk to you about it? You've proved you couldn't live long enough to understand."

"Very well, then," she said, motionless. "That's that, is it?"

"Yes; but there's one thing more, and just now I think it's the worst."

"Well?"

"I happen to like dogs," he said. "I've just heard what you had done to Roggo. I may be over-susceptible to that sort of cold cruelty; but it seems the toughest thing I've found out about you. I can't believe you let him be killed for his own sake, because you thought he was suffering. He wasn't. It must have been because he was shedding hair and being a 'nuisance' round the house. A girl who'd do that to a gay little dog that loved her and had years of life left in him——"

"I——" Her shoulders, compressed as if for protection, straightened somewhat and she lifted her head enough to let her see his face. The look she gave him was not so much inscrutable as it was untranslatable. It was like a word in a language known only to a whipped woman or an injured child, a word that said something clearly yet could be heard but obscurely as a mysterious "No."

"What?" he asked involuntarily.

"Nothing. I mean—nothing."

"All right, I'm through," he said. "I don't suppose anybody ever talked to you like this before."

"No." Her head was down again and her hands came tremulously together in her lap. "Nobody. I didn't know——" Her voice grew fainter. "Of course it means you're going to—to quit me, like the others."

"Yes, you'd think that. I told you that you don't notice people; you haven't seen half the change in me. I'm not a quitter any longer. I'm leaving you; but you can go on letting people think we're going to be married—'after the duration.' I told you I'd go through with it and I will—if I come back."

"If you—what?"

"Oh, hell!" he said. "I mean if I don't get killed. I'm going to where I belong, the good old Army. You can keep on being engaged to me just the same; it makes no damn difference to me. I'll send you a ring you can show around. Good-bye!"

He strode to the door that led into the passageway, opened it briskly and left her.

XXIV

H<small>E</small> W<small>ENT</small> S<small>TRAIGHT</small> T<small>O</small> Rossbeke's inner office, found him
alone and not working but standing at one of the windows and
gazing down at the waterless cold fountain in the courtyard.
"Mr. Rossbeke," Bailey said, "the color we're putting on that
gallery dries in a few hours; we'll have the whole thing finished
and the pictures up again by to-morrow noon. Then, if you
and Miss Jyre approve the effect——"

"Don't worry." The Director turned, showing a troubled
forehead. "Miss Jyre and I have already decided it's an im-
provement."

"Glad to hear that," Bailey said. "I've come to ask you to
look me over."

Rossbeke was surprised but not less troubled. "So it's that,
is it?"

"Yes, sir. I'd like you to state whether or not in your opinion I've recovered from the breakdown that made Colonel
Bedge send me to you."

The mild Rossbeke avoided reference to the "breakdown"
tactfully. "Well, there was your bad leg, you know. Your
wounds——"

"They weren't in question, sir. Dr. Bedge knew it wasn't they that put me in danger of permanent disability. As for my physical condition, yesterday night I walked just under eighteen miles."

"Eighteen miles? Dear me! Eighteen——"

"Yes, sir, and I'd already walked hard during most of the morning. I didn't take my mileage then; but it must have been considerable. Wouldn't you say I'm now a fairly robust specimen?"

"I'd have to," Rossbeke said. "You seem to have got back a lost voice, too, a rather big one."

"I beg your pardon, sir. I'm afraid I was shouting at you."

"Not at all, not at all, Bailey. The change in you's seemed to come with quite a rush."

"To me," Bailey said, "it seemed about a sixteenth of an inch a week. I'm speaking of my nervous condition. Physically I was coming along all right; but nervously—well, I didn't know. Then all at once something happened that I couldn't have expected."

"What was it?"

"I lost my worst symptom," Bailey said. "I just seemed to wake up and be all right. I found I'd stopped thinking about myself every second, night and day, and as soon as I understood that I was putting my mind continuously on other things— why, that was all there was to it. I was well. Haven't you seen that I am? Don't you see so now?"

"I—believe I do."

"You needn't be afraid of not being right about it." Bailey spoke briskly. "Mr. Rossbeke, it's always been understood that I'd go back to Colonel Bedge for an examination at any time when you and I agreed I could probably pass one."

"Yes, that was the layout."

"Of course I wouldn't leave that gallery unfinished," Bailey said. "It'll really be done before to-morrow noon. Mr. Rossbeke, I could get an early afternoon train out of here to-morrow and be seeing Colonel Bedge at the hospital about thirty-six hours later."

Rossbeke looked rueful and also, as if with mixed feelings, befogged——only too plainly wondering what had just happened to the engagement announced that morning. Bailey, grimly observant, left the answer to Josephine; she'd have her damn ring. "Of course," Rossbeke said, "one oughtn't to feel anything except an altruistic pleasure in your pretty obvious recovery."

"Thank you, sir."

"Of course, too," the Director resumed, "we haven't any right to stand in your way."

"I haven't any right not to go," Bailey said. "Nor to delay, either. Mr. Rossbeke, it's what I've hoped and hoped for——and almost didn't dare to hope when I came; but God's been good to me about that. Will you get off a wire to Colonel Bedge, please, saying that in your opinion I'm now sound in mind and body, my recovery's completed and you approve of my going?"

"Yes, I'll tell him that. As you wish, I'll do it at once."

"Thank you, sir. I couldn't ask better."

"I'm not a sentimental person." Rossbeke made the statement with formality. "However, I'd like to say that losing you is going to mean more to all of us than you might suspect. You've been useful to the museum; it's——it's quite a blow. We'd like to think you'll wish to come back——when you can. I believe we could arrange it so that you could do your work here and paint, too. Will you bear it in mind?"

"I'll never forget your having such a thought of me, sir."
Bailey turned to go. "I'll see you again, won't I?"

"Yes; we won't say good-bye now."

"No, sir," Bailey said, and went quickly out of the office.

In the corridor outside, humbly anxious, Harvey stood waiting for him. "Excuse me, Lieutenant sir." The old man made gestures intended to be apologetic, stepped forward and spoke confidentially. "I like say something if you got a minute."

"Yes, certainly, Harvey."

"I wouldn't wish nobody to know I——"

"All right; nobody will."

"Yes, sir," Harvey said. "I don't want to get the name of easedropper. Plenty people does it; but lessen it's about me or the family I ain't go' listen to it. No, sir. How come I to know what happen, you talk pretty loud to Miss Josephine in yonder, sir. I wouldn't like to bear the guilt of me was the cause of it."

"I haven't an idea what you mean, Harvey."

"Roggo, sir. It must been me put you wrong, I don't know how lessen it was when you come to the front door while ago; I must kind of mixed you up. That one thing anyways Miss Josephine she never done."

"What one thing?"

"She never done what done to Roggo. She ain't do that; she was out the house. When she come home and found what got done to Roggo she spoke to her mamma like you never heard and set down and cried bad. She ain't say a word to her mamma since; she ain't speakin' to her. No, sir, no; it wasn't Miss Josephine sent for no vet'nary and got that done to Roggo."

"All right, Harvey."

"Yes, sir. Miss Josephine, that one thing anyways it wasn't her fault." Harvey had spoken with spirit; now he coughed and was meek. "Mr. Lieutenant, you feel so good now you go back where the fightin' is?"

"I'm going to try to."

"I got two grandsons in the Army, one in the Navy," Harvey said. "I wish you well, sir."

"Thank you. I may not see you again. Good-bye, Harvey."

"Yes, sir. Thank you, sir."

Bailey, walking away, had the impression that Harvey stood looking after him wistfully instead of examining the gift that their farewell handshake had left in the old man's clasp; probably he'd have liked to say more. Bailey walked on, but didn't immediately return to his work in the Seventeenth Century Dutch Gallery. Instead, he went to his workroom, found some scratch-paper and wrote a note:

"Harvey has informed me I was mistaken about Roggo. I'll be obliged to you if you will expunge from your memory my remarks on that subject. I regret to have earned your resentment in this particular unjustifiably. Probably you might as well forget also the rest of what I said to you about yourself— I'm not under the delusion that remembering it would be of any benefit. The leopard doesn't change his spots except under pressure of grenades and bayonets. I am leaving to assist again in such a process. Don't be under any apprehensions, however. I shall send you the ring I mentioned and you can keep it on show."

He went down to the basement, found Arturo Meigs smoking a surreptitious pipe, pretended not to see its hasty concealment, made a donation and explained why he did so.

"That's in exchange for a favor, Arturo. Here's a note I'd like you to deliver when you go off duty this evening."

Meigs looked at the address upon the envelope. "Oh, for her, is it? I don't go off till quarter-to-six. I could take it round to their front door right now and——"

"No; there's no hurry. I'd rather you'd just leave it there on your way home this evening."

"Righto." Arturo Meigs put the note in a pocket of an overcoat hanging near by upon the wall and dreamily resumed his pipe as the sound of his visitor's footsteps died away. Bailey rejoined his fellow-workers in the Seventeenth Century Dutch Gallery and had all the walls evenly blued by the end of the day.

XXV

SOMETIMES one of the intricacies of vanity permits the plainest of faces to remain complacent before a painter's true portrait of itself; but even the humblest of human beings must cringe or fight or run away when the portrait is made with words that uncover the worst of the truth. Josephine Oaklin had never yet been humble; for the rest of the day the word-sketch of herself that had been forced upon her produced a dry-eyed daze—the condition known as shock. Late in the afternoon, Mrs. Oaklin rapped and rapped on her daughter's locked door; at last despairingly sniffled through it: "Two people can't live in the same house if one of 'em's never going to speak to the other again! How many times have I got to say I'm sorry about that dog?" Josephine heard this as a noise signifying nothing.

Bailey's note wasn't brought to her when Arturo Meigs went off duty. He forgot it until he'd returned to his rooming-house after the "early show" at a movie and was hanging up his overcoat; then he hurried conscientiously through a drizzle all the way to the Oaklins' front door.

Josephine, urgently reading what Bailey'd written, found it more blackly eloquent than had been even the spoken portrait. She read the note once, she read it twice; the third time she read it the writing was fire. A clatter of protestive outcries presently rose to her lips and she was uttering words that tried passionately to mean something but couldn't. Not gathering toward any semblance of sentences, they hurried themselves into a stammering clamor as fragmentary as the unfinished gestures that jerked along with them. This was true distraction; she didn't know what she was doing.

There was no conscious intention at all in what she did in overwhelmed submission to the impulse that swept her out of the house and into the dark of a wet night. Most of the way she ran, though not to escape from the thickening rain; and she didn't speak intelligibly when a middle-aged orange-aproned woman opened the outer door of The Cranford to her.

"Who?" the woman asked her twice. "You mean Lieutenant Fount? I don't know if he's here or not. Step in; you're all wet, you ought to worn a raincoat. It's Miss Oaklin that wants to see him, isn't it? I'll go up to his room and find out if he's there."

"You needn't, Hannah," a voice said quickly, and Helena Jyre came from the room known to The Cranford dwellers as the "lounge." She stepped into the hall decisively. "He went out about half an hour ago, so you needn't bother to go up, Hannah."

"Oh," Hannah said, and retired.

Josephine stood where she was, near the outer door. "I'll wait," she said.

Helena looked at her formidably, then crossed the hall to the open doorway of the small "reception room." She made a gesture, not an inviting one, toward that charmless interior. "Please step in here."

Josephine did; Helena followed her, closed the door carefully. "You seem in a hurry to see him."

"Yes."

"I wouldn't be, if I were you," Helena said. "You ought to look in a mirror. You'd better go home and change your draggled clothes and get the wet hair out of your eyes."

"No. I have to see him."

"Should I be thanking you?" Helena asked. "These are the first words you've spoken to me in several years, I believe. You've come running through the rain to see him because you're frightened. That's what's the matter with you. You're frightened, aren't you?"

Josephine's wet lashes flickered; her face changed contour, grew oldly longer. Her breathing could be heard and so could Helena Jyre's; the air of that small room seemed not enough for the breathing of the two of them. "Frightened?" Josephine said. "Maybe that's it. I don't know."

"Oh, yes, you do, Miss Oaklin! You're scared half out of your wits. You've just heard he's going back to the Army and it's given you a jolt you've sorely needed all your life! You've come here to tell him he's got to live up to his saintly contract and marry you before he goes."

"No."

"On the contrary, yes!"

"No," Josephine said again. "I have to see him."

"What for?"

"I have to see him," Josephine said. "When is he going?"

"If I knew I wouldn't tell you. If I know I won't tell you!" Helena's wrath gathered strength. "Like to hear why? Because you took advantage of his fantastic goodness and his broken nerves to save face when Murties stood you up. You'd have grabbed any living creature that wore the likeness of a man; but luck sent a splendid one into your clutch. What did you care? You didn't even *see* that he was splendid; but if you had you'd have cold-bloodedly sacrificed him to your egregiousness just the same. *You* don't know what he is or care a tinker's damn! You couldn't. Tell you when he's going? Not I —no, nor will any other friend of his! There's nothing any of us wouldn't do to keep you from seeing him again."

"Why?"

Helena laughed fiercely. "Good God, what a question! To save him from you, if we can. I tell you there isn't a thing on earth any of his friends wouldn't do for that. Ask me 'Why?' again. Because if we can help it we won't turn him over to a creature made up of pride and self-will and hate and contempt and——"

"But I'm not." Josephine found voice to wail out the childlike rebuttal. "I've never been—I'm not. I didn't know how people—I've never hated anybody—not really. I see—I see you do, though. I didn't know——"

"Didn't *know?*" Helena's incredulity was shrill. "Didn't know that snubbing and stinging and ignoring me for month on month and year on year——"

"I didn't—didn't look at it that way. No matter what you say, I really didn't. Everybody thinks there's something wrong about me. This—this morning he——"

Helena took an eager step forward. "He what? What did he do this morning?"

"He—he told me so."

"Grand!" the ruthless Helena cried. "Came out at you with the truth, did he? You got it where it hurts at last, did you? Good for Bailey!"

"I'll have to go." Josephine had begun to weep gaspingly. "I can't stand this. I'll have to go. He's not here, so——" She put forth a wavering hand, found the door-knob. "I'll have to go——"

Helena Jyre was left alone and open-mouthed. Years of well-fed resentment had so distortingly built within her eyes an image of Josephine that they'd ceased to see a fellow-creature and only the image remained. It lacked the nature of a human being, was not flesh and blood nor possessed of a heart that could burn when burned. Some little revelation came to the grim Helena in this not wholly satisfactory hour of revenge. She saw a change in the hard shape to which hate had limited her vision; she began to see something that was, in all fullness and sad kinship with her sex, another woman.

That other woman moved toward home by the impulsion of mere instinct, and, though splashing rain fell upon her, came to an unconscious stop now and then, spoke to herself and went on again. "I'm not," Josephine said. "They think so, but I'm not. I never—it's not the way I am. That isn't me. He doesn't——"

She'd left her front door ajar when she'd come hurrying out of it, and, within the issuing shaft of light that jeweled the raindrops, an elderly man's stoutish dark figure was crested by the silhouette of an umbrella. He was pressing the bell's disk; but turned as Josephine drew near.

"Somebody's left the door open but——" Mr. Horne began, and became exclamative. "Josephine! What on earth?

You rush in and get dry clothes! Haven't you a grain of common sense? What do you mean by——"

"I don't know," she said. "I don't know at all, Mr. Horne."

Helena Jyre, having returned to the "lounge," sat with a magazine open upon her lap and stared at an old couple senilely quarrelsome over backgammon nearer the fire. Often this pair had amused her with voices crackling in personal ferocities; her mind hadn't the ghost of a smile in it now. She wondered why she always held to the mere letter of the truth when she lied. It was true that Bailey had gone out half an hour before Josephine came. He'd gone in a taxi to make sure of his train reservation for the morrow; but he'd returned with his tickets, and Helena'd had a word with him in the hall as he passed to go upstairs to his packing. He was there now; he'd been there, in his room just overhead, all the time that Josephine had been in the house. When she'd said she'd wait, Helena had put her beyond a closed door, had kept her from seeing him, but now knew qualms.

Henry Rossbeke would approve? Helena thought she'd acted as he'd have wished—or at least ought to have wished—but maybe he wouldn't have liked that half-lie? Henry was overconscientious; perhaps he'd have wondered just how far it's safely right for anybody to go toward altering the courses of other people's lives. Could such a thing be imagined as a sane person's coming to tolerate Josephine Oaklin—not Josephine Oaklin in her pomp, of course, but a bedraggled Josephine muttering "I'll have to go——" and stumbling forth into rain without a coat or an umbrella? This was a more and more disquieted hour for Helena Jyre.

Upstairs in his room Bailey'd finished what packing he had

to do and now sat with a strap in his hand, not knowing he held it. What his mind's eye saw was what had dogged it all day— morning sunshine through a many-paned window and, warmly tinged in that illumination, the figure of a girl desolately hunched, taking a beating. He'd thought she'd fight, and at first she did—or tried to—but as he struck harder and harder, she'd just sat there. This was becoming pretty painful to re- member, and it had to be admitted that there was at least one decent thing about her. She'd not had Roggo killed, wouldn't have done such a thing—and she hadn't said, "It was Mother who sent Roggo to be killed, not I."

How far did those two small loyalties go toward redeeming a character otherwise unlovable?—but as this word slid into the thought, he jerked at it, held it and took a look at it. "Un- lovable?" Was he trying to urge upon himself the information that Josephine Oaklin couldn't be loved? If so, then for God's sake what was right now the matter with him? Never in his life had he been so acutely preoccupied with another person. Since the strange hour when he'd seen her frantically abject, twice jilted, she'd held the forefront of his imagination and possessed his thinking. Incessantly, ever more and more brilliantly vivid, her changing gracefulness, every plastic lovely bit of her was before him; all the singular sweet qualities in her voice, every variant tone of it, had been implacably memorized, so steadily re-echoing to him that he felt never for a moment alone. All this was doubled and redoubled: her bright presence was a more poignant obsession than ever, now, in the hour when he made ready to leave her.

"Unlovable?" What a word!

It couldn't be true, then, that we fall in love with only what we believe virtuous and kind. No, since a man can be desperately, miserably, unlimitedly in love with what he knows is neither. "But that's lamentable!" Bailey thought, and the old twist came to mind: that "each man kills the thing he loves." No wonder, since he can love what he hates! He sought to argue that this stingingly undeniable love of his might be a rattled kind of egoism, a perverse form of gratitude, in fact, because she'd broken up his absorption with self, got him out of it and made a man of him again. No, that wouldn't hold water. She hadn't lifted a finger for such a purpose, hadn't given a damn about it.

What of the very self of her? Could a man be in love with that spoiled and selfish spirit because it was cloaked in the resplendent likeness of Josephine Oaklin?

He heard himself break the silence of the room with grotesque laughter. Ought he to tell Doctor Bedge that the right treatment for a soldier with damaged nerves is to put him where he'll fall calamitously in love with a hellion of a girl he despises? Maybe Josephine herself would divine something of this when he'd send her a sharp-cut diamond to keep her engagement finger smarting.

He'd write her not a word. The biting ring would tell her all he had to say.

XXVI

"Yes? what is it?" he called briskly at his door then, a knock having sounded upon it. There was a glimpse of Hannah's departing orange apron as she admitted Mr. John Constable Horne. He came bustling by her, hand extended.

"Not too late?" he asked heartily. "My only chance to congratulate you before you get away. Won't stay but a minute."

"Congratulate——" Bailey spoke doubtfully as the handshake ended. "You'll sit down, won't you?"

"Hardly worth it," Mr. Horne responded, but complied, and Bailey returned to the chair from which he'd jumped up. "Said just a minute, didn't I? Call it ten maybe. Certainly congratulate you—first of all of course on your feeling able to go back and stand up to Rossbeke's friend, Bedge. Grand thing, grand affair! Rossbeke didn't get me on the telephone till quite a while after dinner, so I didn't know till then. Says you'll make it, Rossbeke does; positive you will. So'm I. Pretty pleased with yourself, aren't you?"

"With my health? Yes, sir."

Mr. Horne took a cigar from his waistcoat pocket, looked at

it, returned it to the pocket. "No, if I light it I'll stay longer'n I ought to. Got to be moving on to go see a sick old bird my own age." He chuckled reflectively. "At that high-trapeze age, mine, they're all sick, the few of 'em left. Why I came to-night, I've got to get out early on a morning train, go a hundred miles and be pallbearer at the funeral of another of 'em—classmate o' mine. Won't get back till late to-morrow night. I understand you're leaving soon after noon."

"Yes, I'm all set, sir."

"Great!" Mr. Horne said. "Great, but not too jolly for the rest of us. You've done a good chore at the museum, young feller, yep. Be obliged if you'll remember we'd like to have you back there. Rossbeke says you understand so. Do, don't you?"

"Thank you, sir."

Mr. Horne again brought forth his cigar and this time, as if absently, lighted it. "Now what the devil'd I do that for?" he asked, and explained, "Can't finish it here and can't smoke with any pleasure out in the rain where I've got to go right away." Then he added, in a matter-of-course tone, "Congratulate you on the other main event, too. Fine girl."

"Sir?"

"Your engagement." Mr. Horne made the cigar glow, removed it and said, "Saw the announcement this morning. Fine girl."

"Sir?" Bailey unwittingly said again.

"Surprised *I* say so?" Mr. Horne laughed indulgently. "No wonder! Never heard me do anything but jump on her. Yes, on questions concerning the matter of art she's been hard to hold down. Self-willed, opinionated and's never had the remotest idea that a work of art, especially a modern one, ain't simply and in toto, be-God, precisely what her own contagioned, propaganda'd and often momentary emotions inform her it is. Hell of a way to judge of anything at all, ain't it? Wouldn't use that method to form a critical estimate of a chickadee, myself. It's all the fault of that noble old bonehead, my dear and revered friend, your most magnificent relative."

"Who?" Bailey seemed unable to be anything but monosyllabic.

"That superb and devoted Florentine," Mr. Horne replied. "Thomas Oaklin, this town's greatest benefactor. Not a day since he died I haven't thought about him—and how many hundreds of times with a suffering nasty laugh."

"With a what, sir?"

"Call it a snicker," Mr. Horne said. "The poor old soul was a bubbly container of all of the prosy romanticizing of his deceived generation. Wanted to build a Temple of Art. Temple of Art! Asked me why I snicker, did you? If old Tom Oaklin could have lived to see his temple empty of the uplifted crowds he expected but the grandest place in the world for bickerings, squabblings and general hell-raising, æsthetic and otherwise— me that he trusted doing only too plenty of it, myself——" Mr. Horne let the end of the sentence hang in the air and completed his thought with "Lordy me!"

"He'd be crushed?" Bailey was grave. "I have my doubts of it, sir. One reason I've often shied at 'art talk' is that in art nothing's ever settled, is it? Nothing ever will be, will it? Nobody can call a congress to make laws for it, so it can't have peace. Anyhow, though, just over yonder stands the building the old man made and it's a fine one in its way, isn't it? It stands there. It holds art within it, too; plenty of it, some of it great. I'm of that old fellow's blood; I've thought about him sometimes. We squabble in his temple and the people he gave it to don't take it; but it's not just an ironical joke on him. A mountain's a mountain even if nobody ever looks at it."

"And even if the mountain goats fight one another all over it?" John Horne was almost uproarious; but he supplanted his merriment with an abrupt sigh. "Oh, well! As you Webster-ianly say, there it stands! The bickerings'll pass and so will the bickerers—we're all of us only a little smoke on a big wind—but the works of art and the temple remain. If Tom Oaklin's ghost comes through the old passageway o' nights, maybe it takes some satisfaction unto itself. He did build his temple of art. When he tried, though, to build a human soul to be its custodian——"

"A human——" Bailey began; but, frowning inquiringly, he stopped.

"Golly murder, yes!" Mr. Horne said. "What he put into that innocent child's head! They two spiritually and intellec-tually enthroned aloft, isolated and almost invisible to the vulgar—and doggone nigh everybody else was vulgar. Old High Priest and young High Priestess remotely pontificating together over everything. Soaked it all in, she did—naturally. Fixed her up pretty to lead an agreeable and popular life, didn't he?"

Bailey's silence seemed to utter a sardonic echo: "Popular!"

"What the devil am I doing?" Mr. Horne asked amiably. "Talking to you this way about your kinsfolk, one of 'em your fiancée! Don't think I'm cussing 'em out, though, at this late date. No, nor trying to fix anything all up, make everything look nice and pretty. Everything *ain't* nice and pretty and I'm no crusty old soul, good-hearted at bottom, fairy-godmothering to sweetify whatever looks sour. Understand me, I just like to get somewhere near what's jocularly known as the truth."

"Yes, sir; I understand."

"Hope you do," Mr. Horne said. "No, we'll have to say quick that with the bringing-up she got she ain't popular with upper art ranks; but in such cohorts *every* dumb soul thinks it, too, was born divine—gloriously perfect in æsthetic perceptions. Oh, yes indeed, and in nearly all other perceptions, besides! We're *all* that nearsighted about ourselves, even if we try to keep it a secret. Look at *me,* for instance! So of course she'd fight and we'd fight back at her. Especially the women would. You've seen that going on, of course. You've got your wits about you, haven't you, young feller?"

"I doubt it, sir."

"Good thing, such a doubt." The old man again made his cigar glow; then removed it to let himself chuckle sadly. "*How* the women always *have* ganged up on her, though! Naturally they would. Women's fighting seems to be part of the curse laid on 'em in having to be women. Us thick-headed gents can hear the bloodthirstiest kind of female battle-cries and just think they mean love of righteousness. *We* don't know what it's all about. For instance, take our Helena. Good a woman as God ever made and we all love her; but let her get stung once by some other gal and oh, me! Guess somebody's told you how Helena got off on the wrong foot the very first week she was in the museum. Heard all about that, haven't you?"

"No."

"Funny thing," Mr. Horne said reminiscently. "Come right down to it and it was most likely Helena's fault for starting it. Kind of high-handed, herself, sometimes, in her own way. Had lots of ideas, Helena. Started right in to make new arrangements of the pictures in all the galleries. Your Cousin Josephine hadn't been much off of her up to then; but when she waltzed in and took a look round, she didn't care for Helena's changes. I was there; scared me. The two of 'em wrestled into an argument about art in general, and doggone if Helena didn't snap out at Josephine she'd better go back to school! What *that* didn't do from then on! No, sir, when the ladies get to feuding, we poor blindfolded he-souls seldom know what's really eatin' 'em. On the other hand, take—well, just take this evening." Mr. Horne paused.

"What about this evening?"

"Don't know't it bears on the subject particularly." The shortening cigar appeared to hold the old man's meditative attention. "Probably not. No, I was only thinking about how women are. They're funny. Sometimes a couple of 'em'll manhandle each other like the devil for years, each trying to use us male boobs against the other; then all of a sudden one or both of 'em'll wonder why they ever flung a dart and maybe come right out and spill everything. For instance——" He paused again.

"For instance what, Mr. Horne?"

"Only that I was thinking, Bailey, of something I happen to admire about your cousin and betrothed, Miss Josephine Oaklin. When she fights she does it pretty much out in the open. She isn't good at slyness. When she thinks she's forced to maneuver she's usually transparent; I think it's to her credit. You don't have to eavesdrop to learn her faults; they're like a brass band. Every human being's made up of every kind of thing, a whole lot of it awful; but Josephine—why, anybody can see all of her. A person really knows her. *You* do, of course."

"What about this evening, Mr. Horne? You were saying——"

"Oh, yes, that! Dropped in over there a while ago to felicitate her apropos this morning's announcement. Thought she seemed—well, not like herself. Rather depressed—in fact, a good deal depressed. Yes, quite a little. Reasonable to expect, of course, under the circumstances."

"Under what circumstances, sir?"

John Horne looked surprised. "Why, your going back to the Army. Natural anxiety, of course. Good stuff in her, Bailey. Always been fond of her, no matter how tough she made it to feel that way. Yep, fine girl!" He dropped his cigar in an ashtray on the table beside him and jumped up. "By George! That sick old bird wants to talk to me about his will and here I've been chattering along, forgetting all about him. Left my rubbers and umbrella at the front door—no, rather you'd not come down with me. Hope you'll have at least a few pleasant memories of us; you're leaving nothing but delightful ones of you. Don't be too brave; we want to see you again. Good voyages to you—and good-bye!"

Bailey went back to another reverie in his chair. "Rather depressed," was she? Putting on another act, touching addition to the same old act—engaged girl now unhappy because her fiancé returns to the service? She didn't often entirely fool Mr. Horne, though. The depression might well be genuine. Vanity injured, pride damaged by the discovery that she *could* be "insulted" as she'd been that morning? Scared, too, maybe? Afraid that even when she'd have the ring to show there'd be suspicion of a third abandonment; people might say he'd fled from her as had Murties and that quitter-Captain's shadowy predecessor? "Not like herself," Mr. Horne had said. That might be true, too—for a day or so—but Bailey wouldn't know, because he'd not see her again.

The paintings by the Seventeenth Century Dutch Masters were in place upon the faintly blued walls of the gallery by noon, as he had promised. The whole dwindled staff of the museum came to see the effect of the change and to say farewell to the Assistant Curator of Paintings. Mrs. Hevlin had a hurried word with him aside. "I'll tell her this terrible color isn't your fault," she said. "I'll persuade her they *made* you do it. Trust me!" She gave him a wink, infinitely sly, through her spectacles, glanced over her shoulder, muttered "Murder!" and pattered away.

Everyone else thought the bluishness valuable, congratulated Bailey upon it; and then, with what emotional cheer could be mustered, made much of him, as people do when a soldier returns to the wars. "When you come back to us again——" was often said with a faltering brightness; and Lieutenant Fount, off-hand, responded gayly till he came to say good-bye to Henry Rossbeke.

Bailey got through his final little speech of gratitude manfully enough, however, and turned to Helena Jyre; but she took his arm and went with him out of the gallery and all the way down to the great entrance hall of the museum. There, near the high main portal, she stopped talking of how much she'd miss his help and how happy everybody was to see him in health and strength again.

"There's something—something I don't know whether I'd better tell you or not," she said, releasing his arm but not facing him as they halted. She glanced out into the half-warm sunshine that had followed the autumnal night's rain. "Besides,

your taxi's waiting and maybe you haven't time enough
to——"

He looked at his watch. "I think I have."

"It's about her," Helena said. "She came to The Cranford
last night. She wanted to see you—but—but I told her you
weren't there."

"So? She came there? It must have been when I'd gone out
for my tickets."

Helena let that stand. It saved her from the embarrassing
explanation her conscience had suggested and she felt that she
was doing enough, anyhow. "She'd come running through the
rain, Bailey, and was pretty wet and sloppy-looking; but I
doubt if she knew anything about that. What I wanted to tell
you is that I've felt some compunctions."

"Why?"

"Because of one or two things she didn't actually say, Bailey,
yet seemed to express in a distracted sort of way. I got a feeling
she was sorry she'd been abominable to me so long. I think she
knows people dislike her but hasn't ever understood why. That
seems because she believes she really *isn't* like what most of us
think she is. She was pretty frantic and looked half-sick with a
miserable kind of frightenedness. The truth is, I've been getting
sorrier and sorrier for her all night. She wanted to wait for you;
but broke down and couldn't. I keep remembering how she
looked as she crept out and I wish I didn't somehow have to.
I thought maybe I ought to tell you, Bailey."

"Very well," was the whole of his response.

"There's one other thing perhaps." Helena seemed doubtful.
"I suppose she and I might be called enemies; but last night at
least she wasn't anybody's enemy and was all off-guard and
exposed. She was so rattled I doubt if she knew, herself, what

she wanted to say to you; but, beyond all question, that's what hearing you're going away did to her. Bailey, I don't know if I ought to say this——"

"Yes. Go ahead."

"I can't help wondering if she isn't knocked out this time by more than just another broken engagement."

"Oh, no," Bailey said. "It's not broken."

"What? You say——"

"Yes. Not broken at all."

"But——" Helena was caught in confusions and amazements. "She said you'd told her she—— Then you're going to stop in there to tell her good-bye?"

"No, I did that yesterday." He looked again at his watch. "I've only time enough now to say good-bye to you. Thank you forever for everything, Miss Jyre. Good-bye."

Her mystified voice just reached his ear as he strode between the great bronze doors.

"Good-bye, Bailey Fount!"

Two miles of taxicab to a station have brought to the mind's eye of many a sojourner pictures fond or dark, or both, reviewing a visit just ending. Subject to that old human habit, Bailey could see himself entering for the first time those bronze doors from which he was being borne away. As if he hovered in the haze of that past hot August day, he saw his own timorous figure, limping in spite of every faint-willed effort; saw himself getting himself lost in the museum—as he was lost within his head, lost-minded, lost in numberless apprehensions. He saw himself faltering into the stone passageway to his first sight and sound of Josephine Oaklin; then all of his reviewing pictures were of her and of himself with her.

Hard questions came with those retrospective visions. What part was he now shown to have played? How just and balanced had been his judgments, how right or wrong his actions? To his astonishment he was suddenly convinced that he'd been fair and worthy of respect during only the time when he'd been sick. This was the same as discovering that only when he'd been half-crazy had he been what is called good. Since he'd recovered his strength of mind and body he'd set himself up with sacrilegious certainty as a judging and punishing god.

Whom had he judged and sought to punish? He began to perceive something dimly apparent to Helena Jyre when she comprehended that she'd been hating an image of Josephine. "Fine girl!" Mr. Horne had said, meaning that the image had been sculptured by his dear egregious friend, Thomas Oaklin; so the image was egregious, like old Tom, but wasn't Josephine. She, herself, unchanging and unchangeable, hadn't been altered by the grandfather. To the soldier in the taxicab there flashingly returned that moment when she'd said a vista opened and they *saw* each other. Inexplicably they'd found themselves together in the strange nearness not of images but of selves, and so, fleetingly, he'd known Josephine herself. Fleetingly? No; the thing once done, he'd always know her.

Then what devil had driven him to create that scene of a Petruchio taming Katharine? No; Petruchio was a decenter fellow, hadn't beaten down a woman's head with rawhide accusation and abuse; nor was Josephine Oaklin a simple shrew. Bailey hadn't tamed a termagant; he'd smashed a lonely woman's pride. The discursive hints of old John Horne gained clarity. She and her pride were lonelier every day since Thomas Oaklin died.

Bailey, though young, understood that nobody can skin off

more than the thin top of the manifold truth of himself, or of anyone else, or of anything; he could hope to know only the ascertainable partial truth concerning Bailey Fount. Those ladies and gentlemen of the museum who so kindly thought they knew him had seen a small fragment of his life, a chip different from the rest of it. Had Bailey Fount no baseless prides that should be beaten down—if all were known? In his life had there been no petty treacheries, no spites and shameful small deceptions, no meannesses kept blurred in areas of memory deliberately befogged? If all were known, what human being dare walk with head held high? How lately had he crept about stoopingly, unable to play the man?

Now came the worst of that drive in a taxicab, for he put a knifing question to himself and the answer glared at him. *Why* had he laid Josephine Oaklin low? He'd done it because at his own invitation she used him and would marry him without loving him. If he hadn't been in love with her he'd have held his hand. He'd struck her and what dealt the blow was egoism, the jealousy of a man who loves and is not loved. He'd wanted to hurt her and had hurt her for just that.

What of her coming to seek him last night, drenched, incoherent, unforgettable, nobody's enemy, not even Helena Jyre's? What had driven her? Josephine Oaklin wasn't the woman to fall in love with a big brute for beating her. Bailey knew better than that. Never would she be made to quail, "reformed"; never would she be made obedient for love's sweet sake, a meek rewarding Katharine. If she ever fell in love it wouldn't be because some fool took a whip to her; it would be because she fell in love. Had she tried to find him to try to say —what? He couldn't know and he wouldn't guess; he was on his way to the Army.

As the taxicab's speed slackened on the curve to the station, "That's the way I've got to leave it," he thought. "That's the way it is. That's the way everything is, God help us all!"

The war crowd filled the station. Soldiers, sailors, airmen, marines, cadets, coast guardsmen and strained bright-eyed womenfolk worked toward a gate at the foot of a metal stairway that led to the upper level and departing trains. Through another gate uniformed figures eagerly pushed, emerging to be clasped by radiant mothers, wives, sisters and sweethearts. Enlarged voices of women spoke from iron pilasters, hollowly announced trains coming and destinations of trains soon to rumble forth overhead.

Officers and men hurried upon all the errands of war as Lieutenant Bailey Fount made his jostled way into the close-packed throng pushing toward the steel gate proclaimed the right one for him. It stood open, jammed with service men; and the stairway rising from it clattered under the many feet that had but two more minutes before the packed great train would renew its long thundering southwestward.

"Barely time to make it," Bailey thought.

A white-gloved hand fiercely clutched his arm, and, in spite of people who pressed him forward, swung him about to confront Josephine Oaklin. That elegance of hers was as visible upon her and about her as ever it had been, and was anomalous within this wartime "cross-section"; but no face of any heart-struck woman there was more haggard under strain of the will not to weep.

He was sharp. "I can't lose that train!"

"I don't want you to. Go away and stay! I came to tell you that you'll never have to see me again. Don't send me that ring. Your crazy engagement's broken. I've let you out of it, understand. You're through with me and in the clear. That's all! Go on to your train."

"I will. Good-bye."

They were thrust against each other, and for a few seconds their eyes held to a close gaze in which there was a crisis of defiance—not her defiance of him, not his of her, but most strangely their mutual defiance of all time except these present three or four seconds. The sword hung over them, would be there, above them, they knew not how long, and it might fall; but in this look each fiercely admitted a whole comprehension of the other. Together they comprehended everything, forgave everything, promised everything.

The enchanting new knowledge of each other exalted them; they said not a word. They kissed quickly—then he pushed his way to the gate and strode through it.

Half-way up the stairs, among the last of those who were to reach that train, he turned his head for an instant, looked down and waved a hand. Lingering mothers, wives, sisters, sweethearts were waving from below; but among all the lifted faces, lifted hands, he saw only that palest face and the white-gloved hand extended toward him palm upward—the gesture that means "Come back to me!"